Absolution

Absolution

Alice McDermott

Farrar, Straus and Giroux
New York

Farrar, Straus and Giroux
120 Broadway, New York 10271

Library of Congress Cataloging-in-Publication Data
Names: McDermott, Alice, author.
Title: Absolution / Alice McDermott.
Description: First edition. | New York : Farrar, Straus and Giroux, 2023.
Identifiers: LCCN 2023018757 | ISBN 9780374610487 (hardcover)
Subjects: LCSH: Vietnam War, 1961–1975—Fiction. | Wives—Fiction. |
   LCGFT: Novels.
Classification: LCC PS3563.C355 A67 2023 | DDC 813/.54—dc23/
   eng/20230505
LC record available at https://lccn.loc.gov/2023018757

International Edition ISBN: 978-0-374-61304-4

Designed by Abby Kagan

Our books may be purchased in bulk for promotional, educational, or business
use. Please contact your local bookseller or the Macmillan Corporate and
Premium Sales Department at 1-800-221-7945, extension 5442, or by email at
MacmillanSpecialMarkets@macmillan.com.

www.fsgbooks.com
www.twitter.com/fsgbooks • www.facebook.com/fsgbooks

1   3   5   7   9   10   8   6   4   2

For the friends of my youth

The anguish of the earth absolves our eyes . . .

—SIEGFRIED SASSOON, "Absolution"

. . . but how I wished there existed someone to whom I could say that I was sorry.

—GRAHAM GREENE, *The Quiet American*

I

THERE WERE SO MANY COCKTAIL PARTIES in those days. And when they were held in the afternoon we called them garden parties, but they were cocktail parties nonetheless.

You have no idea what it was like. For us. The women, I mean. The wives.

Most days, I would bathe in the morning and then stay in my housecoat until lunch, reading, writing letters home—those fragile, pale blue airmail letters with their complex folds; evidence, I think now, of how exotic distance itself once seemed.

I'd do my nails, compose the charming bread-and-butter notes we were always exchanging—wedding stationery with my still-new initials, real ink, and cunning turns of phrase, bits of French, exclamation marks galore. The fan moving overhead and the heat encroaching even through the slatted blinds of the shaded room, the spice of sandalwood from the joss stick on the dresser.

Out for a luncheon or a lecture or a visit to the crowded market, and then another bath when I woke from my afternoon nap, damp hair on my neck as I removed the shower cap, a haze of talcum. Still wrapped in the towel, I could feel the perspiration prick my skin. Face powder, rouge, lipstick. And then the high-waisted cotton underpants (I hope you're laughing), the formidable cotton bra, the panty girdle with the shining diamond of brighter elastic at its center. The click of the garters. Stockings slipped over the hand and held up to the light, reinforced toe and heel and top.

We were careful to secure the garter just so. Too close to the nylon risked a run.

You cannot imagine the troubles suggested, in those days, by a stocking with a run: the woman was drunk, careless, unhappy, indifferent (to her husband's career, even to his affections), ready to go home.

Slip, then sheath—small white dress shields pinned under each arm with tiny gold safety pins—then shoes, jewelry, a spray of perfume. I'd be faint with the heat in my column of clothes by the time I came downstairs. Peter, my husband, waiting, newly shaved, handsome in his tropical-weight suit, white shirt, and thin tie, having a first drink and looking a little wilted himself.

And the girls we passed on the street or who met us at the door, or who only moved across my inner eye by then in their white ao dais, were like pale leaves stirring in the humid stillness, sunstruck indications of some unseen breeze: cool, weightless, beautiful.

It was at a garden party on a Sunday afternoon, early in our first month in Saigon. The party was in the elegant courtyard of a villa not far from the Basilica. A lovely street lined with tamarind trees. We'd only been there a few minutes ourselves when I turned to see a young family paused at the entrance, posed as if for a pretty picture beneath a swag of scarlet bougainvillea. Baby boy in the arms of the slim mother, daughter at her side, tall father in a pale suit—another engineer, I learned later. It was much later still, decades later, that I suddenly wondered, laughing to think about it, why so many engineers were needed.

I was twenty-three then, with a bachelor's from Marymount. For a year before my marriage, I'd taught kindergarten at a parish school in Harlem, but my real vocation in those days, my aspiration, was to be a helpmeet for my husband.

That was the word I used. It was, in fact, the word my own father had used, taking both my gloved hands in his as we waited for the wedding guests to file into our church in Yonkers. This was in the bride's waiting room, a small chamber well off the vestibule. I recall a tiny stained-glass window, a kneeling bench (for last-minute prayer, I suppose), a box of tissues (for last-minute tears) on a shelf under an ornate mirror, and the two brocade chairs where we sat. The cool odor of old stone and the fresh flowers in my bouquet. My father took both my hands and held them together on the wide tulle skirt of my wedding dress, which even in the dim light of the tiny room was winking with seed pearls.

He said, "Be a helpmeet to your husband. Be the jewel in his crown."

I said, "I will."

THE LITTLE GIRL WHO POSED so prettily with her parents and her baby brother was you.

She was about seven or eight, in her Sunday best like the rest of us: a crisp yellow dress, nearly gold, with pleats at the bodice, scalloped collar and sleeves. She held a Barbie doll in the crook of her arm, like a scepter. It must have been the first Barbie doll I'd ever seen.

After the family was introduced—my husband knew the husband, had already met the wife as well—I leaned down to ask her about the doll, as you do with children. To tell the truth, I was happy to give her my attention, pretending to be a kindly adult.

I hadn't yet lost the shyness that plagued me then; I had only managed to put it aside—to steady my hands before I extended them and to breathe deeply before I spoke. I wanted to be a helpmeet to my husband, and these gatherings, cocktail parties and garden parties and dinners with embassy people and military people and corporate people and advisors of all kinds, were, as my husband put it, how things got done in Saigon.

The little girl spoke softly, with the manners—she said, "Yes, ma'am"—that were taken for granted in children, in those days. Seen but not heard. Nearly whispering, she touched the doll's little shoes—open-toed high heels—and the pretty floral dress she wore, explaining that the doll arrived wearing only a bathing suit, but that any number of outfits could be purchased: cocktail dresses, uniforms—nurse or stewardess—even a wedding gown that cost, and here she grew breathless with the astonishment of it, five dollars.

From the small purse on her arm she withdrew a tiny booklet, illustrated with all the outfits the doll might wear.

Two men had joined the adult conversation that was just above our heads, blocking me, or so I saw it, from their circle. I didn't want to straighten up and turn away from the child—she was so earnest. Nor did I want to linger on the periphery of these grown-ups, waiting to be invited back in. So I took the little girl aside a bit, to a wicker settee just beyond the trellis of flowers.

Together we turned the pages of the catalogue, and she told me which outfits she already owned and which she was "asking for." Many of these she had already marked with a careful X.

There was an aunt in New York City, she explained. A businesswoman who was the regular source for these gifts. Who, in fact, the child told me, sometimes wore a tweed suit with a matching pillbox hat exactly like the one pictured in the catalogue, an outfit called "Career Girl."

Well, it was all charming to me. I had grown up with broad-faced baby dolls that came with only a party dress or a coat and a bonnet, and my playtime consisted of pushing a doll carriage up and down the sidewalk, or holding to the doll's rosebud mouth a plastic baby spoon of imaginary food. But here was a doll that did not require naps or airings or pretend feedings. A doll meant for a thousand different games: nurse, stewardess, plantation belle, sorority girl, night club singer in a sultry gown ("*très chic*," I said to my little friend), bride.

The girl's mother soon joined us, her plump baby boy in her arms.

Charlene was young and freckled, with thick strawberry blond hair that she wore pushed back with a small headband. Her nose was pert, her darting eyes a deep hazel. There was something both regal and feral about the way the straight line of her scalp met her tanned forehead. I recognized her type from my days at Marymount: she had the healthy, athletic, genetic—as I thought of it—confidence of one born to wealth. The first thing she asked me, in fact, was if I played tennis; she was looking for a partner. I did not.

Then she leaned across her daughter, holding out the baby, offering him to me.

"Would you mind taking him for a sec?" she asked, giving me no option, really. Had I not reached up, she seemed ready to let him roll to the ground. "I have *got* to go tinkle," she whispered.

I'd noticed this before, among girls of her tribe: they knew an easy mark, a girl of lesser means who would be reflexively—genetically—disposed to do for her whatever she asked.

"I'd love to," I said, and meant it. I took the baby from her, a big, warm bundle in his pale blue romper. He was now wide-eyed. She straightened up—"only a sec," she said—and had no sooner gone into the house when his little mouth crumpled and he began to whimper. I lifted him to my chest, held him under my chin. I patted his back to soothe him. He quieted nicely.

We were hoping to start a family of our own—any month now, was how I'd come to think of it—and I felt a surge of confidence. I would be a marvelous mother.

Then the baby hiccuped once or twice, and I felt the warmth of his spit-up on my bare throat. A second later, just as I tried to ease him from my breast, he began to vomit, effortlessly, copiously, as babies do. I felt it running down my dress. That bland, wheaty odor of baby formula—no more awful, really, in that it was regurgitated. I felt it pool warmly in my bra.

There was nothing to be done. I moved the child to my lap, bouncing him a bit, rubbing his back, wiping his little mouth and chin with my thumb. He hiccuped a few times more, seemed to settle, seemed to change his mind—a flailing of his little arms, a sudden stiffening—and then he began to wail. His sister beside me said, "Oh, no," and put her face into her hands as if to withdraw from the scene. "Your pretty dress," she said into her palms. I assured her it was fine, fine, but with the crying child in my lap I couldn't open my purse for a tissue to blot up the mess.

I felt the other partygoers turn to me, pausing in that second in which they remained well-dressed, neat, adult while I became the humiliated child. I saw how the men among them averted their eyes as if I'd just begun to publicly menstruate, while a trio of wives rushed forward with a solicitude that in my embarrassment felt to me like scorn. Some of them brought linen cocktail napkins that they swatted gently at my front, but the material was too delicate to do much good. One woman took the baby from my arms—I felt somehow that this was an indication of my ineptitude—and another, our hostess, put her hand under my elbow.

"Come along, dear," she said. She was a middle-aged woman with short gray hair. Another corporate wife. She put a large pink dinner napkin to my chest, as if my clothes had gone transparent. "We'll get you cleaned up," she said.

We made our way through the increasing crowd of partygoers in the courtyard. I was aware of how they stepped aside as we passed, silent and appraising. I supposed some of them thought I was the sick one. Perhaps they thought *pregnant*, or *drunk*. I tried to say something about this to my escort, but she merely hushed me soothingly, and gently pressed the big napkin to my breasts as if I were a dumb thing, about to babble.

INSIDE, THE LIVING ROOM was wide, cool, nicely furnished. An impression of pink and green silk cushions and rattan chairs. A wide, polished tile floor, fans turning overhead. A house girl appeared from the far end and moved soundlessly toward us.

"Poor Mrs. Kelly here," my companion said—I was surprised she knew my name, although I had learned enough about corporate wives by then to know I shouldn't have been—"has had an encounter with a colicky baby. Poor dear. Let's help her clean up."

And then she gave some soft-spoken instructions in French. I didn't have the wherewithal at that moment to translate the words for myself, though I suspected she was merely repeating what she had already said, for my sake, in English.

The girl nodded sympathetically as my hostess handed my forearm over to her, along with the pink napkin she'd been pressing to my chest. I was led outside and then through the small kitchen, where two more girls were working at a narrow counter, and a burly man all in white, the chef, I supposed, was speaking in a harsh stream. We slid past them and across another courtyard, into an even smaller room, a sewing room, whose walls, on my first impression, seemed to waver, like the inside of a tent. There was that kind of canvas-filtered light. It made the dark bulk of the Singer a silhouette against the one wide window. There was an ironing board with a small black iron, a square, pressed-wood cutting table, bolts of pale fabric here and there. Even with the baby formula spilled down my dress, I caught a scent of starch and newly ironed linen and thought of my mother.

A trifold screen was angled into one corner, a lovely raw-silk cocktail dress in a beautiful shade of green—slim bodice, tulip skirt—was hanging from one of its folds, as if for display.

The girl indicated that I should step behind the screen, nodding and unbuttoning an imaginary dress to show that I should step behind the screen and take off my clothes. I nodded, too, and smiled and thanked her. In my humiliation, I was thanking everyone. There was a small bench behind the screen, a pair of peau de soie heels, water-stained, beneath it. A white ao dai hung from a plush satin hanger, as if in charming counterpoint to the very Western cocktail dress on the other side.

I took off my pearls first. Peter had bought them in Hong Kong, his first trip east, just after we became engaged. I sniffed them, wondering if the odor of baby formula would linger on the thread. I kicked off my shoes and unzipped my dress—it was a narrow sheath in pale blue linen with a silk lining. Very Jackie, I'd thought when I found it at Woodward & Lothrop. Most of what the baby had thrown up was on the inside, all along the scalloped neckline. Ruined, I was certain. I stepped out of the dress. At the armpits, the two white dress shields were like a pair of rolled-back eyes, wildly oblivious.

I wondered just how much I was meant to take off. The lace bodice of my slip was also wet; my bra had caught and held what seemed to me a sloshing ounce of pale vomit.

I was still standing there, all uncertain, when the girl returned with a basin and two white towels. She placed them on the bench and then, as if this were a ritual we had performed together many times, she lifted my slip up over my head, and went behind me to unhook my bra.

I would have been grateful for that big pink napkin then, but she gently eased me to the bench and, after placing one of the towels on my lap—I was wearing only my panty girdle and stockings—she stirred the warm water, the scent of lavender rising out of it, and squeezed out a thick cloth. Then she slowly wiped my neck and my chest, between my breasts, touching them gently. She was a plain, round-faced girl, not one of the beautiful Vietnamese women; there was a plumpness about her cheeks, a broadness to her mouth; her complexion was not perfect; but there was that benign smile, and a sweet, pleasant odor to her warm breath. She patted my skin dry with the other towel and then unfurled a pink silk kimono, on loan from our hostess, I assumed.

"Put on this," she said, whispering. She tossed my dress and slip and bra over her arm, lifted the towels and the basin of water. She smiled at me. Although I think we were about the same age, I felt entirely mothered. "All will be well," she said.

I sat for a few moments behind the screen, not sure what to do next. For the first time, I thought of my husband: if he would be looking for me across the party, if someone had asked him, Was that your wife who was led away? Or if our hostess had whispered to him the whole story of what had occurred, which seemed most likely.

Once again, I felt the utter shame of my situation, knowing it was nothing to be ashamed of, but feeling it all the same. It was a kind of humiliation—worse, a kind of incompetence. Would another woman, a mother, have known how to hold the child to avoid such a mess? Would another woman have anticipated in the baby's twisting lips a coming explosion? I was an only child; my mother was forty when I was born and fifty-seven when she died. My experience with babies was narrow—it was one of the things I worried about as we planned for our own.

I was good with children. I had, I sometimes joked, majored in children. I'd spent the year before my wedding at the kindergarten in Harlem, loving every day of it, because the children were adorable and my competence with them so reassuring—I would be a great mother, I was certain—but infants worried me, babies who, like something rabid or drunk or insane, could not be charmed or cajoled or distracted from their woes with a cookie or a story or a game.

Babies who might pour eight ounces of regurgitated formula right down the front of your favorite dress at a garden party full of diplomats and engineers, economists and generals.

I had a sudden notion—sitting there in the corner behind the folded screen, like a banished child myself—that the baby's mother, the sunny tennis player born to wealth, knew exactly what she was doing when she handed me her child. Tinkle, my eye, I thought. She knew the baby was about to erupt, and she handed him off to me just in time.

I knew her type. I'd met enough girls like her at school. They all had that ability—some kind of noblesse oblige—to enlist the help of strangers without ever seeming helpless themselves. They got other people to take care of them, to lend them a scarf, or ten dollars, or an umbrella, to hail them a cab or pick up their dry cleaning, and then they made their gratitude seem facetious, as if they had merely accepted your favors in order to allay your anxiety to bestow them.

I wrapped myself in the thick silk of my hostess's kimono. It was nice to have the cool material on my bare skin. The little room's odor of starch and fabric had made me remember home—I thought of my mother ironing in her bedroom in our narrow house, the late afternoon light, the tufts of thread on the chenille bedspread where I would lie, watching her—but the silk, and something of the lingering scent of the herbed water on my skin, made me want to reject homesickness and love this place instead.

To love the distance I had traveled and all the strangeness—some of it beautiful, some of it startling—that, up until now, I thought, I'd been seeing as if from the corner of my eye.

I looked again at the lovely ao dai hanging on the screen. So simple and elegant, and sensible, too—no need for panty girdle and garters when you dressed like this. No need either for face powder and lipstick, rollers and hair spray, when you had the smooth skin and beautiful hair of the Vietnamese girls.

No need for the gloved handshake, breath held to convey a steady confidence, when you can instead, more authentically, simply bow your head and lower your eyes.

No taking control of any mishap at your party with a jaunty napkin flourish; no sunburned athleticism that can make a question like "Do you play tennis?" seem the beginning of a moral assessment, if you can whisper, simply, "All will be well" and then move out of the room like a pale leaf stirred by a breeze.

I had worked myself into a good state of anti-Americanism when I heard my tennis-playing nemesis enter the room, asking, "Is she here?"

I stood, pulled the kimono firmly closed, and stepped from behind the screen.

There she was. She let out a laugh when she saw me—a kind of surprised guffaw that she then pretended to smother—and quickly replaced her amusement at the sight of me with contrition.

"I am so sorry," she said. The little girl with the Barbie doll was in her wake. "Truly. How awful. I hope your dress isn't ruined."

I saw her glance through the window behind the sewing machine and turned to see, through the open blinds, that my dress and my slip and my bra were hanging in the bright sun in the drying yard just outside the window. I felt at some further disadvantage that this woman, this Charlene, had seen these things first, before I even knew where they'd gone.

"I hope you'll let me buy you a new one if it's stained. Or better yet"—she turned, just as the house girl came back into the room, a small tray with a glass of lemonade in her hands—"we'll get Lily here to make another one for you. An exact replica. She's a marvelous seamstress."

The girl smiled, placed the tray on the cutting table, and indicated a small settee. "Will you stay?" she asked, and my very American friend shook her head.

"No, dear. I've got to get back to the gathering." She turned to me again. "I've sent the baby home with one of the girls. I am just so *sorry*," but in a jolly way that clearly conveyed that her guilt about the incident in no way diminished her fondness for herself. "It was stupid of me to bring him. Kent so wanted to show him off. I thought that if I fed him before we came, he'd sleep through the afternoon, but I'm afraid, with this heat." She shrugged. "Well, it was stupid of me. And now I've ruined this lovely party for you."

It was really a triumph, the many things she had accomplished in so short an appearance. She had laughed at me—acknowledging that this was the most honest response to seeing me, braless and shoeless, in a pink kimono—and then smothered the laughter with the better angel of her good nature, her pity. She had established herself as an insider here—she knew the servant girl by name, knew she was a marvelous seamstress—and so revealed me as the novice, the stranger. She proved herself a devoted wife to her husband, the doting father, and she finished me off by implying that I'd come not because I understood that these gatherings were how things got done in Saigon, but because I wanted a lovely party.

She was saying something in rapid French to Lily. And then she turned to me again. "You just have to allow me to replace it if the stain doesn't come out," she said, as if I had already insisted on refusing her offer.

"It will be fine," Lily said in careful English. "It will be okay."

"I am so glad," Charlene said, as if the entire incident had come to a happy conclusion. "You'll be back outside in no time." And then her eyes went to the cocktail dress hanging from the screen behind me. I saw a ferocious curiosity, perhaps envy. "Isn't that lovely? For Mrs. Case?"

Lily ducked her head demurely. "For the daughter," she said.

"Of course. So youthful." She turned to her own daughter. "Isn't it lovely, Rainey?"

The girl nodded. "I love the color."

"Really fabulous," Charlene said, without taking her eyes from the dress. Without any effort to engage anyone else in the conversation. In fact, mother and child might suddenly have been alone in the room.

They both reached out to touch the fabric, to peek beneath the hem to the tulle underskirt. A cousin's wedding was mentioned. How perfect for the season, this shade of green. Eventually, Charlene shook herself as if from a dream and said, "Well, I must get back. Kent will be frantic." She turned to leave.

But you remained, the Barbie in the crook of your arm, your little patent leather pocketbook hanging from your elbow.

Charlene seemed hardly to pause as she said, "Oh, yes. Rainey went out to the car when we sent the baby home, to fetch some doll clothes. She wanted to show you." She dropped her brown, freckled shoulders, expressing as she did her polite reluctance to ask this, which was, her smile also conveyed, really a very small favor. "Would you mind terribly? While you're back here, would you mind if she showed you these few things? She's madly bored outside."

"No," I said, "of course. I'd love to see them." The fact that this was true made my tone no less false.

"All right, darling," Charlene said to the child. "Don't make a burden of yourself. Come out to the garden and find Mommy when you're finished."

And now I was reduced to a child's playmate.

Lily followed her out, and you and I sat side by side on the settee.

I have to admit, the clothes were lovely. Tiny zippers and snaps, even mother-of-pearl buttons. You drew three small dresses from your purse and laid them out between us. With what I saw as your mother's humorless efficiency, you also consulted the little Barbie catalogue you had shown me earlier, confirming for me that each dress was a legitimate replica of the one illustrated and described.

And then, as if we had been playmates all our lives, you asked me, "Which one do you want her to try on?"

I selected a long-sleeved sheath with a dark blue sash and saw immediately that I had not chosen wisely.

"Don't you think she'll be warm in that? With this heat?"

You were swinging your legs idly. There was a Band-Aid on your plump knee. I wondered if you had fallen on the tennis court.

"Good point," I said, and selected instead a sleeveless white dress printed with small roses.

As you were undressing the doll, Lily returned with another glass of lemonade. I heard the mother's voice again as you said,

"Thank you so much. Can you place it over there, please," indicating the sewing table.

Lily did so, obediently, and then returned to us, shyly intrigued, I could tell, by the elegant little clothes.

I handed her the rejected choice, the long-sleeved dress, to examine. Lily studied the seams, the tiny snaps. When the doll was dressed in her new, cooler outfit, Lily put out her hand and you asked—your condescension diluted with childish generosity—"Would you like to look see?"

"Please," Lily said. "Very pretty." She turned the doll over in her hands once or twice, Barbie's blond ponytail swinging, and then she measured it against her palm. She was smiling. Her front tooth was chipped. She had a slight overbite.

She nodded. "I'll make you something," she said.

Here it all starts to feel like a fairy tale, in recollection. Me in that fragrant silk kimono and you in your golden garden-party dress, looking on as Lily carried the doll to the sewing table and found a length of white silk and a scissors—in recollection they were comically large, unwieldy scissors—and measured and cut and measured again. Then we were behind her at the ancient black sewing machine. The smell of the motor, a touch of warmed rubber, of oil. The industrious humming. Another recollection from my own childhood.

Beyond Lily's bowed head there was the bright drying yard, my clothes unmoving in the sun.

A fairy tale: the elves and the shoemaker or Cinderella before the ball. Lily's quick and homely little hands, her dark head bowed as she hand-stitched the final touches. You quiet beside me. At one point I felt for sure you were holding your breath.

And then, with an elfin grin—I'm sorry if that sounds like a caricature, but that's how it struck me at the time: elfin—Lily held up the perfect little ao dai—the slim white pants, the long overdress.

"Oh my gosh," you cried.

"Try on," Lily said.

It was quite remarkable, magical even. How beautifully the clothes fit the little doll. You were beside yourself, literally dancing with *thank you*s and *merci*s and *cam on ban*s until you finally added—as if you understood how insufficient the words were to your joy—"Number one dress for Barbie!"

"Something," Lily said calmly. "To take home." And then she left us.

You, of course, wanted to show your mother. You hurriedly packed the doll's dresses into your purse. And then—you were a well-raised child—paused to ask if I wanted you to wait with me. "I don't mind," you added, but weakly.

I told you no, of course. Said I'd be right out to the party, and watched you fly from the room, the doll's ponytail swinging.

Lily returned with my clothes not long after, and although, on close examination, I could see a pale water line on the silk lining, the linen front was utterly restored. I thanked her. Called her—I was trying out some of your mother's self-confidence—"a marvel."

Lily bowed her head modestly. But there was some satisfaction in her demeanor, I thought. She knew I had been given a glimpse of her gifts.

"My name," she said sweetly, laughter in her eyes, "is Ly." She drew in the air. "L, Y. Just Ly."

WHEN I RETURNED TO THE PARTY in the garden, an agreement seemed to have been made that everyone there would pretend I'd never left. Even our hostess only briefly glanced at me as I edged past her in the crowd. She wore a warm smile, of course, but it conveyed nothing. I was looking for my husband, could not find him, and once again felt the flush of embarrassment, incompetence.

There was little I dreaded more than finding myself unengaged, conversation-less, solitary, at one of these gatherings. I had nightmares about this: standing alone in the midst of a happy crowd of elegant and worldly-wise Westerners, my voice paralyzed, my mouth benumbed, my teeth sealed. Humiliated. Inconsequential.

I saw you and your mother chatting with a small group of women. One of them was holding the Barbie, turning it over in her hands as Lily had done, examining the lovely ao dai. I resisted the impulse to use you, my little friend—my only friend, I felt at that moment—as an excuse to end my awkward isolation, but with no alternatives available—all the other groups of chatting Americans seemed impenetrable, my husband was nowhere to be found—I headed toward you anyway.

The trick in walking unaccompanied through these parties was to pretend there was someone just over there to whom you simply must speak . . .

The fear, of course, was that I'd get to the end of the room or the hall or the courtyard and find myself alone and unengaged still . . . my nose bumping against the wall.

Nearing Charlene and her crowd with that wholly false look of determination on my face, I was fully prepared to walk past them.

But Charlene reached out. She drew me into the circle. "Here she is," she said, as if they'd all been awaiting my return. I braced myself to hear her recite some comic version of my mishap with the baby. These girls from wealth, I also knew, were always willing to welcome you into their cliques if you were willing to be a hapless sidekick.

But what she said was "It was Mrs. Kelly's idea. She's been working with Lily. Don't you think it's perfect?"

The woman who was holding the doll, a broad-shouldered woman, perhaps forty, in a bright pink sundress too youthful for her, looked at me, assessing. "How much are you charging?" she asked.

Charlene turned to me—I might say she turned on me, her face to mine, smothering my confusion at the question with a blanket of girlhood camaraderie. "I don't know," she said, speaking into my eyes. Hers seemed to be flashing at the moment. "What did we decide to charge? Five dollars, did we say?"

"For a little doll outfit?" the woman in pink asked.

At a loss, I said—I assure you, I still had no idea what was going on—"They charge five dollars for the wedding dress."

"And this is handmade," Charlene added. I felt her slip her fingers under my elbow. She pulled me closer. We were suddenly, all unaccountably, a united front; for or against what I still had no idea. But I confess to some satisfaction in knowing I had won her over, if that's what I'd done. It was another inborn talent of these privileged girls: they were irresistible, much as you hated them.

"Handmade and utterly unique," she said. "Send these home to your girls in McLean and they'll be the toast of the Barbie set."

The pink lady from McLean turned the doll over in her hands. I could feel you growing anxious beside me. "I'll have to order three," the woman said. And paused. "Make it five. My brother's girls as well. Does it come in other colors?"

Charlene grinned. "Absolutely." She had the smallest, straightest, whitest teeth I had ever seen. There was a flatness to her tanned and freckled face that I was just beginning to notice. It was part of her confidence, somehow, her air of forging ahead, getting done whatever needed to be done; a face pressed to the glass with the assuredness that the glass would always give way.

But also something feral, as I said, fox-like, not only in her determined reddish hairline but in the sprouted thickness of her well-groomed eyebrows. The look of something on the hunt. A face utterly incapable of aligning itself into any expression that might indicate introspection or self-doubt.

Once again, she placed that face in front of mine. "You'll talk to Lily about this, yes?" she asked, and then quickly turned to the others. Had I been another kind of girl, one who knew how to claim an advantage, I would have corrected her—"It's just Ly." But I didn't.

"Lily can easily turn out five," Charlene was saying, "Eight, actually. Peg Smith wants three."

And then she said, "Who else?" And lifted her short nose to survey the party. Still holding my arm—she had managed to move me closer to her, we were joined at the hip—she called out to another wife, a petite blonde in a lime green shift, a maple syrup tan, who moved toward us as if summoned. The women she had been chatting with followed.

"Have you ladies seen this?" Charlene asked, and took the doll from the McLean woman's hands, not rudely exactly, but with the authoritative air of a matron among small children. "Any little girls in your lives who play with Barbie dolls? We've got a fundraiser going."

In only a few minutes, it seemed, she had requests for twenty outfits. Five dollars apiece. The lime green blonde reached into her purse to pay but Charlene touched her arm. "On delivery," she said. "American dollars only."

Another asked Charlene if she should be writing this down, and there was laughter all around. "Photographic memory," she answered.

When any of them remarked on the cleverness of it all, this little fundraiser, Charlene pressed herself against my arm, and gave all the credit to me. Not her idea at all, she said. It was Mrs. Kelly here who saw the opportunity.

And then she introduced me to everyone, not merely as the young wife of a young engineer on loan to the navy but as the passionate fundraiser, the clever conduit to the talented locals.

And then there were just the two of us, you following along, making our way through the party.

I learned in a few efficient sentences that Charlene had started "a little group" of women who brought small gifts to the hospitals and the various orphanages—candy and crayons, baseballs, baby dolls—and she wanted to add something for the nurses and the parents, especially the grandparents, who were often at the children's bedsides. Tea, chocolates, cigarettes would be nice. She had just begun looking for ways to raise some funds for this. And then Rainey appeared with the little outfit Lily had made—"Bingo," Charlene said in my ear.

She added, matter-of-factly (need I tell you at this point that Charlene said everything matter-of-factly?), "I gave you the credit for the idea because everyone here is so tired of smarter-than-they-are me."

WE WERE IN THE LIVING ROOM. And then through the kitchen where we found Lily—Ly—at the sink, breaking up a block of ice. Charlene disarmed her of the ice pick in the same way she had effortlessly taken the Barbie doll from Mrs. McLean, handing it to a startled boy in a white jacket who had just carried in a tray of stubby glasses. "Come," she said to us all.

Back in the sewing room, the French was too quick for me, but the negotiation was clear enough. Lily showed Charlene a remnant of white silk—which Charlene, nodding, slipped into her purse, agreeing, I think, to buy her more. And then the spool of thin elastic that Lily had used for the waistband of the doll's pants, a card of tiny hooks and eyes. I gathered Charlene would provide these as well.

Numbers were exchanged—how much fabric, how much thread, elastic. How much time it would take. How much Lily would be paid. I have no memory for numbers, but, as I recall, it came to maybe about a quarter—twenty-five cents for each outfit. Maybe less.

The poor girl was agreeing to it all, not reluctantly, pleasantly, eagerly, in fact, but with a kind of resignation that looked to me a little like grief. Every now and then, she glanced at you, as if taking a fond last look as she was being swept out to sea on the riptide of Charlene's swift French and indomitable will.

She did manage to say, in English, "I have to ask Mrs. Case. For permission." Which Charlene dismissed. "I'll talk to Marcia," she said. "It will be fine."

She turned on me. "Can you pick them up here, say a week from Wednesday? I've got an engagement. If you can bring them to my house, I'll get them delivered, collect the money. Buy some goodies. I usually go by the hospital on Saturday mornings."

Of course I agreed.

And then Charlene plucked the doll from her daughter's hand and gave it to Lily.

"She'll need this, sweetie," she said—once again, how was it done?—making it seem that she and her daughter were the only two sentient beings in the room. "She needs a model so she can copy the one she made. Make sure they all fit perfectly."

Lily made an attempt to object. "No need," she said. But Charlene's plan was in place. "Mrs. Kelly can retrieve Miss Barbie when she comes to get the outfits next week. Meanwhile, you can pretend she's on assignment."

Charlene suddenly batted her eyes and theatrically touched her chin with her index finger, pretending to imagine. I noticed that although her nails were beautifully manicured, a pale pink polish that matched her lipstick perfectly, they were also bitten to nubs.

"What should it be?" Charlene asked. "A fashion shoot in Paris? Or maybe she's run back to New York to sign a contract." Suddenly she looked at me. We might have been old friends from school, remembering some unspoken bit of shared late-night mischief. "How about this," she said, still talking to the child, but looking at me from beneath those predator's eyebrows. "Barbie's gone north for the week. On secret assignment for the current administration. She's having tea with Ho Chi Minh. Exercising her charm on behalf of the free world."

I laughed with her because we were, somehow, old friends. But Lily seemed puzzled, and certainly there was no mistaking the tears that stood in your eyes. Briefly, I thought I was the only one who noticed this, but then Charlene cupped her hand under your chin, held your face in the V formed by thumb and fore-finger, and directed your gaze into her own green eyes.

"You must be brave," Charlene whispered. No further options would be offered.

I saw you—your face still trapped in your mother's hand—straighten your narrow shoulders, press your lips together, smooth the skirt of your golden Sunday dress. The tears that stood in your eyes, illuminating, or so it seemed, the blue of your irises, withdrew themselves—there was no other word for it. Not a one ever fell.

So that was you. And that was your mother. And that's how we met.

THE NEXT MORNING, before I was out of my dressing gown, a note arrived from Charlene—heavy paper, her three initials embossed on the card and on the envelope. In a lovely hand, blue ink, she invited me to lunch at her villa at eleven.

The house was behind a tall stucco wall, crowned with barbed wire and shards of glass, as was ubiquitous, even then. No doubt you remember. The caretaker—I thought of him as elderly, but I suspect he was not—came to the gate when I rang. He led me past a short green lawn that could have been out of suburban Westchester. There was even a whiffle ball on the grass. We crossed a portico. My memory of the house itself grows vague and merges with any number of villas I saw in my brief time there, but I recall most vividly the living room—the salon, Charlene always called it—and the sense of cool retreat after my short cab ride through the hot and clamorous streets.

The three women were gathered around a low cocktail table. I was immediately aware of the scent of their perfumes. Charlene stood as I was ushered in. She wore a square-necked, sleeveless sundress, polished cotton, I believe, form-fitting enough to remind me again of her slim tennis-playing figure. Her shoulders were tan, but also gloriously freckled—I'm not sure I'd noticed just how freckled the day before.

I recognized the lady from McLean—her name was Helen Bickford, her husband was with one of the big construction firms. The other woman, about thirty, was named Roberta. As I recall, her husband was with USIS. Roberta was wide-bottomed and full-faced. Her dark hair in a small bouffant. She wore a white shirtwaist with a thin black pinstripe, less elegant than Charlene's shift or Helen's signature (I was to learn) deep-pink knit but casual enough to alleviate my dismay that I had underdressed for the occasion: a simple blue seersucker dress with white flats. There was a sheen of perspiration under Roberta's makeup. I liked her better for it.

Charlene introduced me as Tricia. I had been Patty as a child, Patsy in college, Pat to my colleagues at school, and Miss Riordan to my students. Always Patricia to my father. I had no idea how to correct her politely, so Tricia I became.

I had assumed—for no reason—that I'd be lunching alone with Charlene, and I was both disappointed and impatient to learn this would be yet another occasion for steadying my hand as I reached out to greet the other women, for marshaling my best manners, making nervous small talk, for risking another social faux pas—although the evil infant was nowhere to be seen. No sign of little Rainey, either.

The ladies were drinking Manhattans. I'd never had one, but the man who had guided me into the room now carried a single glass on a small tray and held it before me. I suppose I hesitated. In truth, I would have preferred something cool and bubbly—maybe a tall Coke. Although the amber liquid in the small triangular glass looked elegant. The shadowy cherry.

Of course, Charlene saw my hesitation and rushed to ask, "Would you like something else? Lemonade, perhaps?"

I plucked the glass from the tray as if it might be swept out of my reach. "No, this is fine," I said. "This is lovely."

I would not have her make me childish again, not for anything.

The conversation I had walked in on—later I would wonder how it was that the other two ladies had arrived so much earlier than I, though I had appeared at the villa gate at precisely eleven—was about the Episcopal church, St. Christopher's, the church they all attended. A luncheon for a visiting bishop, or some such. What you might now call church lady talk: tea sandwiches were mentioned, tablecloths, the length of the service, the possibility that the ambassador and his wife would attend.

They begged my indulgence as they finished up what they called this bit of business, then directed their full attention to me: How long had I been here, how was I managing, had I learned the art of bartering, did I know the dress shop they all loved, was I being careful about everything I ate and drank?

It was clear that Charlene had already filled them in on my husband (which, it occurs to me only now, might have been the very reason they'd arrived earlier—to be filled in). But still they gave me ample opportunity to tell his story under the guise of telling ours; I think it was Roberta who asked, "And how did you two meet?"

There was no burden in this for me. Not yet married a year, I still sought every opportunity to say Peter's name. Because I was crazy about him. Because my timidity disappeared whenever Peter was the subject of my conversation.

Or should I say whenever Peter was the subject of my praise? Some parallel to the self-obliterating effect of prayer, I suppose.

I told them Peter was, like me, a kid from Yonkers—although we hadn't known each other growing up. He was eight years my senior. He'd spent two years in the navy straight out of high school and then, GI bill, went out to the Colorado School of Mines for his engineering degree. He'd returned to the neighborhood to live with his parents while attending Fordham Law.

"You don't imagine many boys from Yonkers," Helen said, "going out to the School of Mines."

Founded by another Episcopal bishop, the ladies noted, smartly, worldly-wise.

Smarter than them both, Charlene added, "They give out silver diplomas, don't they? Carved in silver. Such a lovely tradition."

"It is," I said. In truth, I knew about this but had never actually seen Peter's silver diploma. I imagined it was somewhere in his mother's attic. His parents, like mine, were first-generation Irish, and so not given to bragging about their smart children. No pleasure for them in making lesser mortals feel inferior.

Peter and I had met on the train going into the city one Saturday morning in mid-December, my senior year at Marymount. Love at first sight, you might say. The train was crowded with Christmas shoppers, and we were both standing, holding the same pole. I was, in fact, standing just under his raised arm. He was reading a paperback, he seemed absorbed in it, and each time he turned a page, he let go of the pole and just barely missed brushing my hat with his sleeve. I was deciding whether or not I should be annoyed by this when he suddenly leaned down to look through the windows. And then he asked me what station we'd just left, our bodies aligned as if for a kiss.

When we reached midtown, we got off and went our separate ways. I was on the street when I heard him behind me, calling, "Miss?"

I turned. I might not have recognized him if it hadn't been for the book in his hand. I was somewhat startled—I thought I'd dropped something. He stood speechless before me. I waited. I asked, "Yes?" And then I saw his resolve melt away—as if, for a moment, he'd lost track of what it was he'd wanted to say. Or—and this actually crossed my mind—he'd mistaken me for someone else. He was only a somewhat handsome young man, handsome in a usual, nondescript way, his pale face a smooth oval under his hat. (He'd prove to be better looking without the hat.) Average height, average build. Brown hair, brown eyes. This was New York City in the weeks before Christmas. Strangers were passing. Our breaths were visible before us. There was on that cold air the burnt smell of chestnuts and pretzels and bus fumes.

He said, "I'm going to spend the rest of my life regretting I never asked you for your name."

Roberta cried, "Oh, I love that." Helen said, "So sweet." Charlene said, "Clang, clang, clang went the trolley," and I knew I should cut my story short.

But not before I had offered these women the prize of my husband's career, his ambition, his future success, in much the same way I had offered these things to my father that evening when I told him I was going out with a young man I'd met on the train. ("A pickup?" he asked. Disapproval was my father's default position in all matters, especially my social life.)

Top of his class at the Colorado School of Mines, top of his class at Fordham Law, snapped up by Esso on Park Avenue at a fine salary for a young man from a middle-class family in Yonkers—it was where he was working when I met him— snapped up again by navy intelligence in Washington, D.C. Telling them this part of my history—and, of course, I saw my husband's history as my own—I was aware of the women's admiration, for his golden future, for my role in it as his helpmeet.

In those days, the war, Vietnam itself, was nothing at all like what it would become. Americans here were cautious, of course, hardly naive—there was barbed wire outside most every villa. There had already been scattered U.S. casualties, and Diem's Independence Palace had been bombed in an attempted coup the year before. We'd all read *The Quiet American*. *The Ugly American*, too.

But Saigon was still a lovely, an exotic, adventure (we'd also seen *The King and I*—in fact, I saw it four times)—and the cocoon in which American dependents dwelled was still polished to a high shine by our sense of ourselves and our great, good nation.

I told Peter's story, which was my own, and felt, what else to call it but patriotic pride. Saw that the three women felt it, too. Bright young men and their pretty little wives rising, rising, immigrant roots and working-class backgrounds be damned. Spine-straightening, tear-inducing, vaguely orgasmic—the Manhattan had its effect (I hope you're laughing)—patriotic pride in an American romance. God, what a country.

You'll have some idea of how uncomplicated our feelings at that moment were when I tell you that when Roberta asked, "And what brings him to Saigon?" I could offer no more detail than "a civilian advisor," and the work being done on the Saigon Electric Power Project. Which seemed to satisfy them. Certainly, it satisfied me.

Another servant, a woman this time, called us into the dining room. Gorgeous soft rolls, which I needed to counteract the alcohol in my empty stomach; a quiche (which I'd never heard of, never mind tasted, before); a beautifully arranged plate of fresh pineapples and mangoes; and delicate little cakes. After the coffee was brought in, Charlene stood, took the tray from her maid, placed it on the table, and then put her arm around the tiny woman. She introduced her with some brief nickname, sang her praises—the rolls, the quiche, the lovely cakes—declared that the entire family "adored" her, and asked us for a round of applause.

We happily complied, the poor woman bowing and grinning shyly.

Oh, I knew shy.

When she was dismissed, the conversation turned to how beloved by these women were the Vietnamese people—the servants especially.

We ourselves, in our town house, had a cook and a housemaid and a gardener who had come with the place, a trio, I must confess, I smiled at and thanked profusely but mostly tried to avoid. Peter was the one who told them what he wanted on those few occasions when what he wanted had not already been anticipated. My father was a high school janitor and my mother had worked for the phone company. And although I'd gone to Marymount with wealthy girls, still something in me balked at the very notion of having my own servants. I guess you could say I was progressive in the era's Catholic schoolgirl kind of way.

My decision to teach at the kindergarten in Harlem, for instance, had not been an arbitrary choice, even though it had annoyed and disappointed my father. ("Do something for the disadvantaged," he'd said, "and get it out of your system.") Preferential treatment for the poor was not a matter of debate, or even nuance, to my mind. It was rather, at that time, both an obligation and an inevitability. The Greater Good. We young Catholic women had only to determine what form of action that obligation would take. Each to her own talents, we'd been told. The kindergarten in Harlem was where I had thought my talents would be put to best use until I had children of my own.

Anyway, I could not see myself as a woman with servants.

I had thought, too, when we first arrived in Saigon, that I would continue the sweet domestic routine Peter and I had established in the months after our wedding, first in our little apartment on the Upper East Side, then in our new place in Arlington for the few months before we left the States. I hadn't returned to teaching after our wedding, mostly because Peter began to consider the job in Washington while we were still on our honeymoon, but also because we knew we'd be starting a family as soon as we could.

And so for those first few married months, I had my days free and my Betty Crocker cookbook (a shower gift) and the blissful (I don't use the word with any irony) determination to be the perfect helpmeet for my husband.

And, oh my gosh—does it even happen anymore?—I was so happy. Newlywed happy. Full of delight. Full of love. In love with the notion of our glorious, successful future together, but also in love with sex, with making love. Holy smoke, I did love it.

I was a virgin on my wedding night, and Peter was patient and dear and funny and gentle.

Of course I didn't ask him if he was a virgin, too—it's only now, after all these years, that I suspect he was not. At the time, I just assumed he had read the right books and manuals. He was an engineer, after all. Top of his class.

Our apartment in New York was tiny, our place in Virginia only slightly larger, but all the better, for me, to enjoy the small intimacies that were so new to us both. To wake in the morning in the same bed, tangled in the sheets I had washed and ironed (yeah, I did that)—the city sunlight across our pillows, across his ear or his stubbled cheek, across my hand on his arm, his hand on my breast, the sound of the traffic in the street only enhancing our sense of being apart from the world, preserved in amber.

And then to observe each other doing the most ordinary things: stretching, putting on slippers, stepping into the small bathroom (for years I ran the water in the sink while I peed), brushing teeth. Peter sang in the morning—it might have been his own way of disguising awkward sounds—but what a delight it was to me, to discover this. He sang mostly to himself, mostly show tunes, but what a rush of joy it was to hear him from behind the bathroom door as I made coffee, poured juice, boiled an egg for this man, this handsome stranger from the subway, who was now bending to kiss me, fragrant with soap and toothpaste. Smooth-shaven, smiling—lips that had given me a whole new appreciation for what lips could do. My husband.

And then, when he'd gone off to work—spiffy in his suit, his slap of aftershave—the day spent preparing for his return. Paging through Betty Crocker and making my shopping list.

Whether to go for one of his favorites or to try something new the biggest decision of the day. Shopping, baking, buying flowers, preparing dinner, setting the table, changing into something fresh and pretty.

But I make myself sound stupid. There were also lunches with college friends, volunteer days at my old school, visits to the library or the movies. Lectures and matinees. I read *The New York Times* every morning. *The Village Voice* every week. I was walking on air in those days, but I was not an airhead.

In the evening, there he was again, my husband, my beloved, sharing this small space. Peter always had a great story to tell from some encounter during the day. Always funny. He had a warm, amused, forgiving way of looking at the human race. Always a little distanced from it, a little puzzled by its many failings. I began to tell my friends that Peter had an Irish sense of humor, but only because I'd recognized something of the same in JFK at his press conferences. Until then, I'd thought the Irish, my relatives especially, mostly a dour lot.

I do believe that Peter was as happy as I was in those days. He'd work in our bedroom for another hour or two while I did the dishes and straightened up. Then we'd watch television in our tiny living room, or play some records, or read side by side. And then his hand on my thigh or in my hair and then naked in bed together—or, more thrilling still, on the couch together. How brazen and beautiful I thought myself, walking without clothes into the kitchen to fetch him a glass of water. We were very young, with a great deal to discover. And, God, I did love it, the newlywed sex—the best hours of the day. (That's plural.)

Looking back on those glorious first months of my married life, I confess I do wonder what ease, what pleasure, women have sacrificed since. Something to be said, I suppose, for the luxurious life of a contented concubine.

Of course, we had our more wholesome obligations as well.

Sunday mornings we took the train to Yonkers, went to Mass with my father, and then had ham and eggs in what I still thought of as my mother's kitchen. Peter would mow the lawn or weed the garden while I cleaned and dusted. Then the three of us would go over to Peter's family for five-o'clock dinner, where a good part of my pleasure was in seeing my father so enjoy the company: Peter's garrulous parents, his many siblings coming and going, new nieces and nephews beginning to appear. To see my widower father, as reticent and shy as I was, being absorbed with quiet affection into this new family of mine was another delight of those newlywed months. A delight that made my leaving him for Virginia, and then Saigon, tolerable.

WHEN WE ARRIVED IN VIETNAM, I thought our domestic routine would continue unchanged, but the housekeeper and the cook and the yard boy were already in place. And there were so many added complexities to running our small household. No doubt you remember some of these as well: tap water had to be boiled and chlorinated, and produce soaked in water and bleach (human feces was used as fertilizer, we were warned), and chicken was probably okay to buy but be careful of beef—might be water buffalo, might be dog. Never accept the first price. Never eat street vendor fare. Only canned fish. Safer to shop at the PX, not the market. Smarter to let the servants do the work.

But I wanted to shop at the market. I wanted to do the work.

I recall our hubris on that first morning in Saigon, our confidence, our Western centrism enhanced, inflated beyond all forgiveness, by our far more conceited, bone-deep New-Yorker-from-Yonkers self-regard.

We were giddy. We were probably still jet-lagged. We took a get-a-lay-of-the-city cyclo tour and spent most of it extolling the far superior vices and virtues of our hometown. That *What's the big deal?* impulse built into every New Yorker's DNA, I suppose. Tu Do Street, we said, looked like the Grand Concourse. The Notre-Dame Cathedral was no more beautiful than St. Patrick's. The traffic was terrible, but, hey, we'd driven through Times Square at noon. The odors, the poverty, sure, but ever been to the Bowery? The Central Market was a thrumming hodgepodge, but certainly no less mad than the Lower East Side on a Sunday morning. The waterfront wasn't the Fulton Fish Market. And the colonial buildings, the wide boulevards, lovely as they were, put us in mind of some of the bigger Mediterranean-style beach houses in the Rockaways, or at the Jersey Shore.

Yes. We said that—giddy and frightened and jet-lagged, viewing the city for the first time with our arms entwined and the Tilt-A-Whirl movements of the careening cyclo distorting, blurring, making a grand fun house adventure of it all.

IT MUST HAVE BEEN THE NEXT DAY when we ventured forth together to the Central Market. I suppose I was still thinking about how I would take up here in Saigon our happy newlywed routine: shopping in the morning, making dinner, welcoming Peter back from the larger world.

The market was, of course—I'm sure you remember—hot and teeming, teeming with people, noise, merchandise, odors: that awful nuoc mam. Peter had never been there either, but he had been to Hong Kong (or perhaps he had once again read the right books), so I accepted his authority as he attempted to instruct me about how to shop among the overcrowded stalls.

I was quickly nauseated—the heat, the din, the push and pull of bodies. I can still feel the wave of horror that nearly knocked me off my feet when I glimpsed a row of slaughtered monkeys hanging from a pole across the length of one of the stalls: milky gray, headless little corpses strung upside down, legs bound as if kneeling—looking for all the world like the pale bodies of sacrificed children.

After only a few minutes, I told Peter I had to leave. He laughed, as I recall, and led the way. He held my hand at first, as I trailed behind him with my head down, sick with the heat.

In the glare of the street—now I felt the throb of sunlight on my throbbing neck—a little girl suddenly stepped in front of me, a palm extended. I had by then lost Peter's hand. I saw her as if through the sound and tumult of shattering glass. Her hair was a tangle, her shirt worn thin as a fly's wing. She was solemn, almost indifferent, but so solidly before me I felt she was soldered to the ground.

I bent toward her, it was instinctual. And then she blinked, slowly, in that lovely way children have. The dirt in the creases of the palm she lifted toward me might have been an indication of her blighted future, her aborted lifeline. I would have been something less than human if I'd been able to push that little hand away. And so I bent, took her hand between my own. It was like cupping a small bird. She seemed too surprised to pull away.

"Here," I said. I reached into the pocket of my skirt (Peter had suggested I not bring a purse), found an American dime, put it in her hand.

In an instant I was surrounded, a sudden onslaught of little bodies, clamorous voices, a tangle of upturned palms, each one as dirty as the little girl's. She was immediately lost to me in this battering, either pushed aside or run away. The children were crying out, plucking at my clothes, pushing, grasping. As I straightened from my crouch, I felt them bumping against me, softly, insistently, touching, poking, my back, my shoulders, my hair. I might have been swimming up through a clutch of small limbs, some blasted, shipwrecked schoolyard.

I heard Peter call out and then felt his hand under my arm. He pulled me forward, but the children followed us. He began to swat at them, shouting objections in Vietnamese until we reached the end of the block and stumbled out into the street, where there were two traffic police—"white mice"—who waved their batons and spoke sharply until the children dispersed.

We walked a few blocks, Peter holding my arm as if we were still being pursued. Finally, he turned and said, no, shouted, "Did you give them money?"

Them. Decades later I hear the word again and know something of what was contained in it, ordinary as it seemed at the time.

"A little girl," I said, already chastised. I could see how hot and flushed he was.

"Never give them money," he said, his voice still raised, perhaps only to be heard above the traffic. Perhaps not. "I thought I told you. Don't give them any money."

It was the first time he'd ever spoken to me not as his wife but as his charge.

We'd only gone a few steps further, rounded a corner, when we encountered another child, rising up from the pavement as we passed, offering another filthy palm. This child was attached by a ragged rope to a very old man seated on a wheeled platform, wearing what I would later learn was a faded uniform from the French war. The man was legless. One of his stumps was touching the pavement, propelling him. The other, stretched before him on the wood, was festering, wet black flesh, green pus, streaks of fresh blood. This child was no older than the first, and whatever future his palm foretold was surely no better than hers. But I recoiled this time. I did not bend down. Peter and I easily skirted them and then hailed a cab.

The argument went that the household staff was accustomed to serving Westerners and knew everything there was to know about bleaching our vegetables and fruits and cooking our mostly Western-style meals. They knew how to protect our American tummies from Ho Chi Minh's revenge. (It happened anyway. It happened to everyone.)

"Just let them do it," Peter said. My talents would be better spent, he said, as a lady of leisure. Shop at the PX if you need to shop. Shop for souvenirs and dresses. Sleep in. Write letters home. Leave the essential things to the staff.

OVER OUR DELICATE DESSERTS, my luncheon companions were now exchanging charming anecdotes about their sweet houseboys and gardeners and cooks—it was hard to keep track of just how many servants they had among them—and although I had by then joined their privileged ranks, it occurred to me that their accounts sounded more like stories of earnest toddlers ("So much starch in his boxers, they could have stood up on their own") or loyal dogs ("And wouldn't you know, there he was, still waiting for me, the rain coming down, an umbrella at the ready. It never occurred to him to open it for himself"). The words they tossed about—"charming," "modest," "generous," "simple," "happy"—began to make me feel, even in those days when ethnic clichés were rampant, sullen and annoyed.

I suppose the effects of the Manhattan, and of the glorious tale I had told about my own (my husband's) rise into the upper echelons, had worn off. Something of the resentment I'd felt while exiled to the sewing room the day before began to rise to my throat again.

I was tempted to interject into the women's blithe praise of these lovely people some comment about that legless old beggar outside the marketplace. To make some mention of all the scrawny children in the streets and alleyways. Or perhaps, I thought, wickedly, I might just start shouting words like "cholera," "malaria," "typhoid," "scarlet fever," all those ancient plagues we'd been inoculated against before we arrived. Or perhaps, I thought—how about this, ladies—I could bring our twittering conversation to a halt by asking them what they made of the distant thudding of artillery we could hear from the other side of the river, even in those days, the distant tracing of fire we could see now and then from the happy confines of our barbed-wired homes.

I had a best friend from my Marymount days, Stella Carney,

an ace debater, a righteous, articulate opponent of what she called the complacent classes, and I longed at that moment to imitate her—to channel her, I suppose you'd say now.

Stella, I knew, would not sit here quietly absorbing this imperialist nonsense. Stella would have had the wherewithal, the historical and political savvy, to speak up, to debate—to make herself unpleasant among these women of privilege and ignorance.

But Stella was a rare bird in those days—and, in truth, as often as I was thrilled by her hubris, she embarrassed and dismayed me as well. Already, not two years out of Marymount, we were growing apart.

Righteous indignation was exhausting to maintain, even as a silent partner.

And you have to remember the times. At the time, my political understanding was inchoate and Saigon was an adventure. And as much as I resented these perfumed, politely chattering women, I wanted to be one of them. If only because I believed that when I held out my hand and made small talk and accepted their invitations (Roberta was having a luncheon at her home the following week, with a speaker, an American-Vietnamese cultural exchange; it would be wonderful if I could attend), I was somehow advancing my husband's illustrious career.

HELEN HAD A DRIVER OUTSIDE and offered the two of us a lift home. We were approaching my very favorite time of day in Saigon, the afternoon siesta, and despite my egalitarian disapproval of hiring household help, I was also anticipating, with great pleasure, what I knew would greet me when I returned to our town house. Our bedroom shutters drawn against the heat and the light. The fresh coverlet turned down. The air conditioner that had been working all morning to chill the fragrant room only recently hushed. The overhead fan moving silently. My dressing gown laid out across the bed. A bottle of cool Vichy water and a short, clean glass on the bedside table. A fresh flower or two in a vase beside them. A lit joss stick on the dresser. Luxurious midday sleep.

But Charlene put a hand on my arm. "Stay for a minute," she said, as the other two ladies offered their cheeks to say goodbye.

She asked, as soon as they'd left, "Can I get you anything else?" in that unholy way she had (sorry if I repeat myself) of making you feel she was doing you a favor by letting you fulfill her any request. She, after all, had asked me to stay, but it seemed now that she was, politely, with infinite patience, indulging my desire to linger.

I assured her that I needed nothing, that the luncheon had been lovely.

She crooked her finger at me. "I have something to show you," she said.

We hadn't far to go. She led me to a small room just off the villa's entrance. Her office. There was a desk before a broad window that showed the shaded portico outside, a couple of rattan chairs, a bookcase containing only a few native knickknacks: jade elephants, carved Buddhas, that sort of thing. Most memorable, however, were the boxes and slatted shipping crates scattered across the tile floor. Some were stuffed with straw. Some packed neatly with books, or folded shirts or dresses—children's clothes.

She waved her hand over the mess. "All my little efforts," she said.

No further explanation was forthcoming.

She moved behind the desk, and I suddenly felt as if I had been called in for an interview. Or a reprimand. As she sat, I saw two things at once. First, Rainey's Barbie doll, sitting up in that slightly obscene, stiff-legged way of dolls without bendable knees, leaning against a stacked pile of cardboard matchboxes. Barbie was still dressed in the white ao dai Lily had made, but now she wore as well a replica of the conical hat all the Vietnamese women wore—magically shrunk to Barbie size. Authentically enough, two thin black strings dangled past her ears with their little pearl earrings.

As Charlene took her chair behind the desk, she lifted the doll to show me.

"What do you think?" she said. She waved it about a bit. Under the hat, the blond ponytail was now immobile.

I was honestly amazed. "Adorable," I said. "Wherever did you find it?"

I was beginning to recognize her only vaguely apologetic smarter-than-you-are tone of voice.

"I happen to know the woman—I call her Weezie—at the market who makes these. Non las, they're called—did you know?"

I said I did, although I didn't.

"So I swung by to see her this morning," she went on. "I'd been out and about. Went by Maison Rouge and bought a lovely bolt of silk to bring to Lily. And then retrieved poor Barbie when I dropped it off at the Cases'. Lily's made herself a paper pattern, so Barbie's modeling duties are over. With Barbie in hand, I stopped by to see Weezie, to see what was possible."

All that went unsaid—how early she had risen and how industrious she'd been in the hours before our lovely luncheon, hours that I had spent trying on dresses and fixing my hair—played about her opened-mouth smile: the unspoken boast we both agreed, without speaking, she had every right to make. "I want to charge two bucks for them. I mean, the outfit now looks incomplete without it. Everyone will want one."

The second thing I noticed, now that Saigon Barbie was aloft in Charlene's hand, was that the pyramid of matchboxes on her desk was not matchboxes at all but pillboxes—the way prescription pills were dispensed in those days (you're too young to remember). There must have been fifty of them.

"Or maybe three?" Charlene asked. "Weezie and I had some trouble figuring out how to make it stay put over the glued bangs and the damn ponytail, but it turns out Barbie's head is quite penetrable." She turned the doll this way and that, lifting the hat a bit to show me how it had been anchored. "A couple of straight pins was all it took."

I suppose I drew in my breath.

I thought briefly of your unshed tears when you learned your Barbie was to stay with Lily. I thought, as I'd thought then, that Charlene had not been the kind of child to imagine full life—with all its attendant affection and compassion and grief—for her dolls and stuffed animals. The kind of child I had been. The kind of child you were.

Charlene laughed at my grimace. "No more painful, Tricia," she said, "than what we endure with our rollers and bobby pins."

As if she had seen me this morning, anchoring those bristled rollers in my hair, burning the tips of my ears under the bouffant cap of my portable hair dryer.

Charlene examined the doll again, adjusted the little hat. "It's what my mother would have called cunning."

And then she looked up at me, a different expression altogether on her pert and sun-kissed face. A sadness, perhaps.

"My mother," she said, "was a fading Southern belle who married a bankrupt Main Line Yankee." She grew quiet, perhaps pensive. Once again, she had managed to become the only person in the room.

I waited. It seemed a peculiar hush. I guess I hoped that she was about to tell me a charming story about her parents' romance, something to match my own romantic tale—perhaps even to mitigate the embarrassment I would feel only a few hours later when I recalled how I had babbled on about Peter. Or maybe, I thought, she was about to tell me something real about herself: a nickel-and-dime childhood or her love for a dead mother. Something we could share.

I waited. The silence grew awkward, wrong. Charlene was looking off into some middle distance, completely still, except for the quick, unconscious way the thumb and ring finger of her right hand were touching, rubbing.

I began to believe this silence was the result of yet another faux pas I had made—I had not managed to keep the conversation going. In a ridiculous kind of desperation I suddenly heard myself exclaim, "You're both Scarlett O'Hara *and* Princess Grace!"

Like an idiot sorority sister waving pom-poms.

Charlene glanced up at me as if I were some harsh light that had just blinked on. I saw her flat face press itself against the invisible force field of my silliness.

There was another kind of silence into which my shouted

words dispersed, disappeared. And then Charlene said softly, businesslike once more, "What I'd like to do is to include the hat in the price and raise it to seven dollars for the whole deal. But too late for that, I suppose." She consulted the yellow legal pad beside her. "I picked up four more orders this morning," she said. And then she returned the doll to its splayed-leg position, gazed at it with some silent assessment, then folded her hands before her, and once more turned her eyes to me.

"How much does your husband make?" she asked me.

Across all these decades, you cannot imagine how rude and inappropriate, even startling, the question was. She might just as well have asked me how I enjoyed oral sex.

I stammered that I didn't really know—I didn't really know—and suddenly she launched into a precise delineation of her own household accounts: her husband's salary, what the company paid for, how much she was given as a monthly allowance, how she spent it, saved it, distributed it among her children and the servants. All of it very precise, and as I said, in that day and age, very startling.

I made some awkward attempt to explain that since we were childless, we were not as strict about our household accounts as she, so admirably, was. When I needed money for something—clothes, perfume, gifts to bring home—I simply asked Peter for whatever I thought it would cost, and he gave me the cash.

She raised those fierce eyebrows. "Just like that?"

"Yes," I said, although, of course, in truth, there would be a playful cross-examination. "Another dress? How many dresses can you wear at once?" Or some vaudevillian riff on why he should have stayed a bachelor. Sometimes he'd croon, "She wears silk underwear, I wear my last year's pair. Hey, boys, that's where my money goes." Fondly, I should add, the prelude to a dance around our bedroom. Although I confess such kidding did prolong the agony of having to put my hand out in this way.

"And spending money?" Charlene asked.

At home, Peter used to leave twenty dollars, a ten, a five, five ones, in my jewelry box every Sunday night. Here, he did the same, but in a mix of American dollars and piastres tucked into a lovely lacquered box decorated with the Xa Loi Pagoda—one of the first souvenirs I'd picked up in Saigon.

"If you want to give me your American dollars," Charlene said coolly, "I can return them to you double their worth. For a small commission, of course."

I was so dazed I actually asked her, "How?"

She paused. "There's a jeweler I know," she began, and then waved her hand. "It's dreary old black-market stuff," she said. "Not interesting at all."

And then once more her eyes went to that middle distance, her two circulating fingertips the only indication that she was thinking—thinking, as I came to see it, ferociously.

Suddenly she said, "I want to do good." She said it with the same calculation and dispassion with which she had said, "I want to charge two bucks."

"There's so much wretchedness," she added.

I assumed at the time she meant in Vietnam, but looking back on it, I'm certain she meant in the world at large.

"It takes money," she said.

She stood, began to make a brief tour of the crates and the boxes scattered about the room. She had a sister in New York, she told me—the businesswoman aunt you had mentioned at the garden party—an executive secretary at Macy's. "We're a two-woman relief organization," she said. "Completely haphazard," she said, although somehow I doubted it. Charlene saw a need and wrote to her sister, and the two of them went about seeing what they could do. Clothes were the easiest things to obtain—her sister could make good use of her employee discount as well as, Charlene said, "the five-fingered kind." Apparently, her sister had a special friend who was in charge of the loading dock for the world's largest store.

She indicated the box of folded children's clothes. These were bound for an orphanage outside the city.

The books, mostly children's books and classics, were for the Vietnamese women and girls that Helen and Roberta—"whom you met today"—and some other ladies were tutoring. "Trying to keep them out of the whorehouses," Charlene said. "Or get them out. Get them real jobs with Americans or Europeans, if we can."

She looked around. "What else can I tell you? Shipping costs are a problem. My sister does well enough, but she also has rent to pay and our aging alcoholic father to look after. If you can give me your American dollars, I'll get you an exchange rate your husband wouldn't dream of. I'll take a little off the top. That— along with your brilliant Barbie fundraiser—will be a lovely contribution to the cause."

"Fine," I said.

She lit a cigarette, barely inhaled. "Tell me what you think of this," she went on, both of us knowing she was not actually seeking my opinion. "If we can store up some funds, I'll ask my sister to send me a few dozen actual dolls—Barbies—at a good discount, of course. We can dress them in Lily's ao dais, pin on Weezie's hats, and sell them for twenty-five dollars at the officers' club."

"Twenty-five?" I asked. It seemed an outrageous sum. It was an outrageous sum.

She shrugged. "We'll only get so far selling these outfits to mothers and aunties. We need a male clientele. And a lot of our American men over here have no idea whether their daughters back home have Barbie dolls or baby dolls. Or cleft palates and missing limbs, for that matter. If we can sell them the actual dolls, already dressed, we won't have to worry about straining their brain cells to recall how old their daughters are and what kind of dollies they play with. No doubt they'll buy one for their wives and girlfriends, too." She lowered her voice and smiled a crooked smile. "Although I do worry about the girlfriend part. I worry about stirring their limited imaginations."

She studied me from under those luxurious brows. She saw, I suppose, that I wasn't quite following. She reached up to flick her cigarette into a silver dish on her bookshelf. "What I'm saying is I just hope they don't get carried away thinking they're buying replicas of their favorite prostitutes." And she shook her tanned, freckled American-girl shoulders, shuddering.

Looking back, I'm amazed to remember how steadily I remained upright through all this speaking about things mostly unspoken of. Our husbands' salaries. Our own allowances. The black market. Shoplifting. Prostitutes. The cleft palates of the generals' daughters. I'd been raised with all the lace-curtain refinements of the era, an era when so many words, so many concepts, were verboten. My friend Stella Carney could talk politics with the aplomb and seriousness of any man, but our conversations about sex were always full of euphemisms, winks, and nods.

And although, as I said, I'd known wealthy girls at school,

and I certainly knew something about fundraising, I had never encountered this kind of—what to call it?—grossly mercenary matter-of-factness. Not in any females of my acquaintance.

Charlene and I both turned our eyes to the seated Barbie. Even with her white skin and her blond ponytail flattened beneath her hat, she did indeed seem a somewhat more buxom replica of the lovely young girls of Saigon. I noticed for the first time that her eyes were almond-shaped.

With a laugh, Charlene cried out, "How sick would that be? Generals beating off on our sweet Barbies. Getting their goo on Lily's pretty handiwork."

Perhaps I did waver a bit then, because Charlene suddenly took my arm, much as she had done in the garden just the day before, aligning our hips, holding her cigarette away as you did in those days when you smoked around a child.

"Lily's making great progress," she said. "So if you'll swing by Marcia Case's villa next Wednesday morning as we planned, pick up the outfits, and drop them here—just give them to the houseboy, I'll be out of town—I'll wrap them up nicely and start delivering to the ladies. Once I've collected the cash, I'll see my money guy. Then, on Saturday morning, we can visit the children and bring our little gifts. You'll come, yes?"

"Yes," I said.

"You go to Mass at the cathedral?" she asked.

I was already too nonplussed to be further nonplussed by this non sequitur. "Yes," I said.

She reached toward the bookcase to stamp out her cigarette. "Of course," she said. "You're the Kellys. What was your maiden name?"

"Riordan," I said.

She laughed her *I'll apologize for laughing at you later* laugh. As uncontrollable as a sneeze. Who can be blamed for a sneeze? "Of course it was," she said.

She pulled me a bit closer. "But would you be my guest at St. Christopher's, our church, this Sunday? You and your husband, of course. We only have the one service, at eleven, so if you wanted to catch a Mass at the cathedral earlier in the day . . ."

She hesitated. "I guess you don't say 'catch a Mass.'"

"No," I said.

She fluttered her fingers as if to clear away the smoke—to clear away any notion that she'd misspoken. "It's just that your presence will give me a chance to sell a few more outfits. I'll have my Rainey put the ao dai in her purse. I don't allow her to bring dolls to church. After the service, I can introduce you to the various ladies over the lemonade and cookies, mention your wonderful fundraiser, and Rainey can produce the outfit. All completely spontaneous. I do hate a hard sell. And if the ambassador and his wife are in town, so much the better. Little Caroline Kennedy just may end up with one of our Saigon Barbies. Can you imagine?"

I barely noticed that as she spoke, she was moving us imperceptibly toward the door.

I said I'd ask my husband. In truth, I wasn't sure Peter would be willing to show up at a Protestant church.

Just as we were about to cross the threshold of her office, Charlene laughed again. "Tricia," she said, with some sudden exasperation—once more we were fond friends from a long-ago girlhood, a history of sleepovers between us—"aren't you going to ask me about the pillboxes?"

Of course, I immediately glanced at the boxes piled behind the Barbie on her desk, even as I said, as if I had no idea, "I'm sorry?"

"You can't be as incurious as you pretend," she said flatly. "Not that I blame you. Vagueness is a wonderful defense." She laughed. "Librium," she said. "Have you taken it?"

I said I had not.

"Calms you down," she said. "I have my own prescription but my sister has another friend in pharmaceuticals. My sister has many friends. I'll make some money on about half of them." And then, as if I hadn't caught on: "Black market," she whispered.

Even still, I didn't swoon. "What about the other half?" I asked her.

She smiled, fondly, still in her *Isn't that just like you?* mode.

"Those are for little ole me," she said. Those straight teeth and those flashing green eyes. "Night terrors," she said. Only the corners of her smooth lips turned down. "I wouldn't wish them on Khrushchev."

SHE OFFERED TO WALK ME to the street to get a cab, but just as we returned to the foyer, you came in through the villa's front door, followed by your father.

You looked up at me, fondly, I thought, if a little startled, and said, "Hello, again." Very adult. Your mother corrected you: "Mrs. Kelly. Good afternoon, Mrs. Kelly," and admonished, you repeated the phrase, holding out your little hand, which felt so hot in mine I wondered for a moment if you were running a fever. I wanted to tell you immediately that your Barbie was home, on the desk in your mother's office and wearing a new hat, but I sensed this was Charlene's news to deliver—or, I imagined, to withhold.

Charlene was explaining that the American school didn't go until three—"as we do back home"—because of the heat. "Which delights this child to no end," she added. "No scholar here."

I saw how you ducked your head under the blow of this maternal jibe. I understood that you considered us equals and did not appreciate being made childish in my presence. I got it.

Kent, your father, was a tall guy who seemed to take up all the space in the wide foyer. He was good-looking, with a big face and straight white teeth to match Charlene's. Despite the glistening sweat across his forehead, he managed to keep a Kennedy-esque wave in his damp hair. He needed a shower—his shirt front was dark with perspiration and his pale suit jacket looked limp, puckered at the armpits. This whiff of male body odor was a familiar scent in those days. People forget. (I hope you're laughing again, although it's true.) He carried a leather school-bag, which he handed to you before he shook my hand.

That scent of leather, of manly sweat, can evoke for me, to this day, my time among the American men in Vietnam as much as the smell of diesel fuel or fish sauce brings back Saigon itself.

Charlene introduced me as "Peter Kelly's wife," and although Kent said, "Of course, Pete," he gave no indication that he remembered me from the day before. Or that he had seen his baby chucking up all over my dress.

And then, as if I had conjured the child, one of the servants entered the salon behind us with Charlene's baby on her shoulder.

Kent's face lit up. It's a cliché, but there you go: that's what happened. "Hey, there he is," he exclaimed, and seemed ready to leave us behind. But Charlene took his arm. "Tricia's just leaving," Charlene told him. "Will you walk her out and get her a cab?"

He bowed. "Of course." But the faux gallantry could not hide the fact that this was the last thing he wanted to do.

I objected. Charlene insisted. And then Kent made a joke about who wore the pants in this family of his. A familiar married-man joke. In response, Charlene ducked her head in much the same way her daughter had just done: aware of the attempt to diminish her in front of a new friend. Acquiescent but not happy.

"Sunday, then," she said to me. She did not lean forward to air-kiss or touch cheeks as the other ladies had done. I was just as well pleased. "I'll look for you after the service."

And I plunged into the midday heat with her husband clasping my elbow.

As we crossed the portico he said, "Pete tells me you've settled in Virginia now, is that right?"

"Hardly settled," I told him. "We had only a few weeks before we came here. My sister-in-law is minding the house till we get back—"

"I grew up in Virginia," he said, speaking over me as if he hadn't heard a word I said. Perhaps he hadn't—he was very tall. "Both Virginia and New York." (I promise you I did not foolishly cry out, "Thomas Jefferson! Al Smith!") "Virginia is much nicer. Make Pete keep you in Virginia."

We'd barely left the gate when a noisy little Renault pulled up to the curb. Those ubiquitous blue-and-white taxis. You remember, I'm sure. Kent opened the door for me and then reached into his pocket to pay the driver. I tried to object, but he held up his hand as he leaned into the window, said a few quick words in French to the young man behind the wheel. Over the noise of the engine, I shouted my thanks, and he replied with the full charm of his good looks and straight teeth and wilted JFK pompadour.

"Just don't let Charlene lure you into her cabal," he said. And the cab pulled away.

When I leaned forward to give the driver my address, he waved his hand as if to brush a whining mosquito from his ear. "I got it. I got it," he said.

And took me to our door. I guess I wondered at the time how it was that Kent did not know that Peter never went by "Pete"—no more than I had ever gone by "Tricia"—and yet he knew where we lived. It was a mystery I never bothered to explore.

AFTER SOME INITIAL DOUBT—of the *How will it look?* sort—Peter agreed to attend the Episcopal service. A gesture in keeping, he reasoned, with the good pope's move toward (a new word for us) ecumenical understanding. As long as we sat in the back and didn't receive communion. And went to the earlier Mass at the cathedral, of course.

We would not have believed, in those days, that a Protestant mass was a legitimate substitute for our Sunday obligation. Mere bread and wine versus actual body and blood. Mere ceremony versus miraculous transubstantiation. That sort of thing.

The president of the United States was a Catholic then and so, still, was the president of Vietnam and his family. Years later, really toward the end of his life when he spoke about these things more freely, Peter told me how important it had been to him in those days that the U.S. was supporting a Catholic regime in Vietnam.

There was to his mind, then anyway, something divinely ordained about Diem and his brother and even Madame Nhu, as crass and vain as some of us found her.

Personally, I never forgave her for her "barbecue" remark after the first Buddhist monk set himself on fire—what was it she'd said? One can't be responsible for the madness of others. And yet, she had banned contraception and abortion and closed the dance halls, as a good Catholic sovereign should.

It was a rough alliance, Peter admitted, our shoring up the Diem regime, full of compromise, but an alliance that seemed to portend the redemption he so believed in then. Redemption not just for the Far East but for all the world, for all of us in it.

BEFORE WE WERE MARRIED, Peter's mother had shown me a small gift she was waiting to bestow, "when the time comes." It was a diaper pin—does your generation even remember there was such a thing?—with a pale blue plastic cover at the top and a tiny blue medal attached to the circle of steel at the bottom. A medal so small that it took me a moment to decipher it: an image of the Virgin Mary, a Miraculous Medal, in the parlance of our times.

Peter, she told me, had been dedicated to the Blessed Mother at his baptism, and had worn this medal on his diapers until he grew old enough to wear a larger version around his neck. I was familiar with this larger version. He wore it every day under his clothes.

I'm not sure, to be honest, what people know anymore. So much that was common knowledge back then is a cipher now. Do you know what I refer to when I say Fátima? A small village in Portugal where the Blessed Mother appeared on multiple occasions to three peasant children. This was during the First World War. The Virgin asked the children to tell the world to pray the rosary. She promised that if Russia could be consecrated to her sacred heart, communism and all its pernicious errors—atheism, materialism, war and persecution and moral confusion—would be defeated. Satan's "diabolical disorientation"—as the nuns at Marymount used to put it—would not overwhelm us.

Peter owned a copy of a full account of the apparition at Fátima, published in the late 1940s and written by a priest who seemed to have interviewed all the participants and witnesses—those still alive, anyway. Peter brought the book to our first apartment. It was dog-eared, the spine nearly broken, even then. It was one of the first books he asked me to read.

And it led to one of our first spats.

Early in the account, during one of the apparitions, Lucy, the oldest of the three children and the chief spokesperson (we'd say now), asked the Blessed Mother about two little friends of hers who had recently died.

Mary answered that one of the girls was with her in heaven, but the other was still in purgatory.

I remember telling Stella Carney about this when we met for lunch in Manhattan, not long after Peter and I returned from our honeymoon. Stella was already expecting her first child—the culprit, as she called him, who had kept her from being the matron of honor at my wedding, since, in those days, pregnant women were not allowed to walk down the aisle.

Stella argued that it was highly unlikely that a small shepherd child in Portugal who had died so young could have sinned enough to earn herself a stint in purgatory.

Maybe, Stella said in her own smarter-than-everyone way, the dead little girl had been a rival, and Lucy's report that the

Virgin said the child had not yet made it to heaven was only a bit of petty girlish revenge.

Girls—especially Catholic girls, Stella added—can be so catty.

"Don't you and I know it," she said.

That night, laughing, I told Peter about Stella's theory.

He was not amused. In fact, he plucked the worn book from my hands. Threatened to withhold it from me until I had "gained some faith."

I was a bit startled, but nevertheless full of regret. I loved him all the more for this unaccustomed glimpse into his very serious soul.

HARD TO UNDERSTAND IT NOW, I suppose, but my husband, for all his education and his worldliness—the navy and Colorado and law school and Esso on Park Avenue—had a deep and abiding, old-fashioned kind of faith. God become Man and the seven sacraments, transubstantiation, our infallible pope, and our immortal souls. His own life dedicated at birth to the Mother of God.

He believed entirely in the promise of the apparition at Fátima, that Russia would be converted. He believed communism would be defeated, in Russia, in China, here in Vietnam, not merely by the superior military power of the West, not even by mankind's own yearning to breathe free, but by the intercession of Mary.

How peculiar it must seem to you—not only that Peter believed entirely in the promise the Virgin had made, but that he believed fully in the apparition itself, believed that the gentle Mother of God had appeared on earth in 1917, in the same body that had given birth, in the very usual way, to the Savior of the World.

Thinking of Stella, my irreverent friend, I wonder now if Mary appeared at Fátima in a matronly body, a belly pouched by childbirth, downward-turning breasts, a laugh line or two, or was it the trim, immaculate body she had inhabited before the angel appeared? A postpartum body or a pre-? As I recall it, the priest's account of the apparition at Fátima said the children claimed the lady was beautiful, but how to interpret that beauty now? How to gauge the opinion of children who had never seen a Disney princess, or a Miss America, or a dewy movie star on the silver screen? It seems quite possible that a mother's body, a mother's careworn face, would have been more beautiful to these peasant children than a slim teenage figure not unlike their own.

I'm pretty sure that if there is indeed a resurrection of the body, as we Catholics are meant to believe, then my own mother will not appear at our reunion in the spectator shoes and permanent waves of her youth, but as I knew her in the brief time we shared: softly plump and weary-eyed, plain and dear.

Faithful as he was, Peter believed that a Catholic regime in this small country, a charismatic Catholic president in our own country, were indications enough that Mary's promise, the hope she had offered in that spongy Portuguese grazing field, was slowly but inexorably moving toward its fulfillment.

I guess you could say our sense that we were a part of the one true faith was pretty solid in those days. Or maybe I should say that mine was solid because I so trusted my husband to be right.

I'M RECALLING NOW something Peter told me in this regard—again, this was many years later. He said when he was first recruited for intelligence work, he was both intimidated and impressed by the men who were offering to make him a colleague. They were WASPy Ivy Leaguers, uniformly fit, born to privilege and yacht clubs and, to his mind, old money—old, he said, but still virile enough to keep reproducing itself effortlessly. (That was Peter's sense of humor.) Even the secretaries, he said, were beautiful girls from the best schools.

Made him feel something like a clodhopper, was how he put it.

And yet he was told in an early interview, by a man who had been recruited for the OSS by Wild Bill Donovan himself, that it was Catholics they were seeking. Who better understood the threat of godless communism?

In the middle of their conversation, Peter's interviewer had reached into his pocket and placed a black rosary on the desk before him. Wordlessly, Peter did the same.

The Catholic Intelligence Agency was the joke.

PETER DIDN'T MUCH LIKE CHARLENE. When I told him she wanted us to come to the Episcopal service in order to expedite the selling of the Barbie ao dais, and thus to raise funds for all her good little works, he said, "She's a dynamo, isn't she?"—not as a compliment.

Uncertain as I was about the word "cabal"—there was no dictionary at our town house—I never mentioned to Peter your father's peculiar warning. Neither did I mention the black-market money exchange, or the pillboxes, or the Manhattans, for that matter.

I was aware that it was not like me—not like us—to keep such things hidden from each other. I knew, in other circumstances, I could have made a funny story out of the luncheon: Helen Bickford's girlish pink knits, the tortuous celebration of that shy housekeeper. I knew we would have speculated about what kind of guy Kent really was, or what Charlene was after—all the delicious mysteries of other people's marriages. But I didn't say a word. Maybe this strange, small silence was the beginning of my loyalty to a new woman friend. Or maybe the first small fissure in our post-newlywed lives.

Anyway, Charlene picked up twenty new orders in the hour after church. Enough to keep Lily busy for another week.

And you, Rainey, as I recall, were a charming little saleswoman. Every bit your mother's daughter.

I SHOULD TELL YOU MORE about my friend Stella Carney. She was like your mother in so many ways. Her precursor, I suppose.

Stella drove a kelly green, utterly ramshackle Volkswagen bug. She'd bought it, "used and abused," she said, from a newspaper ad, repainted it herself, and then christened it FIFAL: Freedom, Independence, Flight, At Last. She drove it across the Queensboro Bridge every morning with the passenger window stuck open, the hole for the missing cigarette lighter crossed with electrical tape, and the interior scattered with books and notepapers, discarded tissues, candy wrappers, tickets.

Seeing the little car squeezed into various parking spaces around the Upper East Side was for me somehow akin to running into Stella herself, since she, too, was always half-buttoned, disheveled, her smudged glasses repaired with tape and her books and papers an unwieldy bundle in her arms. She was tall, rangy, square-hipped, and pigeon-toed. There was always ink somewhere, on her fingers or her blouse, the corner of her mouth. Up close, she gave off a scent that was something like pencil shavings.

In the classes we shared at Marymount, Stella was ardent,

argumentative—leaning in to every discussion, sixty years before that term referred to anything other than one's posture. I remember how her large hands left puckered sweat marks on the lined pages of her notebooks. How her voice rose and fell in various registers of outrage or irony as she questioned whatever was being offered: the interpretation of a poem, the accuracy of a historical account, the end result of a complex equation.

She read everything, accepted none of it unconditionally. (She's the one who got me reading *The Village Voice*.) She volunteered for JFK's campaign but called him a phony baloney, a cold warrior, a rich jerk. She rode Fifal downtown two or three times a week to volunteer at the *Catholic Worker*, but said everyone there was a creep, an idiot, or a hanger-on. She told me Dorothy Day had no sense of humor.

In class, whenever anyone asked if she was a Democrat or a Republican, she said neither. She was irritated.

I recall a morning, before I knew her well, when the city held one of those duck-and-cover air-raid drills that now seem such a relic of the era. To be honest, I loved these drills, the drama of them. I loved the thrilling way the sirens permeated the atmosphere, as if from some godly source, a sky-wide soundtrack that sent all the bustling world—my father at work in the Bronx, our neighbors in Yonkers, strangers in midtown, even businessmen on Wall Street—into the same quick, obedient pursuit of shelter, whether basements or subway stations or the undersides of kitchen tables.

At school, we slipped beneath our desks or lined the tiled corridors and crouched against the wall. We prayed out loud during the eight minutes until the all clear sounded. Even as I prayed, I entertained a heart-thudding vision of my postapoca-lyptic life: hopping heroically over a smoking, smoldering waste-land, rescuing from the ruins small children, frightened puppies, a series of only mildly injured but passionately grateful young men.

On that spring morning when the siren sounded through Manhattan, our freshman English class dutifully stood and headed for the hallway. But Stella remained in her seat, calmly reading. When the instructor asked her to comply, she looked up from her book, licked her finger as if in prelude to turning the page, and said, to him and to those of us who lingered long enough to see what would become of her, "Don't you know this is ridiculous?"

A simple enough thing to say, I suppose, although until that moment I'm not sure any of us was truly aware that we did know this—knew that the whole exercise was ridiculous.

The teacher did his best. Fines were mentioned, the possibil-ity of arrest, the risk to the college community, the importance of national unity. Stella merely shrugged. With the siren echo-ing, the poor man locked the classroom door, Stella still inside with her book, and joined us on the floor of the corridor. He was a sad, slim young man, always in the same dark suit and narrow tie. Stella told me once that he would have had a happy life if he'd never read a poem. I recall his lavender socks as he hitched up his pant legs and squatted among us, avoiding our eyes. We, his stu-dents, we Marymount girls, tucked our loafers under our bot-toms and pulled our skirts over our knees, fully knowing, now anyway, that this was, of course, a sham.

Somehow or other, Stella and I became fast friends. I suppose she was grateful to discover one girl in the school who didn't find her opinions dismaying. I was grateful to find someone who demanded to know what I thought. Stella wanted a sparring partner; I wanted someone who understood I was smarter than my shyness made me appear.

Anyway, we became a pair.

Once, I followed her to City Hall Park, for an annual demonstration against these very same ridiculous air-raid drills. Dorothy Day and a few other *Catholic Worker* "weirdos" had initiated the protests, Stella told me, and in years past they'd been arrested and released. But then they were sentenced to thirty days in jail. Dorothy had written about her experience, and, according to Stella, the publicity was not good for the powers that be. "An old lady like that," Stella said. "Thrown in jail with hopheads and lesbians."

Stella's own plan was for us to go downtown to this year's demonstration, to refuse to take shelter, and to get ourselves arrested instead—sacrificial lambs, she called us.

"They'll want to arrest somebody," she told me. "They have to. But they won't want Dorothy again. We'll let them take us."

I was reluctant—I worried what my father would say—but I was also, in those days, easily led. And much as I parroted Stella's courage and outrage, I was pretty certain that no policeman was going to throw girls like us into a paddy wagon, nice Catholic girls in pedal pushers and ponytails, our First Communion crucifixes on thin gold chains around our fair necks.

That morning, we parked Fifal somewhere downtown and made our way to City Hall on foot. I had convinced myself by then that we would quietly secure a bench in some leafy part of the park and then sit stubbornly but pleasantly, our hands

folded in our laps, as the sirens sounded and the rest of the obedient city went underground. I imagined saintly Dorothy Day
(my father called her a communist, but Stella knew better) on
another bench nearby. I imagined she would catch my eye ap-
provingly, send me a serene smile.

But as we approached the park, we saw that we were not to be
the protest's sole sacrificial lambs. There was a crowd, in fact, already well spread out onto the surrounding streets. Many looked
to be university students like ourselves, many others looked to
be their professors. There were also what Stella called the usual
placard-carrying kooks, some of them crazy-eyed and malodor-
ous, others looking like businessmen and secretaries.

And young women, lots of them, young mothers, to be precise, many with children in strollers. Well-dressed young mothers
who stood in tight groups, laughing and gossiping (it was Stella
who accused them of gossiping), the tangled wheels of their
strollers making our way impassable. Young mothers just taking
up space. (Stella's words again.) Some of them told us as we tried
to push through that a police line had already been set up. Dorothy Day and the others were inside the park—Norman Mailer
was there, someone said. But we could get no closer.

I was no doubt relieved. There was a carnival atmosphere, a
sense of triumph even before the sirens began. But Stella grew
furious as we navigated the crowd. She bounced impatiently
on her tiptoes, trying to see over heads and shoulders. She
abruptly—rudely, I thought—touched the backs of strangers to
move them out of her way. She ranged impatiently this way and
that, a tiger in a cage, sometimes pushing me ahead of her, sometimes leaving me to catch up.

At one point, we made it to a curb where there was a police

barricade. Stella suddenly ducked to go under it, but a young cop gently blocked her way, simply by placing his hand on the top of her head. He said, pleasantly enough, I thought, "Come on, sweetheart," touching her elbow to get her upright again on the proper side of the barricade. He was a redhead, with piercing blue eyes under the rim of his cap, crooked teeth in his grin. Not much older than we were. I know I smiled at him, even as Stella flailed to get his hand off her arm. I followed her as she turned back into the crowd. Everyone else was smiling, too.

AS WE CROSSED THE BRIDGE late that afternoon—I was sleeping over again at her parents' house in Woodside—Stella banged the heel of her palm on Fifal's steering wheel (a dirty bone white, as I recall it, like something out of a reliquary) when I remarked that the size of the crowd was surely an indication of the protest's success. She disagreed.

Of course she disagreed.

Shouting above the traffic that roared through the stuck-open window, above Fifal's farting engine, she quoted Stalin at me, "If one man dies of hunger, that is a tragedy. If millions die, that is a statistic."

A gathering of the masses was not what she had hoped for. The voice of the masses, she shouted, is an incoherent din. One person is what is needed. One, *one*. Again she struck the wheel.

One person bloodied, arrested, photographed by the *Daily News*, named, interviewed, sent to trial. That's what was needed. Crowds are a joke, she said. Mass protest is a joke. (She was nearly crying.) Who cares if a thousand marched today; they were no more real to the rest of the population than the thousands who drowned in last year's monsoons, or died in China's famine, or were obliterated at Hiroshima. Their very numbers smeared them—"smeared," she said, squinting through her glasses into Fifal's dirty windshield—smeared them into meaninglessness. Their faces become a blur, their message a blot.

One person is what is needed. One face. One story. "One," she shouted. "One, one."

"I disagree," I said evenly, although given the open window, I suppose I had to shout as well. This was the articulate sophistication I was able to call forth only in Stella's presence. "One person is just a voice crying in the desert," I said.

She kept her eyes on the road. After a pause, she laughed. "You just made my point, Patsy. One voice crying in the desert about one man who would change the course of history." She couldn't resist a grin. "One," she said again.

"And who's the one in this case," I asked her. "You?"

I saw her fair skin, which had grown bright pink with her fury, now darken to an unpleasant shade of maroon.

"No," she said, "Not me."

I saw how her inherent Catholic girl humility was vying mightily with her Catholic girl hope of martyrdom. "Not necessarily me," she added.

And then she cried out, striking the bone white wheel, "But everyone else is so goddamn timid!"

I can imagine Charlene saying exactly the same thing.

IT WOULD HAVE BEEN EASY enough to believe that the Americans living in Saigon in those days had come over simply to go shopping. And not just the wives. Every American you saw on the street, man or woman, carried a shopping bag, or had two or three of them surrounding their feet at any café. Shopping was the one thing we all talked about at our parties and lectures and luncheons. Shopping for souvenirs, for clothing, for jewelry, radios, cameras, quarts of Johnnie Walker. And cigarettes, of course. All so cheap and abundant.

You didn't travel, in those days, without bringing back a souvenir for everyone you knew, so we all had long gift lists to consider. Something nice for Stella and Robert, who were on the West Coast by then. Something for their baby. I also had Peter's big family to shop for, as well my own friends from high school and college and my kindergarten year. And my father, of course, and Mr. Tannen, his best friend from his boyhood days on Tremont Avenue. All of my mother's neighborhood girlfriends as well.

It was one of the ways I shaped my idle days, even found some sense of satisfaction with how I'd spent an afternoon— determining just the right gift for just the right person.

Something to take home with you, as Lily said.

AS I IMAGINE YOU and your husband have begun to do, I long ago went through that winnowing of *things*—clothes and books and papers, excess kitchen gadgets, knickknacks, so many souvenirs: the Saigon souvenirs, and the Paris souvenirs, London, Ireland, San Francisco—souvenirs I had bought myself and all the souvenirs I'd been given by family and friends, who were also, one by one, being winnowed from life.

Evidence of where we'd been, stays against forgetfulness, I suppose.

The process—the privilege of a long life—fills you with the lingering sense of uncertainty. Why did I buy this in the first place? Who gave it to me, anyway? What am I keeping it for?

You have your children to pass the most precious, or perhaps the most practical, items along to—although a friend once said giving such stuff to your children is only a shifting of responsibility (let the kids be the ones to finally toss the thing when they come to their own sorting)—but with no children, I was free to be somewhat ruthless about all we had acquired. First when we moved from our house to the condo, then from the condo to this place.

I had letters from your mother. They were brief and chatty, maybe half a dozen of them, no more. All on her heavy stationery—she hated air-mail tissue paper. Notes mostly from just after we left Saigon, and then a few more scattered across the years. They were brief, as I say. I can't imagine Charlene writing a tome like this one.

I should have sent the letters to you then—it did cross my

mind—but there were boxes and boxes of paper to be sorted through, letters, receipts, cards, and invitations—what was I saving all this for?—and I had no idea where you'd landed.

I did find the few letters my father had written when we were in Saigon. He of course would only use those regulation Par Avion sheets with their careful folds. His letters were also brief, reticent: the weather in Yonkers and the neighbors who were moving away, a word or two about the advancement of communism in the Far East, and then a reminder to be safe, a touching but uncharacteristic closing: I keep you and Peter in my prayers.

These I still have—let some stranger toss them. But your mother's letters I sent to the shredder with everything else.

I'm sure you have your own letters from her. I'm sure they survived your own first sortings. Still, I'm sorry I don't have them to give you.

I suppose all this—this saga or whatever it is—is my way of making amends.

And, of course, of answering your question about Dominic. Small world, right? Although in truth it seems to me that it's not the world that's small, only our time in it.

O N SATURDAY MORNING I took a cab back to Charlene's villa, my third trip, then, after I'd delivered Lily's doll clothes that Wednesday. The houseman let me through the gate again, but there was no one in the foyer or the salon. He gestured that I should follow him into the dining room, where, once again, Charlene's lovely family seemed poised for a pretty photo. Kent at the head of the table, in an open-collared, short-sleeved dress shirt, pale blue, crisply ironed. (Oh, our marvelous servants!) Charlene at the other end in a sleeveless shirt-waist, pale yellow—the same shade as the sunlight that came through the lightly curtained windows. The baby in a high chair to her right. Little you and—new to me on that morning—your brother on the left. Kent stood and the boy stood the moment I appeared. Both came forward to shake my hand. Ransom. Rainey and Ransom. Twins. "Nice to meet you, ma'am," he said.

I hadn't known you were a twin, and, I suppose, Charlene hadn't thought to mention your brother before this. Apparently, he'd been at a friend's birthday—bowling—the day of the garden party. Another handsome child, slim and blond.

I felt the envy, the ache of it, that would become so familiar.

That very morning our plan to start a family any month now had been set back once more.

I felt, too, the smallest tug—no, that's not the word, but "cut," "pain," is too strong; a "whiff," a "curl"—of another disappointment. How little Charlene and I had really shared.

"Am I too early?" I managed to say. I must have been blushing.

Charlene touched her napkin to her lips and stood. "No, no," she said. "You're right on time."

She turned to her family. A female servant came in to clear the plates. Another, younger one followed to take the baby away. "You all be good for your father and have a lovely morning," Charlene said. She went to the other end of the table and leaned to kiss Kent's cheek. I saw him pat her hip, but when she turned away I saw, too, a weariness on his face, beneath his robust tan, more an absence than a mark or a dark line or two—just some former health or youth subtly missing. Maybe it was the end of the long week. Maybe it was life with Charlene the dynamo.

As we crossed through the salon, I heard Ransom tell his father, "But she was gone yesterday. All day."

I followed Charlene out the door and across the portico. I thought we'd go through the gate to hail another cab—I also wondered where our gifts for the children were—when she led me around the villa to a narrow driveway where a jeep was parked: military green cab, beige canvas canopy over the truck bed. The kind you usually saw transporting baby-faced Vietnamese soldiers. This one, however, Charlene explained, belonged to the company. "Kent sometimes finagles it for our errands."

"Are you going to drive?" I asked.

She gave me that brief *Looking through your cluelessness* stare. "Of course," she said. And then, "Behold!"

She lifted a flap of canvas. There on the floor of the truck, between the two narrow benches, were four large market baskets, like Easter baskets but bigger, painted in bright colors, lined with pastel calico, and each one fitted tightly, beautifully, with small toys and gifts, candies, whiffle balls, little stuffed bears, tins of tea, packs of cigarettes. "See what Barbie's earned us?" she asked. "So many goodies. I usually barely fill two of these."

As we climbed into the cab, I saw her elderly houseman waiting to open the gate at the end of the drive. Charlene waved to him. Inside, she found the keys in her purse, tucked her purse behind the driver's seat, and turned the key in the ignition. I recall she wore some rather flashy sandals, no stockings, but with her tan she didn't need them, a perfect pedicure.

She pressed the clutch, shifted, turned to look over her shoulder, and with steady speed backed the truck through the gates, steering with one hand while with the other she leaned on the horn—for so long I was tempted to put my hands to my ears. We bumped over something (a curb, I wondered, a pedestrian?). And then we were in the street, cyclos and small Renaults, bicyclists, buses, more military vehicles swarming around us. Charlene shifted again and we were moving with them.

Every ride in Saigon traffic was a wild ride, but as a New Yorker who seldom drove herself (I had a license but never used it), I was accustomed to climbing into the back seat of a taxi and pretending the chaos was of no matter to me—that it pertained only to the stranger gripping the wheel.

I can't account for it, that taxicab oblivion, but I'm sure it's the very blithe, trustful ignorance that allows couples in New

York to, well, *couple*, in speeding taxicabs, allows young girls and old matinee matrons to gossip happily in their back seats, allows ambitious businessmen to make deals, to make complicated plans, all while an absolutely unknown person—whose face you have seen only in a postage-stamp-sized photograph, a person who is in truth only the back of a head and a pair of shadowy shoulders—gets you where you're going, your life and health, your future, for whatever time it takes, completely in his hands.

Peter and I had brought that happy New Yorkers' faith in back-seat immunity, invincibility—or is it fatalism?—to Saigon with us. We had been well steeped in it during that first cyclo tour. But now, with Charlene, I was up front, at the dashboard, right beside an utter madwoman. Fearlessly, amid the speeding flotsam and jetsam of this crowded city, she steered us through the chaos, into the careening roundabouts, where the white mice were waving their batons with abandon but achieving no visible organizing effect.

I was certain we would die. No, certain that I would die, because, well, that was how the relationship between women like me and women like Charlene went. I imagined my last words—spoken through broken teeth and smashed windshield glass and her own *I know I shouldn't laugh at you but I can't help it, if you could only see how you look* laugh—would be a breathless apology for keeping her from her appointed rounds.

I held on to a strap in the door as a thousand different vehicles veered toward us, veered away—or was it vice versa? Tried not to show her how terrified I was as I braced my feet against the floorboards, straightened my spine, gasped a little, and even—more than once—cried out.

I suppose it's to her credit that Charlene said nothing at

all—no obscenities tossed off to her fellow travelers, no sounds of impatience or even delight. I suppose it's to her credit that she drove with full concentration, leaning over the wheel. But also with utter confidence.

I don't recall how long it took us to get to the hospital. I can only gauge the distance by the length and breadth of my imaginings: my father at Idlewild, receiving the coffin that contained my broken body. A funeral in the church where we'd been married not a year ago. Peter, distraught, giving up our place in Arlington, returning to his own parents' house, riding the subway to work once again, reading a lonely paperback as he grasped the pole. Excuse me, miss. Clang, clang, clang went the trolley.

I might have wept, thinking of what a cute widower he was going to make.

THE MAIN PART OF THE HOSPITAL was in a French colonial building, still lovely if a little worn looking, with a dusty sweep of sparse lawn before an elaborate entrance. Charlene parked in what looked like a small lot, where Helen (today in a polished cotton blouse and skirt, warm pink) and another woman were waiting for us. Charlene handed out the baskets—my hands were still trembling a bit, and I was, I realized, soaked in perspiration under my clothes. The four of us walked toward the hospital with our bright baskets hung over our arms like, I don't know, milkmaids? cigarette girls? candy stripers? colorful matrons out of some colonized Toyland?

The place was rather sprawling, as I recall, but Charlene led us through the gate, through one building and then out again, across another hot and dusty courtyard and into what seemed a somewhat modern concrete building in need of repair.

She greeted a number of Vietnamese nurses and physicians, as well as one or two Americans, along the way: bonjour, bonjour.

At that time, my experience of U.S. hospitals was limited to an appendectomy I'd had when I was seven, and while the strong odor of ether brought those days back to me, nothing else seemed to match what had been my expectations for a children's ward. For one, it was terribly noisy—crying, chattering, rattling carts.

(I remembered from my own surgery a sacred hush soft enough to hear the squeak of white nursing shoes on the hallway linoleum, or the sound of my mother approaching in her heels.)

And crowded.

(There had been only two other children in my room.)

The two long rows of cribs and small beds were squeezed together, barely enough room for the parents—or, as Charlene had said, grandparents—who sat at the foot or the bedside of so many. Barely enough room for the few nurses, for that matter. Or for us with our silly baskets.

Helen and the other woman, who knew the routine, sailed down the center of the room, nodding and smiling at the nurses, skirting the carts, gathering in their wake a trail of small children who were not bedridden. When they reached the far end of the ward, they turned and began to offer their goodies, smiling and nodding to the children around them, expertly sidling along, their hips turned as they made their way between the tiny cribs.

Charlene indicated I should take one side at this end of the room, she would take the other.

Smiling, soaked with sweat, I approached the first mama-san, who was leaning over the chipped white railing of a crib, waving a paper fan over a sleeping child. She was a tiny woman in the ubiquitous black pajamas, hers faded to a dusty gray. She wore a long gray braid. It was impossible to tell if she was a hunchback, or if it was only her weariness, as she leaned over the child. I had the sense she had been leaning there for hours. There was the odor of cooking grease about her. An odor of urine about the crib. I said bonjour and she turned and grinned and answered in Vietnamese. She bowed a little but never paused in her fanning. Her teeth were stained with betel nut.

The child, perhaps about three, was on his back, sunk into that deep oblivion with which only small children can sleep. The curled fingers, the dark circle of his tiny mouth. He wore just a diaper; I could see it was wet. Under it, and up to his waist, he was wrapped in overlapping bandages. I felt a strange, delusional (I'm sure) hand of God in the meaningless coincidence of this.

I asked the grandmother, "Appendix?" Gesturing toward my own middle and grinning as if to convey "Me, too"—as if our identical experience, the sleeping child's and mine, were some supernatural revelation of our shared humanity.

But she only turned away from me to continue gazing into the crib. And in an instant I went from feeling amazed and ordained to feeling idiotic and intrusive.

I touched her arm. Hoisted the basket that was hung from my elbow, offered the array of its content. She looked. Nodded. And then plucked from the crowd of goodies a pack of red licorice and a pack of cigarettes. She nodded her thanks and turned back to the child. I felt she had merely humored me. With something of Charlene's persistence, I took one of the small teddy bears from the basket and placed it at the foot of the crib. I said, in English, "For when he wakes up," and then squeezed my way over to the next bed.

A child with the lower part of her face wrapped in gauze, the aftermath, I was to learn, of a repaired cleft palate. A child listless with fever. With typhoid or tetanus or diarrhea. (At one point during this visit, or maybe another, my toe struck a full bucket of waste that had been pushed under a bed, the odor of it rising, turning my stomach.) Congenital malformations of limb or skull. Malformations from polio. Abscesses. Burns.

I am conflating here, of course. I trailed Charlene on these missions of hers during the next few Saturday mornings, until I began to suspect we had finally (as Peter put it) hit the mark, and we both agreed a children's ward was no place for a newly pregnant woman. We might have said American woman. And then I began to join her again after I lost that pregnancy. So what I'm describing here is an amalgam, of course.

What stands out in my memory is the noise, the odors, the heat, the dim walls that more than once we women considered painting ourselves. (We never did.) And, of course, the suffering of so many sick children.

I mentioned there were burns. On a few occasions, Charlene learned from the nurses that a child had been scalded in a household accident, or splashed with hot oil, or hit with the coals of a sidewalk cooking fire. But there were others whose burns were spotted, oddly placed, a hand and a hip, for instance, the side of a face and the opposite leg and foot. These burns were raw, but with a distinct shape. I knew very little about napalm then and don't claim to know now that this was what I was seeing there, among these children. In fact, I only made the connection years later, when that terrible photograph of the little girl first appeared. But neither were the answers forthcoming when I tried to understand what had happened to these children, how such odd, accidental burns could have occurred. I confess I wondered briefly if they were indications of some terrible ritual I didn't understand. Or even manifestations of a new, unmentioned disease.

I guess you could argue, if you're so inclined, that I was right on both counts. Metaphorically, anyway.

One girl in particular stands out—no doubt the very child I remembered when I later saw those heartbreaking photos from the war.

She was wailing when we came into the ward that morning. A child who had not been there the week before. The sound of a child wailing was not unusual, someone was always bawling, but her cry was sustained and unwavering, almost adult. My father would have said she was wailing like a banshee. The poor girl was about halfway down the row of beds, on the side of the room I was attending to, standing in a crib that was too small for her. From the moment I began my rounds, bed after bed, I was aware of how I was slowly approaching her—moving toward that unrelenting cry of distress, misery, pain. In truth, I was dreading the approach. I'm sure I even lingered a bit longer with the children and the grandparents as they chose their little gifts, shouting my bright *bonjour*s and *merci*s and *you're welcome*s in tortured Vietnamese (*com pah yeah*) over the little girl's terrible, sustained keening. Wanting, in all honesty, to pass her by.

But there was nothing to be done. Soon she was my next patient. She wore only a small shirt that barely covered her taut belly. Her size made her nakedness all the more difficult to see. The slim hip and thigh, not quite adolescent, but not mitigated

either by a toddler's plumpness. The folded bud of her bare pri-
vates. The sweet tenderness of her undamaged skin. Her back-
side and the backs of her legs bore most of the burn, which was
not new but perhaps only just beginning to heal, bordered as it
was with the spotted, yellowish scar tissue that seemed to illustrate the moment of contact with the heat, the moment the flesh
was melted away—I'm thinking here of the cinematic image of a
match lighting celluloid. Terrible to consider. Her hair was cut
raggedly short—there were also burns on the back of her neck.
She was standing up, gripping the metal railing, her mouth open,
her dark eyes—which she immediately turned on me without
any change in the pitch and volume of her voice—were terrified,
there is no other word.

Although she'd been crying since we'd arrived on the ward,
no one had come to attend to her, so I knew this must have been
going on for some time, this terrible lament. I knew it must have
been her steady state. I gathered that everyone in the ward had
somehow come to the understanding that she was inconsolable.

I showed her the basket on my arm. Her eyes went to the array, and then back to me with no change in the fear and the outrage they contained. Still she wailed. I ran a hand over the gifts.
Lifted a teddy bear, made it dance before her, then a small, soft
baby doll in a pretty pink dress, a bar of chocolate, a Pez dis-
penser with the head of a clown. Unrelenting, even as her eyes
went to each item and then went right back to me. She was tall
enough that the bar of the crib came to just below her waist. Another child could have climbed out easily, but there was no sense,
it seemed there was no possibility, that she would ever change
this stance. She would be here endlessly, clutching that bar,

turning her terrified eyes on the world, giving wordless voice to her outrage and her pain.

I lowered the basket to the floor and took her in my arms.

It was an impulse from my days of teaching, I think, but not something I had ever done here before. We were careful, especially with the burn patients, to avoid any touching—just smiles and soft words, and little gifts. But I put my arms around her on desperate impulse and felt her immediately tuck her head into my shoulder. Still she would not be silenced. I felt her hot breath against my neck, but her wailing was unchanged, or changed only in that the sound of her voice was now right in my ear, painful, drowning out everything else.

I held her. In those few minutes she became—it must sound strange to say—wholly physical for me, a body, human, distinct, whereas, I think, until just a moment before she was in her misery a problem to be solved, a child in pain, yes, but also a wailing to be stilled, a sound to be soothed or smothered, something pathetic but wholly other. I had, in truth, dreaded approaching her.

But now, holding her in my arms for however long I stood there—not long—I understood that the sound of her cries was only a continuation, a reverberation, of her initial scream, perhaps days or weeks ago, when she felt the first touch of the flame, as if her initial, desperate flight from that pain was somehow coiled still in her thin bones. I became, overwhelmingly, aware of this small body: her bones and tender flesh, her heartbeat, her pulse, and then, somehow, of the bones, the pulse, the heartbeat of those who had brought her into life, who had formed her, as well as bone, flesh, pulse, voice of those who had formed them. And so on.

I'm not making myself clear.

I held this child in my arms and felt the crouched, the coiled struggle, the agony, of what she'd been through, the outraged, muscular insistence in her little body as it had fled that first touch of pain. But I felt, too, insistent life: bone, pulse, voice, flesh— terror and outrage, yes, but also demanding, human, distinct, determined life. I felt the relentless repetition, the unending lineage, life after life after life, that had formed this child. I was aware of the push, the urge, the demand to breach—what's the term?— the bone gates, to give birth, in agony, over and over and over again—the very instinct, the very unspoken exhortation that had brought into life, howling, this child in my arms, her hot breath now on my neck, her cry painful in my ear, overwhelming.

I recall it so vividly.

Maybe because I was pregnant myself, without knowing I was, as I held her. Or about to be, perhaps. The exact month or week when this happened has become unclear. Maybe it occurred after I'd lost that first pregnancy, had already experienced that loss, and so I held this small child in my arms with some sense of what I had not managed to achieve, but with some new, unformed understanding of the impulse, the insistence, the push for more life.

Anyway, for one brief second, she stopped. Grew silent. I still felt her hot breath, her wet mouth, still open on my bare neck, but briefly, so briefly, she was silent. I hoped she had fallen asleep. I suspect she had only paused to inhale, to form again a new cry. A nurse approached—I don't think she was pleased with my holding the girl like this, threatening her healing scars. I quickly removed my arms and stepped back, retrieved my basket. The child was wailing again—or perhaps she had never really stopped. The nurse was hushing her, unwrapping her fingers from the crib's bar, urging her, I supposed, to lie down. To quiet down.

As I stepped away, Charlene was there in the aisle between the beds, her nearly empty market basket on her arm.

She said, over the ear-piercing din of the girl's cries, "She's Rainey's age, the poor thing. My daughter's age." And then she added, "My own."

Was it napalm? It's possible. The French had used it in their war. That year, the war in the north was driving many into the city. America had begun to aid the south with deforestation. Napalm. White phosphorous. But I can't say for sure that's what it was. Who was to blame for that anguish.

CERTAINLY, AND I'M GETTING TO YOUR QUESTION, there were American soldiers at the children's hospital in those days. Not many, but Charlene, it seemed, had befriended them all.

I recall especially Lieutenant Welty. Wallace Welty—who could forget a name like that? A tall, lanky kid, couldn't have been more than thirty. Had just finished his pediatric residency back home. One of those gentle Southerners, from Georgia, I think, who had the knack of looking you in the eye with instant, affectionate interest—without being creepy. He was Charlene's "partner in crime," I was to learn. She often brought him to the orphanages she visited, and now and then he allowed her to tag along—unauthorized—when some of the medical corpsmen drove out to a leper colony on the coast.

I recall as well that there were older American and British

doctors, older to me anyway, serious men who came to work with the surgeons on staff. Part of the Hearts and Minds initiative, I suppose, although I don't remember anyone using that term. A number of interchangeable young GIs, some assigned to the hospital for practice or training, others there on their own time, for the kids. Or maybe it was more Hearts and Minds PR. In truth, I found all these younger guys, just boys, so cheerful, and funny, and so good that I believed they were all volunteers. More tear-infused swelling of my patriotic heart.

Dominic was one of these.

He was nineteen or twenty. Squarely built, not tall. He told me once he'd gained twenty pounds in Basic—"all muscle," he said, joking, pointing to his close-cropped skull—but he still moved with the goofy, loose-limbed abandon of a chubby kid.

An open, pleasant, all-American face, blond and blue-eyed. Happy-go-lucky, I want to say. A cliché in every way.

Charlene informed me immediately that he was a CO, which was why he'd trained as a medic. "More Catholic than your pope," she said.

But I could tell right away that Charlene was fond of him. Or at least that she approved of him—an emotion that seemed to come to her more readily than fondness. He would on occasion take some kids who were mobile, mostly boys but not, as I recall, exclusively, out to the courtyard for a game of whiffle ball. Charlene regularly made sure he had a new set, bat and ball still in the cardboard covering so he could make a show of unsheathing it, running a hand over the smooth bat, the unscathed plastic of the ball. He did sportscaster commentary over the kids' heads as he pitched, or—I was the pitcher that day—when he stood behind the batters and taught them how to hit. Did an excellent rendition of the roar of a crowd.

Of course, the kids had no idea what he was saying—no matter how often he threw in bits of his high school French or Vietnamese phrases more mispronounced than my own—but they were delighted by him nonetheless. These games usually ended with Dominic stretched out in the dust, the kids swarming over him. Or a triumphant return to the ward with some poor lame or bandaged kid on his shoulders, newly christened Mickey Mantle, Roger Maris, the Sultan of Swing, the Emperor of Ice Cream.

He had a small record player and brought it along with a stack of 45s. Taught the kids the Twist. He retrofitted a puppet he'd found in some shop—a dragon marionette—and set it dancing to "a one-eyed, one-horned, flyin' purple people eater." The kids went nuts, those who could. It became a kind of anthem. A sweet and charming guy.

But, in truth, they were all great with the kids, these playful American boys, even when they were giving shots or taking blood. We women were welcomed by the children, the papa-sans and the mama-sans, mostly, we knew, for the gifts we brought. But the young GIs were thrilling to them, even the bedridden kids. They were superheroes, movie stars. And were always greeted as such.

We felt no envy, we do-good American ladies. We liked men better than women as well.

I'm recalling now a morning we arrived at the hospital with our baskets and found Dominic asleep in a chair in a far corner of the ward, a toddler in a full body cast also asleep on his shoulder. Charlene learned from the nurse that he'd been there since the day before. We learned from Wally Welty that Dom had held the child all through the night, had risked being AWOL until Wally intervened.

As one of the nurses lifted the kid from Dom's lap, I could see how the awkward weight of the cast had left deep, striated ridges along his pale forearms. There was a crimson mark on his cheek as well, where the child's head had rested.

Charlene took a candy bar from her basket and held it out to Dom, who was still in the chair, looking like a sleepy kid himself. "That was over and above," she told him.

But he shook his head, grimacing, feigning paralysis. He said, in a rusted Tin Man kind of voice, "Can't move. Can't move anything but my eyelids." Making a joke of what he had done.

We ladies rushed to help him, giving him our hands as he stood, telling him to stamp his feet, to rub the pins and needles from his arms. Charlene remained apart, barely smiling. Her narrow-eyed approval a far superior prize, we knew, than all our twittering affection.

He had a wife at home—in Maryland, where he'd grown up. (I confess to a very, very brief wave of disappointment when I first noticed his wedding ring—no need to examine any further that particular feeling.) But it was on that morning that I learned, from Charlene, that Dominic's wife was expecting their first child. "First of ten, I'd wager," Charlene said in her *you people* way.

Dominic Carey—although I would not have been able to recall his last name. From what you say, Charlene predicted right.

I'M GOING TO TAKE A MINUTE now to see if I can get my dates straight. Peter and I were married in June of 1962. Moved to Arlington in November, and Peter told me we were going to Saigon in early December. We left for the West Coast in February 1963. Arrived in Saigon right after Tet. Early March, perhaps, when I met you and your mother at the garden party. A week or so later I began to join her on the hospital visits. I recall how disappointed I was that first morning to find I was not yet pregnant.

Another month when I began to hope. A few more weeks, then, when I dared to say a word to Peter, and we agreed the hospital visits should end. I didn't want to tell Charlene just yet, so I begged off with various notes sent over to her villa: a cold one week, Peter and I entertaining one week, taking a drive, that sort of thing.

My first doctor's appointment in May, after my second missed period, a doctor at the navy clinic most of the dependents used. Peter had gotten his name. I was too superstitious to ask any of the women I knew for recommendations. Not yet.

The doctor assured me we'd hit the mark. "The rabbit died," is what we said in those days, although I don't think any rabbits were actually involved. It was, the doctor pointed out, the year of the rabbit. A good omen, he said.

And I recall Peter asking later, "How is a dead rabbit a good omen?" We had a laugh over that.

Peter's assignment here was meant to be for nine months to a year, so chances were good I'd be home for the delivery, but Dr. Navy (cannot recall his name, no doubt I've suppressed it) said he was perfectly capable of delivering our child for us should our plans change. And, he added, nursemaids were so cheap over here, why go back to the States where you'll have to do all the care and feeding yourself?

And think of it, he added, all his life your baby will have an intriguing tale to tell about the exotic place where he was born. All his girlfriends will be checking their atlases.

I had the sense that he'd said this to other women, that it was one of his standard, avuncular attempts at a charming bedside manner, but still the words gave me, for the first time, permission to exhale, to begin to imagine our child's long life.

Early June and I was dressing for another party. A reception at the American embassy, then dinner with three other couples at a Chinese restaurant we liked, a floating restaurant on the river—you must remember it, a popular place for families. My Canh.

Maybe because it was a popular place for families, it was bombed by the Viet Cong only a few years later. There was another photograph, as I recall, not as well known as the little girl fleeing the napalm, but the kind that sears your memory nevertheless: an impossibly bloodied child—impossible because her body was so small—in the arms of an American man—the eyes of both, man and child, blank, somehow, utterly expressionless.

Shock, I suppose. You can only imagine what those eyes had seen.

But that was some time later, as I said.

We were still keeping the news of my pregnancy to ourselves, but I was sure knowing glances would be exchanged among the other women when I refused a cocktail. I recall I'd had a new dress just delivered from Maison Rouge. A silk floral with a full skirt. I was looking forward to wearing it, wondered how long before I outgrew the fitted waist.

I was in the bathroom just off the master. It was a fairly large Western-style bathroom with a lovely soaking tub. I was in my slip, waiting until the last minute to put on my new dress. A sudden sense of vertigo, and then a small cramp. Nothing dramatic. No more than the bottoming-out sensation of an elevator dip, followed by a brief stab, like a runner's knot, in my center. Followed immediately by an utter sense of devastation: the collapse of something precious and irreplaceable, that gale of disbelief that follows the news of any loss, that follows the sudden, slipped-from-your-fingers loss of something invaluable.

But that was brief as well. I shook it off, finished doing my makeup. Sprayed my hair. Used the toilet one more time and saw the spot of blood.

It seems strange to say it now, it even seemed strange to me at the time, but my first thought was that I did not want to be the sort of woman who had a miscarriage. Didn't want to be a part of that simpering sorority, a keeper of that shameful secret (for so it was considered at the time), that failure. Until that moment, I was on the side of healthy, fertile women who gave birth easily to robust and beautiful children. On Charlene's side.

Now, with the small circle of blood, I was on the side of the stumblers, the weak, those sick and troublesome, bedridden women in pin curls and satin bed jackets who gave their long-suffering husbands nothing but grief and disappointment.

I wanted to put on the new dress, pretend this wasn't happening, carry on regardless, and it might have been only the memory of my humiliation at the garden party that made me hesitate. I had a vision of blood staining the seat of my skirt, soaking through the gorgeous silk while solicitous but subtly scornful women came to my aid with linen napkins sympathetically placed.

Poor Mrs. Kelly here has had an encounter with a bad pregnancy . . .

When Peter called to me from downstairs to say we were really running late, I asked him to come up. His particular expression of husbandly indulgence and impatience—he was, I could tell, prepared to tell me I looked fine, any dress was as good as another, we're late—fell away as soon as he saw me, now in my dressing gown, stretched out on our bed.

"What's wrong?"

I said I'd had a wave of nausea. Said perhaps the morning sickness I had so far avoided had finally found me here in the late afternoon—maybe it was confused by the time zone.

He took my hand. Said we'd cancel our plans.

But I told him to go. Told him I only wanted to sleep and he'd be here all night with nothing to do. We'd already sent the cook and the yard boy home, as we usually did on the nights we dined out, and Minh-Linh, our housekeeper, would return to her quarters out back as soon as she'd prepared our bedroom for the night.

I told Peter to ask her to stay, maybe she could bring up some tea once I'd had a snooze. I remember he was wearing a new suit, too—I'd gotten the name of the tailor from Helen Bickford, whose husband was always impeccably dressed. He was freshly shaven, I could smell his signature bay rum. Behind it, a touch of the gin and tonic he always had as he waited for me to get ready. He seemed so boyish sitting on the side of the bed like that, and I was so in love with him that I whispered, without thinking, "I've had a little blood." And then wished I hadn't.

He flushed. "Is that bad?' he asked.

I knew so little. "Not really," I said, with an authority I completely lacked. "It happens."

I saw him glance, surreptitiously, from my face to my breasts, hips, then legs. And then he quickly looked back again, as if everything below my neck—that territory he had so expertly explored over these many months—had suddenly become alien to him, somewhat disconcerting.

We came up with a compromise: he would go to the cocktail gathering, then come back to see how I was doing. We would decide then whether or not we would go out to dinner.

I suppose I slept heavily for a while. When I woke—the cramps were now full-blown menstrual style—the lights in the room had been lowered, the air conditioner was humming, and a joss stick burned on the dresser. I went to the bathroom, more blood, but nothing copious, and when I crawled back into bed Minh-Linh appeared with a tray: a teapot, a delicate cup and saucer, a plate of rice crackers.

I hadn't known until that moment that she knew I was expecting.

She was middle-aged, thin, with a quiet industriousness about her. She looked humorless on first encounter, but we'd quickly learned that she laughed easily. Peter claimed that she understood English very well and was also fluent in French, but I hadn't had much occasion to speak with her at length. She'd been taking care of whoever occupied this house for years, and my impulse had always been to accede to what I thought must have been her well-established routine.

She placed the tray on my bedside table and poured a cup. I sat up to take it from her. Then she went to the window to turn off the air conditioner, and then turned on the overhead fan. She knew this was how I preferred the room when I napped. She came back to the bed and asked, "Feeling better?" I only shrugged, too exhausted and worried to be perky. She patted her flat stomach.

"Much pain?" she asked.

I nodded. And then raised the teacup to my lips to keep from blubbering. But the tears came anyway.

Gently, she took the cup from me. She ran a comforting hand over my hair, still stiff with going-out hair spray. I suppose it felt odd to her. She went into the bathroom and found my brush. Then she nodded that I should move over. She sat beside me, slightly behind, and slowly brushed my hair until the hair spray was combed out and I'd cried all I could cry. And then she gently pulled my hair back over my ears and braided it neatly. When she was finished, she returned the cup to me. I drank the now tepid tea, ate a tasteless cracker. She fixed the pillows behind me and said, "Sleep, please."

I recalled Lily's "All will be well." Which Minh-Linh did not say, but conveyed nonetheless. I thought, as I slept again, that my sincere affection for these women was surely purer, less condescending, less self-satisfied, less colonial, certainly, than that of the other female dependents here in Saigon. Another kind of American hubris, I suppose.

I woke again when Peter came in, my navy doctor just behind him. They both had their jackets off. Peter wore a white short-sleeved dress shirt, his collar was opened and his tie unknotted. The doctor was in his military beige. They both filled the room with the smell of cigarette smoke and sweat.

Peter said, cautiously, "How are you feeling, honey?" He stood at the foot of the bed. He seemed a little shy, maybe embarrassed, and I suddenly touched my hair—Minh-Linh's French braid coming undone. Not a look he was accustomed to. I suppose it made me look weaker than I felt. I struggled to sit up. I knew I was bleeding heavily now.

Dr. Navy moved into our bedroom with more authority than my husband had, tossing his jacket on the bed, coming toward me as if to make some small adjustment to my head and neck that would restore proper order. He felt my forehead. His hand was large and soft, the backs of his fingers covered with manly fur. I felt a rough callus or two. A golfer or tennis player, I thought. He wore a handsome wristwatch.

"No fever," he said, and then sat heavily on the side of the bed. "Any pain?" he asked.

Reluctantly, I told him I was a little uncomfortable. Not much.

"You can take some aspirin," he said. "It won't hurt the baby."

I knew he was drunk. I could see how he struggled to keep his eyes properly focused, and yet his words filled me with hope. If he believed the baby would not be harmed by an aspirin, then he believed the baby was still there, still headed for his birth in this exotic place.

"There was some blood," I whispered, and glanced at Peter, who glanced away.

The doctor waved his hand. "It happens," he said. "My wife was always springing leaks when she was expecting—we've got five."

He showed me his palm, fingers spread and wiggling, as if to illustrate five plump children with hair on their backs.

"Nothing unusual. You first-timers fret about everything."

He patted my thigh. "Get yourself some rest, little mother," he said. "Take an aspirin if the pain gets bad." He gestured toward Peter. "I'm going to take this man of yours out for a good meal. Things will look better in the morning."

Peter asked, "Do you want me to stay?"

I waved him on. He'd probably had a few too many himself. "No, go," I said.

In truth, I wanted them both gone so I could get to the bathroom and see the extent of the blood. I wanted to take that little bit of assurance this drunken doctor had given me and hold it up against the fact of whatever it was my body was determined to do.

They lingered a bit longer. Discussed bringing something back for me to eat, some soup or some pho. Peter told me he had already asked Minh-Linh to stay close. She'd spend the night in the second bedroom. She'd offered to cook some eggs.

I said, perhaps impatiently, that I was fine. Rest was what I needed.

The navy doctor said, "Absolutely. R and R. The best medicine."

As they left the room, my husband asked the good doctor, "Is that a Rolex?"

I waited until I heard them go out through the gate, until I heard the car—it might have been waiting—take them away.

In the bathroom, I saw the blood was copious. And then I saw, in the midst of it, the small sac of the embryo. I reached into the toilet, into the water and the blood, and scooped the tiny thing out. Held it in my cupped hands. It was so small, but still I recognized the pale seahorse shape from college biology texts. The curve of it, the dark indication of an eye. I slid it from my palm to a folded towel on the side of the sink, washed the blood from my hands, changed into another nightgown, and went back to bed.

So now I was a woman who had had a miscarriage. So now we would begin again, the monthly hope and disappointment, now with a little more caution, a little more fear. Now the easy, fertile future—my part in our successful life together—was no longer so easy. Or so assuredly mine.

I heard from downstairs the buzzer at our gate. Heard Minh-Linh go out. Heard her voice as she returned, intertwined with—I felt another elevator drop—Charlene's. I heard Charlene come up the stairs.

She wore a sleeveless cocktail dress of the same deep green shantung of the dress Lily had made for Mrs. Case's daughter. It had a slim skirt, a V-neck in front, and a raised collar in the back, regal. She'd been right: it was the perfect color for the season. Her hair was up in a French twist, her diamond earrings sparkled. Her hazel eyes were now deep green. She really was, in that dim light, remarkably attractive. Some cross between Grace Kelly and Maleficent.

I was braced for her reflexive sneeze of a laugh, but all she said as she came into the dim room was "Kiddo." It was neither maternal nor condescending. It was—for lack of a better word—businesslike, efficient, authoritative, even. Queenly. "What's going on?"

I told her, without weeping, that I had miscarried. That I'd been almost three months along.

She said, "Shit."

In those days, I was not—I dare say most of us were not—accustomed to hearing women like Charlene curse like that. It startled me, but also made me want to laugh.

She frowned. "You're sure?"

I nodded toward the bathroom and she went right in—she was wearing strappy black heels—businesslike, as I said. When she returned, she had the towel that held the embryo folded in her hands. She sat beside me on the bed. I sat up, leaned forward. With hardly a thought, hardly a doubt, I put my cheek to her tanned and freckled arm, which was surprisingly cool. There was the metallic tang of perspiration just beneath her lovely perfume.

Charlene placed the towel on her lap, over the gorgeous green silk, and unwrapped the little thing, barely distinguishable now against the blood-soaked cloth. We looked at it together, silently, for what seemed a long while. I was aware of the click of the fan above our heads, the encroaching heat, some distant sound of traffic and voices in the street, Charlene's flesh against my own. The joss stick had nearly burned down, but the scent of it was certainly on the air.

And I suppose it was this scent that made me aware of both how far from home I was, how strange and exotic this place was, and yet how confined and familiar everything now felt, as if, with my own small failure, my own small grief, the world had shrunk, distance had lost its meaning. Nothing was foreign. No one was a stranger.

I mean, here was Charlene, beside me in my own bedroom, my cheek to her bare arm.

Gently, she placed the towel into my hands. She reached for the half bottle of Vichy water on my bedside table and poured a drop into her palm. She wet the fingertips of her right hand and made the sign of the cross over the tiny thing. Softly, she said, "I baptize thee, in the name of the Father, and of the Son, and of the Holy Ghost."

Then she bent her head and whispered an Our Father. I joined her—pausing awkwardly as she spoke the final, Protestants-only (as I thought of it) phrase "For thine is the kingdom, and the power, and the glory, forever and ever."

They seemed very grand words for a such a small gathering of cells.

She took the towel from me, folded it over again.

"What should I do?" I asked her, not wanting to say, "What should I do with it?" But I knew she knew this was what I meant.

Charlene said, "Let's think for a minute."

She carried the towel back into the bathroom, rested it again on the edge of the sink.

When she returned, she emptied the bottle of Vichy water into a glass. Then went to her purse and found one of the small prescription boxes, slid it open, and shook out a pill. She handed the pill to me, with the water. Said, when I hesitated, "You might as well." I swallowed the Librium and some water. She seemed satisfied. Took the glass from me and then bent down to whisper in my ear.

"I hate this," she said, hissing the words. "I just hate it."

There was a small bamboo chair in the corner of the room, and she carried it one-handed over to the side of the bed. She sat down, kicked off her heels, rubbed her stockinged toes. Casually, casually gossiping, she mentioned who had been at the party that night. The usual suspects, she said. I think it was at this time that the American ambassador was off to the Aegean on a family vacation and the chargé d'affaires was acting ambassador. Charlene couldn't say his name, Trueheart, without some venomous irony coloring her voice. "Like something out of *Ivanhoe*," she said.

The gossip in those days was about a new ambassador—there was an American delegation in town, perhaps related to this. I remember Charlene telling me that the Washington contingent couldn't stop perspiring.

She kept talking. She'd taken orders for six more Barbie ao dais. Lily had enlisted the help of a friend, a girl named Phan, another seamstress with a Singer sewing machine of her own and two small children, as well as a pair of elderly in-laws and a husband gone missing.

She said Lily was already helping Phan to stay afloat financially, passing along her Barbie earnings. "So like our Lily," she said.

Charlene had told her that Phan could help out, could run up the little clothes on her own machine, but she had insisted Lily still do all the hand stitching. It was the beauty of Lily's stitching that everyone noticed, the thing that made the outfits so unique.

What else did she say during that long night? I recall how she leaned across her lap and spoke in the tone you might use (I myself had used it) to distract a small child from a chicken pox itch, a scraped knee, a fever.

She'd caught a glimpse of Madame Nhu somewhere: beautiful, tiny. Maybe a bit heavy-handed with the eyebrow pencil.

"The Dragon Lady," I said, to show I was grateful for her efforts to distract.

Charlene gave me her cool, assessing green eyes. "Don't fall for it," she said. "She's a woman with spunk. Which is why men want to hate her."

She went on: a higher-up at one of the U.S. agencies—USIS, USOM, I can't recall—had been at the party with his unhappy wife. Apparently, he'd been off in the countryside for six weeks, something to do with the rural hamlet program, and the wife had been left alone in Saigon.

Charlene insisted I'd met the woman somewhere—she'd introduced us, she was certain, on one of our hospital visits. "She's a clotheshorse," Charlene offered. "Tonight she was wearing Guy Laroche, two pieces, coral pink. Would have been lovely if it fit her right." She shook her head—what to do with these women?

"Girl spends a fortune on clothes," Charlene said. "But not successfully. It's all higgledy-piggledy. She doesn't want the clothes. She just wants her husband to pay for them." She arched a brow, amused. "Revenge spending. She's bought ten ao dais already, and she's only got a son, in boarding school in Virginia."

At one point during the party tonight, Charlene said, this woman's husband took her elbow to turn her toward an introduction, and "the poor girl" pulled away from him as if she'd been scorched. He cursed her under his breath. Everyone heard it. Everyone saw it. Awkward for all.

"Plenty of rocks in that marriage," Charlene claimed.

And Helen Bickford had a tale to share. Charlene leaned over her skirt. "This is just between us."

Apparently, Charlene said, Helen had a friend back home, who had a friend at the Pentagon, who was the friend of a woman there who projected the draft call numbers for the Joint Chiefs. Five years out.

"It's quite complex," Charlene said. "She takes all kinds of things into consideration. Retirements, re-enlistments, men who'll be drafted and then rejected, all overseas deployments, of course. And she needs to project five years out. Across all the services. She needs to be extremely accurate. It's quite a job."

I tried to attend. I know I asked, "A woman does this?" But as she spoke I was listening, too, for Peter's return, hoping this time he would not bring the doctor with him. I was considering whether I should show him the little embryo. I decided no, I should not.

I was thinking of how naive we had been, he and I, over these many months, believing that all our fun, our passion and delight, would lead only—joy upon joy—to a healthy child in our arms, our own.

Charlene was saying that Helen Bickford told her tonight that last month this woman at the Pentagon was asked to go back and recalculate her projections for next year, 1964. This never happens, Helen said. These are careful numbers, carefully calculated five years out, there's never a need to reassess. Pretty clear the order had to come from the White House.

This friend from McLean told Helen Bickford that this woman at the Pentagon was ordered to recalculate next year's draft projections based on a full withdrawal from Vietnam. Everyone. All the brass, all the GIs, pilots, MPs—all. All out of here by the end of next year.

"Picking up our marbles and going home," Charlene said.

"Not just the troop reduction JKF's been talking about. Total withdrawal."

I moved uncomfortably in the bed; a cramp was cresting. I was remembering, too, adding up the extent of my disappointments, that this was the week I was going to write to my father, to tell him the good news about our baby. His grandchild.

With my father in mind, I asked, "What about the communists?" Hoping to prove I was listening.

Charlene stood, walked around the room until she found an ashtray. She took a cigarette from her purse. "What about the peasants?" she asked, lighting it. And then, with a laugh, "What about Brown and Root? What about Esso? What about the porcelain-faced Madame Nhu?"

She came back to the chair, shrugged, went on talking.

She said she'd looked for me at the reception. Found Peter, who told her I was under the weather. And then, of course, she saw him leave with Dr. Navy.

"Don't go back to that guy," she said, "Next time around. The last thing you want is a navy doctor. They hardly know what they're looking at. They get your feet in those stirrups and their ears between your knees and suddenly it's all *Up Periscope*. They spend the rest of the exam trying to figure out what's port and what's starboard. Wondering where the hell the penis is."

I smiled. Still shocked, but growing less so, by Charlene's use of words.

"I went to a Frenchman for little Roger. He's had a practice here for years. All the elites see him. He came right to the house for the delivery. Kent wanted me to go to Hong Kong, but I wouldn't hear of it. Leave the twins alone here?"

She brushed the suggestion away with a wave of her cigarette.

"Go to my guy. He's getting on in years, but he has a deep and abiding love for women. It's delightful. I'm thinking of getting pregnant again just to see his brown eyes above my belly. You'll swoon."

She paused. I had the sense that she was taking charge of this part of my life, gently wresting it from my clumsy control.

"Next time," she said.

When Minh-Linh came in with her tray, more tea for us both, she asked me if I would like some eggs, and Charlene replied, "Good God, no." Which was my sentiment exactly. I was happy to let her speak for me.

Minh-Linh poured the tea and handed us each a cup. I saw her glance into the bathroom; she seemed about to go in to tidy up when Charlene said something to her in quick French. Minh-Linh paused, then glanced at me. Then nodded. She said, softly, "I understand."

She went out with her tray but returned later with another joss stick and what looked to me at first like a small gray stone. She lit the stick and placed it in the little sand-filled pail where we burned our incense. And then she placed the stone before it. It was in fact a small, smiling Buddha.

Sharp-eyed Charlene, smarter than everyone, said, "Jizo?" And Minh-Linh shook her head. "Dizang," she whispered.

Charlene nodded. "Very sweet," she said. "Thank you."

When Minh-Linh left again, Charlene looked at me and frowned. She did not like to be corrected. "Same difference," she said. "It's Jizo in Japan. Dizang here. A bodhisattva. Protector of travelers, but also of stillborn or miscarried children. Very sweet of her."

She told me then that she and Kent were in Tokyo when she miscarried after the twins. A Japanese friend had given her a similar little statue. She was five months along.

"I'm sorry," I said, but Charlene shrugged and sipped her tea.

"Poor little thing was a mess," she said. "Hadn't developed right at all. She looked like a glove turned inside out. A little monstrous." And tossed off a small laugh. "Although I guess that's true of us all. Inside out, we're all monsters."

She shrugged again, nodded toward the bathroom. "Mother Nature disposes." And then added, "The bitch."

I was strangely comforted by this news. I had not yet taken into consideration that there had been an imperfection. Or if I had, I believed the imperfection was mine.

I thought of how lovely Charlene's twins were, you and your brother. Such a handsome family.

"Apparently, Jizo, or Dizang," Charlene was saying, "watches out for the little souls that have not lived long enough to accumulate good deeds. Who can't cross over into the spirit world—permanently neither here nor there. Left only to pile stones endlessly on the edge of the riverbank. Just this side of the river Styx, I guess you could say. What you Catholics call limbo. Not exactly purgatory because there's no hope for change."

"How sad," I said.

Charlene squinted at me through the smoke. "It gets worse. It's a limbo without mercy. Apparently, there are demons in this place, this place on the riverbank. I guess so the little ones don't get deluded into thinking they're in heaven. The demons torment these lost souls, scatter their piled stones. Jizo, Dizang, protects them, hides them under his robes. A hint of benevolence in a place of eternal stasis."

She paused, picked some tobacco from her tongue. "Or some such," she added. "As I understand it, Jizo's a bodhisattva rather than a Buddha because he's elected to serve the underworld before reaching enlightenment himself. A kind of martyr, I guess. Assigned to the saddest and most futile of projects. Doing whatever good he can for these hopeless ones. What inconsequential good."

I saw her rub her thumb and ring finger together under her cigarette. A sign, I was beginning to learn, of her own quick thoughts. "Or something like that," she went on, suddenly dismissive. "Buddhism is charming but I can't say I truly get it."

"Minh-Linh's a Catholic," I told her.

Charlene shook her head. "So's Madame Nhu. But she was a Buddhist first." She squinted again. "Or maybe Minh-Linh finds it politically expedient these days to call herself a Catholic. With all that's going on."

I knew this was possible, but still I said, "I've seen her at Mass."

Charlene laughed her laugh. "Well then, Tricia, you've been given your first little Buddha by a Roman Catholic."

And then she added, softening, "But that's Vietnam. A mishmash."

She stood, plucked the little figure from the dresser, and examined it carefully. Then she padded over in her stockinged feet and handed it to me. It was plump and sweet-faced, of course, smiling, eyes closed. The outlines of small children were carved shallowly into the stone hem of his robe. There was something comforting about the way this happy little bit of cool rock fit into my palm.

I hefted it and felt another wave of tears.

Charlene reached for her purse again, induced me to take another Librium with my tea. She took a few as well. Knocking them back with the dregs of hers.

A T SOME POINT THAT NIGHT, our conversation led us to her night terrors.

They'd plagued her since the twins were born. Not nightmares, exactly, she said, because she knew when they were happening that they weren't dreams, and, moreover, she knew she was not asleep. And yet, she said, whenever she tried to explain them—to Kent, to the doctors he'd sent her to—she always reached first for some description of darkness. These terrors were, she said, infused with a terrible sense of waking darkness. Something like what the newly blind must feel. Or the newly buried.

Impenetrable darkness with its attendant disorientation, missteps, clutches at the air.

And yet there was also this tremendous certainty on her part that something truly worthy of her fear, something as solid as it was horrific, was there, in this darkness. Something terrible within it, or maybe just beyond it. It was not sleep, not dream, not nightmare, and she always felt afterward that if she had just managed to pursue it, terrified but resolved, she would have discovered a glitch in that dark veil, a tear in it. She would have glimpsed . . . she couldn't say what.

"It sounds awful," I told her. We were both speaking drowsily by now. The hour, I suppose, or the Librium.

"Yes," Charlene said. She waved a languid hand as if to dispel all consolation. "Absolutely awful."

She was on the little chair beside my bed, one leg pulled up under the lovely green silk of her skirt, the other swinging childishly. We were once more two girls, schoolmates, sleepy and a little high, exchanging late-night confessions.

She said she only sometimes cried out during these episodes. Mostly, she sat up suddenly in bed, or—and this disturbed poor Kent even more—quietly rose, eyes wide open but utterly without sight—and stood stiffly in the dark, or sometimes with a hand held out before her, barely breathing, although when he touched her, he said, he could feel her pulse racing in every part of her body.

And when she woke, her heart, too, would be racing. She would have to struggle to catch her breath. Like a third-rate actress in a two-bit horror movie, she said.

"Our doctor at home prescribed the Librium. Recommended a psychiatrist. Anxiety, he says, something to do with childbirth. Although I suspect he told Kent I'm completely batty." She paused. "I know it sounds ridiculous. No one likes waking up soaked in sweat. But I'm not sure I want to be rid of them. They're telling me something. About myself, I suppose. Who I am." And then she laughed. "They're telling me what my little old mind is capable of."

I'm recalling now the wailing little girl in the hospital crib. Recalling Charlene's attention to the sound. I'm wondering now, in this long retrospect, what Charlene had recognized that day when she said, "My own."

"I'm not a fool," she added, suddenly sober. "And I won't be patronized." She paused, looked into the air, but this time I knew her impatient, green-eyed appraisal was not directed at me. "I mean to see what I'm meant to see."

"Like what?" I asked her.

She ran her eyes over the four walls of our bedroom. There was a bright little gecko in the shadowed far corner of the ceiling that suddenly scrambled away, as if her gaze pursued it.

"Demons," she said. "Demons who want to topple the little stones I'm piling up here."

"In Vietnam?" I asked.

Her cool gaze fell on me again.

"In limbo," she said.

LATER, WELL BEFORE PETER CAME HOME from dinner—he was very drunk—we did something, Charlene and Minh-Linh and I, something I've never told anyone about.

We took that bloody little embryo and slipped it into the emptied prescription box. Charlene cleared a space in the pail of sand on the dresser and placed the box there. We added a few paper tissues and some broken-up pieces of another joss stick. We said another prayer.

I said a Hail Mary in English while Minh-Linh said the same in Vietnamese. (I recall glancing at Charlene, as if to say, See? She's a Catholic.) Charlene knew the prayer, but only in French. Together, we lit the little pyre and watched it burn.

The smell of sandalwood overtook the room, and the brief

flare of the flame caught the sweet stone face of Dizang, protector of my little sufferer, companion of my brief and ill-formed hope of a child.

BECAUSE SHE WAS FROM QUEENS, and because we both bought our clothes at Klein's, I thought when I first met Stella Carney that she was from a working-class family like my own. I was partly right. Her father was a retired fireman, but her mother's family was something like Charlene's, perhaps: once-wealthy Southerners, from New Orleans, as I recall. There was a prestigious writer whose name I have forgotten somewhere in their lineage.

Once, in a U.S. history class, Stella announced rather dramatically that while her father's "people" were Polish, Italian, and Irish immigrants, her mother's were French slave traders. "So I've got that to deal with," she said, as if the burden were hers alone.

Before the war (the second world one), Stella's mother had come to New York with her sister Lorraine—Lorraine to study art, Stella's mother, who was once beautiful, to model. I guess she had some mild, limited success, mostly showroom stuff. The story went that when Stella's mother was dumped by a wealthy boyfriend, Lorraine marched her past the nearby firehouse. It was a stifling summer evening on the edges of Greenwich Village. The firemen were sitting outside, trying to catch a breeze.

The two girls walked past, stopped for an ice-cream cone at the corner, and then walked past again.

By that time, the young men had had a chance to devise their opening lines. One of them asked, "No ice cream for us?"

Not very original, as Aunt Lorraine later told it, but enough to change the trajectory of a life. Although—Aunt Lorraine told us this, too—her intention had been only to get her broken-hearted sister a restorative roll in the hay.

FOR ME, STELLA'S CROWDED HOME LIFE was a delight. The kind of busy household I began to imagine for myself, in some not-far-off future.

Times Square, she called it.

Stella was the second of six—there was an older brother away in the marines—and along with her younger siblings the household contained a tiny Polish great-grandmother, a Polish Italian grandmother (her daughter), and a grandfather, Pop, who was, he said, straight-off-the-boat Irish, although he'd been in the States for fifty years.

Stella's room was in the attic of the narrow house—hot as Hades in the summer, and full of whistling drafts all winter long, but a place, she said, where at least she could hear herself think.

The four younger siblings, two boys and two girls, shared the one large bedroom at the back of the second floor, the room divided by a clothesline hung with beach towels; her grandparents shared a little room off the same hallway; and her parents had the bedroom at the front. Babka, the great-grandmother, slept in a small nook off the living room, although, in many ways, the entire first floor was hers—the couches and chairs were covered with her crocheted doilies, her clothes hung in the hall closet, and her nightgowns and underwear (Stella showed me this when I first visited, laughing) were tucked into the drawers of the dining-room server, where another family might have kept the good silver and the table linen.

The two grandmas did all the cooking—all day long, it seemed to me—moving slowly around each other in the narrow kitchen and producing pierogies or wedding soup or Irish soda bread, stuffed cabbage, roasts, meatballs, cookies, iced layer cakes. Like chefs in some commercial kitchen, they cooked constantly, in no particular order and with no particular meal in mind. Just the endless turning out of something good to eat.

Stella's father was a quiet guy—"What choice?" Stella asked. You could tell he might have been good-looking when he was young, still dark-haired and dark-eyed. But bent and shuffling now with chronic back problems. There was an outdoor lounge chair, webbed with plaid tape, set up in the living room for those days when he could not walk at all. When he was mobile, he spent most of his time with his old father, listening to a ball game or to the static of police and fire dispatchers on his "special" radio, either down in the basement or out on the stoop. Other men, mostly friends from his firehouse days, were always stopping by.

These were the men who would kid us as we stepped past them on the stairs, or met up with them in the kitchen as we reached for something fresh out of the oven. The college girls, they called us, Stella and me. Or Mike and Ike. Lucy and Ethel. The Bobbsey Twins.

Stella's father was always polite, even deferential to us both. On the wall above the dining room server, where Babka kept her clothes, were half a dozen or so framed citations from his time as a firefighter—"beyond-the-call things," Stella said, dismissively. Proud, though, I knew.

She was equally dismissive of the two carefully preserved pages from the *Daily News* that also hung there. One showed her father in full-dress uniform, receiving a citation from a white-hatted captain. (The fire that ended his career, Stella explained. Two discs shattered in his lower back.) In another front-page photo, he was a younger man in full firefighting gear. It was late at night on some city block, and he was holding a barefoot and pajamaed little girl. The girl's arms were around his neck, her face buried in his shoulder, and he was looking seriously at the photographer. ("You want to get out of my way?" was what Stella told me he was thinking.)

It was clear that smart Stella was the apple of his eye.

She was as free with her opinions at the family dinner table as she was in our classrooms at Marymount, but her father never disagreed or contradicted, as mine would have done, only listened and nodded and told the rest of the family, "She has a point."

Stella's mother, on the other hand, would shake her head ruefully, interrupting her daughter to say, "Softly, dear." Or "There are two sides to everything, Stella," or, more passionately, "Why must you be so disagreeable?"

Her slight Southern drawl perhaps the most incongruous sound of all in this quintessential Queens household.

No doubt Stella's mother had grown quite plump since her modeling days, but she still had a lovely face and luxurious auburn hair. Even in this small, overpopulated house, there was an air of elegance and detachment about her, a runway posture. Stella complained that she was always cleaning, but I only saw her moving through the rooms in a pretty shirtwaist, waving a soft cloth—an old baby diaper—over every surface, the lemony smell of furniture polish following her like a dowager's Chanel No. 5.

IN STELLA'S ATTIC ROOM, we ate whatever the grandmas had offered, and drank ginger ale or iced tea (summer), hot tea or cocoa (winter), and talked, and read, and discussed, and argued. Khrushchev, Castro, Gary Powers, Dorothy Day or the Dalai Lama, the Greensboro Four or the Mercury Seven, the viability of mass protests, the evils of the military-industrial complex, preferential treatment for the poor, the pope, the Church. Oh, my. Stella was eager, a hungry mind, and I scurried to keep up.

Thanks to George Orwell and Arthur Koestler, Joseph McCarthy and the radio sermons of Bishop Sheen—as well as the nuns who'd taught us most of our lives—we were well versed in those days about the horrors of communism.

It was a favorite fantasy of ours, up there in Stella's room, to imagine what would become of us if the communists won. God eliminated, of course. Statues and crosses banished. Our glorious cathedrals—St. Patrick's, even!—turned into palaces for the ruling class. Even our humble parish churches and chapels beset by barbed wire and armed guards.

We women would have to go to work. Our children, even our

infants and newborns, dropped off every morning at some massive brick or concrete government institution. Our aging parents and grandparents sent off as well to desolate warehouses—no sweet Babkas squeezed in among your loving family, your daily life—all so that we would be free to take up our duties in office buildings or factories or construction sites. (We'd seen the photographs of stout and solemn-faced Soviet women in babushkas sweeping Moscow streets.)

All sense of family obligation erased so we could go to work—work being, in this godless world, our only source of happiness, our only reason for being, our sweetness and our hope.

I'm sure it all seems absurd to you. It does to me. How earnestly we imagined that bleak future—the diabolical disorientation that would transform our innocent lives.

Although, recounting it now, it dawns on me that there are four hundred old souls in my assisted-living facility. No resident under seventy. I don't know a single one of my contemporaries who lives with her family.

The parochial school where I'd taught was shuttered years ago. The school I attended as a child is on the verge of bankruptcy, what with declining enrollment and reparations for clerical abuse.

The old Brooklyn cathedral where my parents were married, where I was baptized, is a condominium now. Quite pricey.

So maybe our dystopian fantasies were not so far-fetched after all.

What's the line from Emily Dickinson? "While we were fearing it, it came."

That's a joke. Born of this old lady's nostalgia for a lost world, flawed as it was.

IN THE SPRING OF 1961, our senior year, the Freedom Riders were all in the news. Just before we graduated, Stella learned that some of the Marymount nuns, the ones we most admired, would be in Birmingham all summer, registering voters, advocating for integration, joining arms with those seeking justice long-denied.

In June, she talked me into driving down to join them.

She had it all planned. Two weeks, more if things went well. Both of us had part-time summer jobs—mine was at Klein's on Central Avenue, hers at Macy's in Herald Square—and "real jobs" that would begin in September. I would teach at that parish kindergarten. She would start as a secretary at the Foundling Hospital in Manhattan.

Stella argued that we could juggle our sales clerk schedules with co-workers for at least two weeks, and if we decided to stay longer and got fired, so what? Summer jobs were a thing of our teenage pasts.

We would drive down together. Fifal was up to it, she was certain. Our first overnight would be in Charlottesville, Virginia, where Stella's aunt Lorraine now lived, married to a professor at the university. A two-day drive should do it.

Knowing my father would worry, knowing even better that he would disapprove ("Nobody in this country has it easy" was all he had to say about civil rights), I told him that Charlottesville was the end point of our excursion. Two weeks of touring antebellum mansions and hiking in the Blue Ridge, I said. A vacation before I started working full-time. It was an easy enough lie.

When Stella pulled up in Fifal early on that overcast morning, my father, as men of his generation were obliged to do, walked me out to the car, carrying my small suitcase. As we approached, I saw Stella suddenly begin to clear the debris from the front passenger seat, tossing more books and papers into the back, as if it had just occurred to her that I would need a place to sit.

My father asked me, "She knew you were coming, right?"

I said, "I'm not sure."

Once I was inside, he leaned down into the opened window. His broad Irish face was freshly shaven. He wore a short-sleeved dress shirt, though he wasn't going anywhere. He was sixty-six that summer, newly retired. "You girls be careful, please," he said.

And Stella smiled. "I will take very good care of her, Mr. Riordan."

I knew he was making an effort not to get teary-eyed. Since my mother died, tears came easily to him. "You take care of each other," he told us.

He stood on the curb as we pulled away. I looked back, waving. I knew it caused him some pain, this adventure of ours. It caused me some pain, too, thinking of him alone in our house for the two weeks I would be away.

"He'll be fine," Stella told me. She read me easily. "He'll eat cake for breakfast and walk around in his underwear the whole time you're away. He'll love the freedom."

I shook my head. "He'll iron a shirt every morning just to walk down the driveway to get the newspaper. He'll set the table for one and peel three potatoes instead of five every night for dinner. He'll say 'pardon' if he burps, even with no one there."

"The High Episcopal refinements of the working-class Irish Catholic," Stella said.

"Don't make fun," I told her, tearful myself.

On the floor by my feet was a roll of heavy plastic and a roll of masking tape, provided by her own father and meant to close up the passenger-side window should we encounter a heavy rain.

But by the time we were through New Jersey, the morning clouds were gone. The day was warm and sunny and perfectly June. Stella kept her own window rolled all the way down, and as a result, those back-seat scraps of loose-leaf paper, notebook paper, candy wrappers, as well as the ruffled pages of her jumbled paperbacks and library books, flapped and swirled and rose and fell behind us as we drove, as if the car itself were powered by their roiling dance.

I suppose it was this tumult, as well as the rush of the air through the two windows, not to mention the less than purring sound of Fifal's engine, that kept us mostly silent throughout the ride. We were by then both dating the men who would become our husbands. Stella's beau, Robert (never Bob), was a graduate student at the Rockefeller Institute, studying infectious disease, the catalyst for the trajectory of Stella's own peripatetic future—the West Coast, Sweden, Africa.

Robert was skinny, serious. He had a dark crew cut, even darker horn-rimmed glasses, not the best teeth. But he was a nice guy in his own distracted way. They'd met on the sidewalk on East Seventieth Street when he paused to watch her maneuver Fifal into a parking space that was—she claimed—no bigger than a sleeping cat. When she climbed out of the little car, books bundled in her arms, Robert stepped forward to express his admiration of her skill.

I was dating Peter.

In just over a year's time, we'd both be married women. And yet I don't remember us talking much about our boyfriends on the way to Charlottesville. Maybe it was the noisy car. Maybe it was the momentousness of what we were about to do: we had seen the photos of the burning Greyhound bus, the bloodied faces of the Freedom Riders; we had already decried—in Stella's attic—Bull Connor! tear gas! martial law in an American city! in literature's storied South!

Or maybe—is this only historical revisionism?—we said so little about the future because we suspected, both of us, that once we were married we would not know this kind of friendship again.

We took only one detour—into Washington, D.C., to drive past the monuments. I'd been to D.C. before, on a high school trip, but on this bright day it appeared to me to be an exquisite city, sunstruck white and green and somehow golden under a benevolent blue sky. Orderly, elegant, clean, and, compared to New York, still looking like something newly built. A little unreal in its familiar postcard perfection. Giddily, we stuck our arms out the windows as Stella called, "Wave to Mr. Lincoln," "Wave to Mr. Jefferson," "Wave to Jack and Jackie!" and at the Capitol, "Wave to the boys under the dome."

We thought this tremendously funny, intoxicated as we were with freedom, independence, flight, at last.

WE ARRIVED IN CHARLOTTESVILLE in the late afternoon. Aunt Lorraine's house was very large, at least to my eyes, but old and shabby. A wide front porch and a sloppy, high-ceilinged interior that was sparsely furnished with slouchy chairs and threadbare couches. The pale green, dingy walls were covered in modern art—mostly big, stark paintings, the kind I'd seen only in museums. There were books and magazines piled on every flat surface, no rugs, a lovely staircase with at least half a dozen balusters missing from its railing. There were big dogs, three or four, I think, but maybe more, who seemed to circulate through the rooms in a constant state of joyful anticipation, tails wagging, nails clicking on the worn floors. The place smelled of warm sunlight on old books, and of dog.

Aunt Lorraine was tall and big-boned like Stella, although heavier, with searching, deep-set eyes. She must have been in her fifties. I immediately saw how much she resembled Stella's beautiful mother; there was no mistaking that they were sisters, although in Aunt Lorraine some delicacy, some finesse had been lost. What was lovely in one was disappointing in the other: the nose a touch too wide, the chin slightly weak, her cheeks freckled and pockmarked, as opposed to peaches and cream. Actually, Aunt Lorraine was very close to being homely. Thinking about her later, I found myself, for the first time in my life, grateful that I had no siblings. No mirror-image sister to correct and accentuate my flaws.

She was gracious and welcoming. She immediately showed us to the room we would share: twin beds under flesh-pink chenille spreads, a bathroom with a claw-foot tub. Cut lilacs in a big vase and a crystal carafe of water with matching glasses, which I thought very elegant.

When we came downstairs again, she led us out to the back porch, where a table was already set—rose-patterned china and linen napkins and a small candelabra not yet lit. Her husband, the professor, was mixing drinks at a wicker cart. "Mint juleps, no less," he said, by way of welcome, the mint—he held a bunch in his hand—plucked from a mess of it growing wild beside the back steps.

He was old. I was so surprised to see how old he was—maybe seventy—mostly bald, with those little white tufts of baby hair that some men end up with. An uncombed patch of it stood straight up on the top of his shining head, proclaiming him, to my mind, a man who never looked in a mirror. He was paunchy, round-shouldered, bespectacled. He wore a white shirt with an open collar and a baggy seersucker suit.

But what shocked me even more than his age was his accent. I suppose I was expecting either Tennessee Ernie Ford or Tennessee Williams, but he sounded just like my father. Or, more accurately, he sounded like my father's best friend, Mr. Tannen (Mort to my father, but always Mr. Tannen to me). A jokey, complaining, charming Jewish guy from my father's boyhood on Tremont Avenue. His Hebrew double, as Mr. Tannen liked to say of himself. Proof positive that the Irish were the lost tribe of Israel—that was my father's joke. Gallagher and Shean they called themselves. Brothers from different Testaments: Old and New.

I recall a wave of vague confusion: this battered antebellum mansion, Aunt Lorraine's gentle drawl, the icy, sugary taste of the bourbon and mint—Stella proclaimed it toothpaste with a kick—and the delicate, crustless pimento cheese sandwiches set on a wicker coffee table placed in the midst of our floral-cushioned wicker chairs. There was even a slow-moving fan above us, a Black maid ("colored," we would have said politely) wearing a pale blue uniform. The buzzing of katydids, the three or four hounds moving in and out of the French doors . . . and then there was us: three New Yorkers, talking about New York.

The professor knew my neighborhood in Yonkers; he'd once gone door-to-door there, selling magazine subscriptions. He knew the Bronx high school where my father worked. He knew the bus and subway lines I took from Yonkers to Marymount. He knew a great little dive downtown near the *Catholic Worker* offices—Stella knew it, too. And a kosher cafeteria up by Columbia that we'd like since we liked the one near school. We had the same favorite restaurants in Chinatown, on City Island.

I remember the professor crying out—at the conclusion of a funny story about how he'd been "gypped" by a local—"And me, a doctor of philosophy, a smart guy."

When dinner was served, we moved to the elegant little table. Aunt Lorraine called it a cold summer supper: slices of roast chicken, a cool tomato aspic, potato salad, pickled snap beans, freshly baked biscuits warm in my hand. There was also white wine in delicate crystal glasses that the professor made sure we never emptied. As everyone talked, delightfully—this was when Aunt Lorraine told us the story of that fateful summer stroll past the firehouse—I felt my own silence, my usual shyness, melting away. Felt welcomed to this brave new world of large houses and colored servants, modern art, brilliant minds. No doubt the mint julep, and the Riesling, had much to do with it, but at some point I heard myself say to the professor—this smart guy— "You know, you are the spitting image of my father's best friend, Mr. Tannen." And then added, showing off, "His doppelgänger."

The professor's glasses might have flashed in the lovely candlelight.

"Is that so?" he asked, as if charmed by the notion.

I was somewhat astonished, and yet thrilled, by my own sudden leap into loquaciousness. "You might even be related."

Aunt Lorraine smiled, too, no doubt aware of the source of my sudden garrulousness, my foolish *I know another old Jewish guy* repartee. She said, "Tell us about your father. What subject does he teach?"

Here I hesitated. I had said, earlier, before the alcohol had loosened my tongue, that he worked at a high school in the Bronx, but I had not said he was a janitor.

Stella interceded. "He's not a teacher," she told her aunt. "Patsy's father actually works for a living. He's a custodian at the school."

"Ah," Aunt Lorraine said pleasantly.

"He used to be a stevedore," I added. It was my mother's word; she had preferred it to "longshoreman." "Same as his brother was. But after his brother was killed in an accident, on the docks, *très tragique*"—proving that I was a college girl—"my mother asked him to give it up. To work at something less dangerous."

"And was your mother Irish, too?" Aunt Lorraine asked, letting me know she knew my mother was gone—that Stella had already offered her this much of my biography.

I said, "Her parents were." In those days, it was my way of saying "No, American."

Aunt Lorraine asked if I had siblings. And when I said no she asked, "Are there cousins about? Aunts and uncles?"

Stella spoke up again. "Patsy has the luxury of living alone with her father. Just the two of them." And then she added, dramatically, "You have no idea how much I envy her."

"A large family is a blessing," Aunt Lorraine said.

"I'm not going to have children," Stella declared. "Only parakeets."

Last I heard from her, she had five. Children, that is.

Once more the professor filled our glasses.

As the dishes were cleared by the maid, Aunt Lorraine steered the conversation to our plans for tomorrow. The professor had mapped out a route for us, and she had arranged for our lunches to be packed, sandwiches and a couple of Cokes, so we wouldn't have to "be diverted" into small towns along the way. The pillows and sleeping bags she was lending us were already in the hallway.

This was the first I realized that we'd be sleeping on the convent floor.

Aunt Lorraine had the address and the phone number of the Sisters we were staying with—she actually knew one of them—but still she wanted us to assure her ("Please assure me" was exactly how she put it) that we would not go wandering off by ourselves. Especially at night.

"There's been some violence of late," she said, "as you well know."

"Of course we know," Stella told her.

"And despite what's being said by young Mr. Kennedy"—she meant Bobby—"I don't believe there's been much cooling off."

"It's going to get worse," the professor added, speaking softly, as if to himself, and Lorraine replied, continuing some conversation it was clear they'd already had, "Yes, it's going to get worse, I'm afraid."

There was a pause in which we all seemed to consider this.

And then Stella said, "I hope it does. It needs to get worse."

The maid returned with small dishes of vanilla ice cream

scattered with strawberries and garnished with more mint. We all thanked her, remarked on how lovely it looked, and then Aunt Lorraine said when she was gone, "I'm not out to dissuade you, girls. What you're doing is very brave. I'm just asking you to be careful."

"It's a different place," the professor added. "The South." He leaned forward. "Two bits of advice," he said. "If you go to any sit-ins, write our phone number, in ink, on your forearm here." He indicated his seersucker jacket sleeve. "If you get arrested, God forbid. You call us. Second"—he shrugged with Mr. Tannen's shrug—"take some dog biscuits with you. Put them in your pockets. You never know. Police dogs. They might get hungry."

I probably laughed at this more than I should have. There were many aspects of this trip I hadn't much thought about.

The maid returned with a plate of shortbread. Once more we all murmured our thanks, and Aunt Lorraine said, "I'll get the coffee, Sonia. You take yourself home now." And thanked her for the wonderful meal.

I saw Stella's eyes following the woman back through the French doors, into the low lights of the house. I knew some objection, some argument, was forming behind her eyes, going into a crouch along her spine and shoulders.

Aunt Lorraine said, growing serious once again, "There's more violence coming. I'm sure of it. I want you girls to be careful."

Stella raised her chin, pushed her smudged glasses back on her nose, and said, "Why's that?"

In her voice, the familiar sound—familiar to me—of a struck match. A match struck, held hissing to a short fuse.

"Because I want you to be safe, " Aunt Lorraine said simply. "I don't want you hurt."

"Nothing will change if we're all keeping safe, " Stella told her. "If no one gets hurt."

I saw the professor smile at this, glance from Stella to his only mildly bemused wife. Something in his manner said he had identified a promising student.

"No doubt that's true," Aunt Lorraine conceded.

But Stella suddenly slammed her fist on the table. The little ice-cream bowls jumped and the candlelight shivered. "I am the descendant of slave owners, Aunt Lorraine," Stella proclaimed. "And so are you. The original sin is ours, our family's. We don't have the option to stay safe. Not anymore. A sin like that can't be absolved"—and here she turned up her lip, waved a hand in the air as if to flick from her fingertips something sticky and distasteful—"safely."

Across the table, I saw how the professor, his arms folded over his chest, raised an eyebrow, wrinkling his bald forehead.

"Yes, I know," Aunt Lorraine was murmuring, full of sadness. "Of course I know this."

Stella leaned toward her. "No, you don't," she said steadily. She clasped and unclasped the hand that had struck the table. I saw that the white cloth was damp under the edge of her palm. She said, her teeth clenched, "A family that once owned slaves should not be hiring colored maids."

"Oh, honey," Aunt Lorraine whispered, gentle, conciliatory.

But Stella hardly paused. "As atonement for past sins, if nothing else."

Aunt Lorraine glanced at her husband. But he was sitting back, admiring Stella still.

"The issue is complicated," Aunt Lorraine said softly.

But Stella was at the height of her Stella-ness. "No, the issue isn't complicated," she said, full of fury. I saw how she was moving her hand over the pale tablecloth, touching the rim of her ice-cream dish, as if to feel around it. For a moment, I was grateful that Sonia had collected our dinner knives.

"I'm sick to death of hearing how the issue is complicated." Bold. Brazen. "The issue is actually quite simple: there has to be a break with the past, there has to be retribution." The candle-light might have caught, or caused, the tears that were suddenly standing in her eyes. "Nothing breaks without violence, Aunt Lorraine. There's no retribution without blood." Her eyes shifted toward me. Shifted back. "This is exactly why we're going to Birmingham."

There was a pause. Into it, I might have asked, "It is?"

But Aunt Lorraine and her husband were studying Stella with appreciation and concern.

"You are full of passion, young lady," Aunt Lorraine said finally.

And then the professor whispered, "Tikkun olam." He smiled at us all. An ancient midrash, he explained. "Your Mr. Tannen would know it," he told me. "It means 'repair the world.'"

He gazed at Stella across the candlelight, a favorite student. "The Jews know that everything God has created is in need of repair, flawed and imperfect." He gestured. "Kind of like this house. Fix one thing, for certain something somewhere else is already broken."

Aunt Lorraine laughed quietly, her eyes cast down.

"Easy enough to live with this when you're old like us," he went on, "but when you're young," and he paused to run his hand over his bald pate, his little apostolic flame of white baby hair. "When you're young, it's fuel to the fire of a sympathetic heart."

He smiled at Stella again.

"Tikkun olam," he said. "Go forth and do likewise."

AT SOME POINT during our time together, I gave the phrase to your mother. It might have been the only thing I ever gave her. I watched her turn the words over in her mind. In my memory, I see her turning it over, quite literally, in her hands.

I also see her—more fairy-tale recollection—tossing it back to me playfully, like one of our whiffle balls or pink Spaldeens.

"Repair the world." She shook her head. Said something both condescending and admiring about the hubris of the Jews.

And then she looked at me with her smarter-than-everyone smile.

"But don't you know, Tricia," she told me, "the Buddhists say, 'Mend yourself.'"

Isn't it awful, really, how days and dates disappear, how the bright routines that absorb our attention for so many hours of the living day fall away so easily over the years, obscure and confound memory's precision. Was that last Monday or last Tuesday? Last month, the month before? Sometime last year? Some season of my childhood?

I regret now that I never kept a diary while we were in Saigon, but I suppose I believed the letters I wrote, filling each folded side of those delicate blue pages, were record enough. Not because I thought they would be returned to me (at twenty-three, I would never have imagined myself grown so old that my girlish jottings might become artifacts, even treasure), but because I had made some record of things, and that record, I assumed, had been read. By my father. Or by Stella. By Peter's parents or his siblings or our New York friends.

How innocent it seems now: to have ever believed that words written for, read by, one alone, only one, were sufficient unto themselves. Sufficiently shared. Sufficiently saved.

But the public record is helpful, as I struggle to get the dates clear.

Late in the same month as my miscarriage, good Pope

John XXIII died in Rome. There had been a few days of world-wide vigil—for us Catholics, anyway—and then he was gone. I remember bowing my head at Mass that Sunday, tears falling on my folded hands. I recall the sound of other women weeping, a soft echo through the cathedral—a faraway grief folded into my own.

It was June as well when the first Buddhist monk set himself on fire in front of the Cambodian embassy. I was at home when it happened, but Peter was nearby. He heard the nuns praying, caught a whiff of the gasoline, even saw the black smoke rise above the crowd. Peter told me that as the man burned, another monk spoke into a microphone, a surreal narration in that hollow, open-air echo that was to become so familiar to us in the years ahead, especially when we took a Sunday stroll along the Mall. The sound of some protester's voice, amplified and indistinct, littering the air with anger or imprecation, slogan and cliché.

"A Buddhist priest burns himself to death," the monk chanted into his portable mike. "A Buddhist priest becomes a martyr."

One witness said it was astonishing to see how swiftly a human body could melt out of existence.

I shuddered as I listened to Peter's account—we all shuddered, of course, when we saw the terrible photo.

But in the days that followed, Peter was sweetly, even boyishly, puzzled by the suicide. He thought he understood Buddhism. He had taken two semesters of world religion at Fordham. He'd read Thomas Merton. He understood the Vietnamese Buddhists to be a gentle people who cherished life.

The Western cliché in those days was that a Buddhist

wouldn't crush a biting flea or swat a buzzing fly, and Peter believed this. He believed the Buddhists understood better than
anyone the brief nature of our lives, and so they eschewed all
politics, certainly all political protest.

He couldn't reconcile this image of a gentle, deeply spiritual
people with the photograph of that dark figure engulfed by
flames, or with the eyewitness accounts of how the younger
monks had helped the stumbling old priest from a car, carried the
gas can for him, doused his head. Peter's usual wry, forgiving,
good-humored sympathy for what he called the naturally occur-
ring inconsistencies of the convoluted human brain gave way in
this instance to a stubborn skepticism, a childish objection that I
thought was somehow inadequate, even irrelevant, to the horror
of the tragedy. The awfulness of it.

"It just doesn't make sense," he told me again and again in the
days that followed, resentful as an adolescent of a world that had
not conformed to what he was certain he knew.

I recall a dinner party with some American friends when he
turned briefly, almost rudely, adamant about it all. An apartment party, as I recall it, all of us gathered around a small coffee
table with our drinks, hand-carved souvenir bowls of mixed
nuts and potato chips before us, everyone newly showered and
powdered and shaved, the wives tucked comfortably beside
their handsome husbands.

Religious persecution, Peter pronounced, persecution against
the Buddhists or anyone else, had never been a problem in Vietnam. This was a country, after all, that included the Cao Dai, the
Hoa Hao, the "pagan" Montagnards, Confucians, Catholics,
Protestants even.

"A mishmash," I might have added.

There were Buddhists in Diem's cabinet—"for heaven's sake," Peter said.

There were Buddhists everywhere you looked, pagodas galore. The Buddhists moved freely about the city.

"How are they being persecuted?" he asked our friends. "Where are they being persecuted?"

"Hue," someone answered—where Buddhist protesters had recently been killed by Diem's troops.

But Peter argued that even the facts of that confrontation were in dispute. It was an explosion, a bomb, that had killed the protesters, not government bullets.

And—he was raising his voice now—Diem himself had launched an investigation into the incident. Reparations had been paid to the families of the dead and injured.

So what, he asked our American friends, or the men among us anyway, "what in God's name," was the old monk's awful suicide really meant to prove?

And why was the young monk with the portable microphone reciting his chant in English if it was Diem's government he meant to address? Why had the monks invited the AP to attend?

The other men—how young we all were—merely shook their heads, amused and unserious, unwilling, I suppose, to disrupt the evening with debate. They dismissed Peter's arguments with a laugh, or the single word "kamikaze."

Solicitously, sociably, they explained to Peter that suicide was easy for a Buddhist, a shortcut to a better next life.

"A brief bonze fire," someone said, "and you come back as Rock Hudson."

I suppose I was the only one among us who saw how quickly,

how adeptly, Peter responded to this: how he checked himself, tamped down his voice.

He smiled gently, dipped his chin (it was his way), offended by their dismissal, I knew, but utterly, politely, conciliatory. "I may be wrong," he told them, smiling. "I may be missing something."

I suppose this was his natural instinct: to defer, to deflect, to remind his betters that he knew his place by a humble display of good manners. A habit born of his lace-curtain upbringing, I suppose, as well as the time he'd now spent among the Ivy Leagued.

A false humility, in truth.

Because when we were alone that night, in bed, he took up the argument again, speaking vehemently into the dark.

The Jesuits, I recall him saying, require twelve years of training before a man can make his vows. But in Buddhism, anyone can shave his head and become a priest. So how easy would it be for the communists to infiltrate a few pagodas, to infiltrate and then to encourage, even to coerce, certain others to commit suicide in this public and horrific way?

How better to turn the West against Diem, to undermine his war against the North? How better to embarrass Diem's American allies?

Buddhist protesters, he argued, should be an oxymoron. "Communist infiltrators is more like it," he said.

Of course I took the Buddhists' side—sounding like Stella, I'll admit. I must have reminded him of Madame Nhu's notorious barbecue remark. Or her husband's secret police. Or Diem's icy indifference.

I know I made the case, cribbed from *The New York Times*, I believe, that the Buddhist protests in Saigon were akin to the Civil Rights Movement at home. A repressed people trying to draw the world's attention to their plight.

Which led me to recall for him our dinner in Charlottesville, Stella and me—our great adventure. A way to distract him from his seriousness so we could go to sleep.

But Peter would not be distracted. When I'd finished my tale, he patted my thigh and muttered something like "Good for you."

But all civil disobedience was not equal, he declared. "American Negroes," he said, "want reform, even restitution, and rightly so, but the militant Buddhists"—another oxymoron, he pointed out—"want only chaos."

I told him he was beginning to sound like my father, who called every righteous outlier a communist, not just Dorothy Day but Eleanor Roosevelt, Martin Luther King Jr., Norman Mailer, even Peter's own guy, Thomas Merton, who my father thought was both a communist and a "bit of a kook."

We had a laugh over this, finally, side by side in the dark.

PETER BELIEVED FOR THE REST OF HIS LIFE that the Buddhist suicides were political theater, part of a communist effort to embarrass Diem, to turn the West against him.

He told me once, toward the end of his life, that the tragedy of the U.S. role in Vietnam had at its roots an insidious kind of anti-Catholicism: a Catholic administration, a Catholic intelligence agency, so anxious to prove their impartiality that they all too readily abandoned a fellow Catholic president in Vietnam because he was getting bad press.

He called it a kind of self-immolating reverse discrimination, turning against an ally like that precisely because he was one of our own. An ally who had been, Peter remained certain, that beleaguered country's best hope. Even if that hope lay in Diem making an agreement with Ho Chi Minh to divide their country between them. A pact with the Devil, as Peter saw it, that nevertheless would have saved so many lives.

I guess you could say that the miraculous, portentous, historical alignment of the stars that had so inspired my husband before we got to Saigon—two Catholic presidents standing together to defeat the march of communism, to fulfill Our Lady's promise at Fátima—had become in retrospect the very thing that sent our good intentions all awry.

They never saw the hand of God in it, Peter later said of his superiors in Saigon. "But they made useful fools of those of us who thought we did."

DURING THAT SAME SUMMER, Jacqueline Kennedy was pregnant with her third child.

Of course, I was always studying her clothes and her hats, her long shoes and her breathy voice. Now I studied her demure smile and the delicate hand she placed on her growing belly. I allowed Charlene to remind me that Mrs. Kennedy, too, had suffered a miscarriage in years past.

This was at a christening party in July, a party your mother threw for the Vietnamese orphan whom Roberta and her USIS husband were taking home. A lovely gathering—all your mother's parties were lovely. Tiny American flags on toothpicks anchoring the canapés.

As I left, Charlene walked me out. You came along, too, as I remember, in another pretty pastel dress. I recall how you slipped your hand into mine. We had shared some playtime during the party. There were new Barbie clothes, just arrived from the aunt in New York. Once again, I was grateful to give you my attention. A way to avoid taking Roberta's new baby into my arms, as all the other women were doing. Protecting my dress, I told myself.

We were at her gate when Charlene mentioned that Jacqueline Kennedy had had a stillbirth and a miscarriage—did I know this? I nodded, reluctant to say more about it in front of you. The mechanics of childbirth—from bedroom start to bloody finish, so to speak—were not a fit subject for small ears. Not in those days.

But Charlene didn't hesitate. "And now here she is," she told me. "Pregnant again. About to deliver her third child."

I smiled, nodded, holding your hand.

"Hope springs," your mother said. As if she were making me a promise.

WHEN I WAS READY to join her again on the visits to the hospital, Charlene offered to drive to our place to pick me up. The wheels and the underbody of the truck were spattered with rust-colored mud. The rainy season had begun—your mother liked to call it "Rainey's season" because there was nothing you liked better than to stay indoors with your Barbie and your books.

Not a tennis player at all, I had learned by then.

I assumed the truck had been used during the week at one or another of the construction projects Kent's company was involved in, but I think the sight of it, or of me climbing into the cab, was a shock for Peter. As we pulled away, I saw him looking warily from behind our gate.

Dominic was among the first to welcome me back, and I asked him right away how his wife was. I thought maybe Charlene had told him something about my miscarriage, because he blushed deeply under his already sunburned cheeks. She had, just days ago, been delivered of a healthy baby girl.

I told him I was delighted. I tried to mean it.

B Y MID-JULY, the foreman of the loading dock at Macy's in Herald Square had secured—"Don't ask me how," Charlene said, "my sister is a woman of incalculable charm"—four cases of brand-new Barbie dolls, something like thirty-six to a case.

Each doll was in a narrow cardboard box. In two of the cases, they had those glued ponytails and curled bangs, and were dressed in a strapless striped bathing suit. In the others, the dolls were dressed in red bathing suits and had short bouffant hairdos—a bubble cut, Rainey informed me.

The blondes looked like Marilyn Monroe, but the brunettes looked like Mrs. Kennedy. I gathered they were meant to.

Charlene had befriended—in her own inimitable, dare I say "transactional" way—an American woman who worked as a manager of sorts at the Brink, the officers' club.

She was another American dependent, the wife of a major, as I recall.

I was beginning to know these military wives. They were stoic and efficient. They would, at the easiest provocation, or no provocation at all, recount for you (at garden parties and cocktail parties, over lunch or after lectures at the Vietnamese-American

Association, even sunbathing by the pool) their husbands' various postings, to Guam, to Hawaii, to North Carolina, Germany, Italy, Colorado, the Philippines, wherever, easily enumerating the years of each deployment, each settling in and each uprooting, with benign sufferance. They seldom expressed a preference for any particular place, but neither did they offer any complaint. Good soldiers all.

The understanding among them seemed to be that their peripatetic lives were simply the inevitable result of their marriages to these particular men, their fate: part accident, part unintended consequence, all inescapable. The unpredictable fruit of any American romance. Yet another ramification of *clang, clang, clang went the trolley.*

And while some of these women instantly embraced wherever they found themselves—studying the language, bartering in the market, going to every State Department lecture, every cultural exchange—others simply brought their stateside lives with them, packed hermetically into whatever family unit they traveled in; some even brought the family dog, the family station wagon—well contented with themselves and the utter impenetrability of their American lives.

According to Charlene, the major's wife was one of these. She absolutely hated Saigon, the food, the heat, the noise, the people. Once she'd settled her three children in the American school, set up her furniture from home, joined the proper social club (Le Cercle Sportif), and disabused her cook of any notion of providing them with native cuisine, she'd found this job at the Brink billet, the bachelor officers' club, because, she told Charlene, she was accustomed to being a working woman.

She arrived at the Brink early every morning and stayed as

late as she could each afternoon in order to convince herself, for as many hours of her day as it was possible to do, that she was still living in New Jersey. Or so said Charlene.

She was nice enough. Marilee was her name. She was tall, broad-shouldered, thick-armed, somewhat homely. These days you might wonder if she hadn't been born a man. She kept her dark hair carefully curled, wore cat's-eye glasses on a chain, a cardigan over her shoulders, neat skirts, and sleeveless blouses. Charlene and I met her for lunch at the rooftop restaurant of the Caravelle, and I sat mostly quiet as Charlene made her pitch. She wanted to display our Saigon Barbie on a table at the Brink, with a simple sign-up sheet that Charlene would gather every morning as she delivered the previous day's orders. The money—American dollars only, of course—would be left in a marked envelope. The honor system.

"If we can't depend on an honor system in the officers' club," Charlene said, "then where?"

Marilee eyed the doll. Without much interest, it seemed to me. Charlene had propped up the Barbie in her ao dai and her non la on the little wire display stand that came with each doll. I thought our Saigon Barbie looked quite, well, cunning, and noticed a few of the other ladies who lunched, many of them military wives, glancing over as well. But Marilee was not charmed. I feared for a moment that what was crossing her mind was some version of Charlene's crude suggestion about our generals and their whores.

But what Marilee said, after a dramatic pause, was "The poor you will always have with you." She said it gravely, but also with some smug condescension. Which I suppose is exactly the way Christ said it, too. And everyone since.

I was taken aback but—my own default position—simply smiled. Charlene ducked her head. She was holding a lit cigarette in the hand she had rested on the tablecloth, and I saw her rub her thumb and ring finger together impatiently. I knew that gesture.

"I admire your good intentions," Marilee went on. "But, honestly. How much are you two going to raise and how much good will it do? The American taxpayer is already supporting this country in an exorbitant way. And for what?"

Her husband, she told us, had just shown her an article about the Commercial Import Program, which, she hoped, the U.S. was—or so rumor had it—about to suspend. When Charlene and I made no intelligent response to what was clearly for Marilee a delicious possibility, she took on the burden of enlightening us.

The CIP, she informed us, involved our government pouring American money into Vietnam's economy. American taxpayer dollars that the Vietnamese would change into piastres and then—"Can you believe the gall?"—sell back to us at a distorted rate.

I glanced at Charlene, who kept her head down.

Free money, essentially, Marilee exclaimed. American taxpayer money that the regime, as well as the wealthy exporters and importers, were using however they pleased. Not to help the country but to help themselves.

She mentioned the cheap electronic equipment available in Saigon. How much her son had paid for a certain camera. I confess I began to lose the thread.

Marilee repeated the phrase "free money." I could imagine her and the square-shouldered major squawking about it over breakfast. "We've built them roads," she went on, "dredged their ports. Given them schools, orphanages. Ammunition. Our best and brightest are here to advise them. Have you ever seen so many generals in one place? And what are we getting in return? They're taking potshots at our boys. Turning a blind eye to their murderous communist friends."

I was beginning to suspect that Marilee was the kind of woman, numerous in those days, who strove to parrot her husband—not as an act of fealty, not even of admiration or love, but as an attempt, I think, to appear masculine herself. Strong and wise. A kind of verbal cross-dressing. Talking down to other women in this husbandly way was just a part of it.

She informed us of Vietnam's recent history—something else she and the major had read about together. They'd tossed the Chinese out. Tossed the French out—despite all the lovely buildings the French had given them. "What makes you think they aren't going to throw us out, too?"

Charlene and I both shrugged.

"And charities?" she asked us, laughing at the absurdity of it all. "How many charitable organizations have stepped in? And still the place is a mess, and getting messier, if you ask me. Diem's a crook. His brother's worse. And his wife!" She held up her hands. "The Vietnamese don't care about their war. You saw what happened at Ap Bac." (In truth, I'm not sure I had.) "My husband says they're the first to disappear when any fighting starts. Our pilots call the guys from the ARVN who go up with them 'sand-bags.' Dead weight in the cockpit. And the officers! They aren't soldiers, they're the spoiled children of the elites. They care more about their pretty uniforms than their troops."

She brought her fingertips to both edges of the tabletop, as if seeking to steady it against the wobbly spot of earth on which it stood, and leaned, chest first, toward us both.

"Honestly," she said with amused frustration. "How much good can we really do here? How much good can the two of you do?"

With her head still down, her fingers moving, Charlene said, "Very little."

"Exactly my point," Marilee said, satisfied.

I was beginning to think she would have made a pretty good major herself, her chest a broad calico field for the pinning of medals. She was very sure of herself, of her husband, of what she'd just been reading.

"Look," she began again. I could tell she was enjoying the opportunity to set us straight. "I'm happy to help out." She gestured toward our Barbie. "These are very cute. I'll definitely get one for my daughter. But why not raise the money for the American school instead? Let your own children, and mine, get some benefit. You know as well as I do, Charlene, the classrooms are overcrowded. Why not give the money to the American school and save us mothers from all the bake sales we've been having? I mean," and here she seemed to make an effort to soften her expression, "the children here—I have the deepest sympathy for them—but they aren't going to have their lives improved by a toy or a lollipop. Let's face it: their fates are sealed. Their fates were sealed the moment they were born in this godforsaken place. Arrange an airlift, if you really want to help. Get every newborn out of here. Get them American parents." She laughed at her own absurdity. "Why kid yourself? Nothing less will do any good."

As Marilee made her pronouncements, Charlene's short, well-groomed, but nevertheless painfully cropped fingertips, flickering impatiently under her cigarette, were the sole indication of her fury. But no other was needed.

Marilee saw this, too. The woman's breast was on the rise. The little bit of dark cleavage that showed above the top button of her blouse seemed to edge closer to her chin. And then, as if Charlene had offered some rebuke—though she'd said nothing—I saw Marilee's face grow stony; her mouth, her rose-colored lipstick, drew itself into a firm line. She was an opinionated woman, certain of her opinions—that is, her husband's opinions—and she was ready to talk some sense into us.

She took off her cat's-eye glasses, left them to dangle over her décolletage. Without them, her eyes seemed palely innocent, undressed, but in a sweet, even childish way. "There's a real danger here," she said, and paused to let that sink in. I wasn't sure if she meant here at this table or in the country at large. "There's a real danger in the bestowing of gifts upon the hopeless only to inflate the ego of the one who does the bestowing."

She paused, as if to admire the way she'd put this. She might have grown a little cross-eyed.

"A real danger," she said again. After she'd let that sink in, she added, "It encourages self-righteousness in the one even as it destroys self-determination in the other."

Or so, I thought, says the major.

Marilee returned her glasses to their perch. Paused to let her eyes refocus. She executed an elaborate squint, like a man flexing his fists after he'd struck a triumphant blow. And then she added, one more jab, "The road to hell is paved with good intentions."

With her head still bowed, Charlene put out her cigarette, straightened her spine, adjusted the napkin on her lap. (I saw

Stella Carney's own revving-up in the gesture.) Then she glanced at me, the slightest trace of her smarter-than-everyone smile.

Charlene brushed back her hair, although it was already well tamed under a wide headband. Drew in her breath as if to accept wearily the burden she bore. Then she looked up and aimed her green eyes at Marilee.

"On sundry days, mostly Thursdays," Charlene said, nearly whispering. We both had to lean forward to hear her, clever girl. "I've been visiting a leper colony out on the coast. It's a beautiful place, run by some French nuns. Some of our boys, our medics, have been going out there to do what they can. To do some good. Surgeries when our surgeons are available, but palliative care for the most part. And now and then I've gone with them. I shouldn't. I'm not authorized. But they indulge me, let me tag along, because I bring a basket or two of our inconsequential little toys for the children. Little somethings for the adults as well, sweets and cigarettes. For the lepers."

She smiled. I was certain she'd added the subtlest drawl to her words.

"You can't imagine two things more incongruous, Marilee, the absolute beauty of the place, the beach, the blue water and the white sand. The lovely trees—tamarind, pine. And the wonderful flowers, orchids and hibiscus, the scent of jasmine, even roses. The buildings are lovely, too, Marilee. French-built, as you say. Open corridors. Beautiful tile floors. All of it immaculate. The Sisters keep it very well. And you can't imagine how incongruous all that beauty is when you meet the patients themselves. The lepers, Marilee. The terrible distortions to face and limbs. The grotesque transformation of the human form. The human face. You recoil. It can't be helped, Marilee."

And then she turned to me. "Isn't that right, Tricia?"

Of course, I had never been there. Never even knew until this moment that Charlene had gone. "Yes," I said.

Marilee shot me a look. I moved my head, not quite a nod, a vague confirmation. Marilee's own, unplucked eyebrows might have been arranging themselves into the one word "unauthorized," in careful cursive; her thoughts were that apparent.

Charlene raised her elbows to the white tablecloth. Gestured with her open palms. "And that recoil, Marilee. That perfectly reasonable impulse to turn away, to gag, you might say, to close your eyes at the sight of this suffering is, to my mind, Marilee, a kind of evil."

The poor woman made some sound of rational objection— she might have said, "Come now," or "Really"—but Charlene stopped her with her palm.

"It's a very small evil, of course," she said pleasantly enough. "That impulse to turn away. It's not murder. Nobody's getting corrupted. It's not even something we can be blamed for, really." A breath of a laugh. "Surely we can't be held responsible for the madness of"—she waved her fingers—"*creation.*"

She seemed to consider for a second the insufficiency of the word.

"Turning away," a gentle indulgence now in her voice, "it's an honest reaction, isn't it?" As ever, she did not pause for reply. "But it's an indication nevertheless of what we're capable of, it seems to me. We're capable of turning away. We're capable of despising the sight of something so awful, something so incongruous to the good order we prefer. The beauty we prefer. I mean, Marilee," she added with a huff of breath, "*suffering.*"

She made the word itself sound like a fashion faux pas: like white shoes after Labor Day. An ill-fitting Guy Laroche. "Honestly, Marilee. Who wants to gaze at suffering?"

And then she smiled sympathetically across the table. "Do you see what I'm saying?" Conveying as she said it the full confidence that Marilee did not.

A flush had begun to spread from under the neat collar of Marilee's starched blouse, across her ruffled breast. "I thought we were talking about raising money," she said, and then added with a small laugh, "for little toys."

"We are," Charlene said, utterly patient. "It's just that you said there's very little good we can do. In this place. And I agree, I do. But that very little good might be just the thing required to stand against that very little evil—that impulse to turn away."

Marilee laughed again, vaguely. "This is all very philosophical." She paused. Made her own spine a bit straighter and threw back her broad shoulders as if to show she would not be drawn into these emotional, female, arguments.

"I thought you said you wanted to make some money, with your dolls," she said sensibly, "for your little gifts and things."

She suddenly glanced around at the other tables, aware, I think that she had raised her voice.

"I don't know why you're talking about lepers. Of all things. Like something out of the Bible." She made an attempt at light-heartedness. "My goodness, ladies. Forget the little toys. Maybe you should buy yourselves some paper parasols. You've gotten too much sun."

I laughed, politely.

But Charlene grew languorous, full of tolerant sympathy. She brought her forearms to the table, folded them together, and leaned down, as you might do to help a child struggling with her homework. Again she glanced at me but this time as if, together, we'd often had this very conversation with multiple other fools. And then she turned back to Marilee.

"I'm so sorry," she said. She let out one of her softest *Forgive me for laughing at you* laughs. "I let myself get way ahead of you." Classic Charlene.

She said we were, in fact, looking to purchase more than toys. She said I had been inspired—"It was Tricia's vision," she said—after visiting the lepers, after working with Lily on our Barbie clothes, to do more than bring our little gifts and toys to these poor, suffering people.

"Tricia said to me," Charlene went on, without the slightest indication that the majority of us at this table knew she was lying, "'What if we could raise enough money to make the same lovely ao dais for the women and girls at the colony? Perhaps some nice silk tunics for the men as well?' Tricia thought that bringing such gifts to these poor people, the lepers, would be the clearest indication we could give them that they, too, were beautiful in spite of their disease. Still beautiful. Still human. And we will not look away."

As Charlene spun this noble fiction, I was aware of Marilee glancing at me from across the table. There was a transformation taking place. I saw I was being reevaluated: when I shook Marilee's hand outside the restaurant, I'd been Charlene's petite young friend, pretty enough but with a shy woman's bad posture, a hardly memorable girl Charlene had brought along to lunch. As we ate, I became what I was quite certain Marilee would later describe to the major as a quiet one, remarkable only because I had an impressive young husband with a law degree and an assignment here with the navy, since my only real contribution to the conversation thus far had been my usual recitation of Peter's accomplishments, as well as some anodyne agreement that the Central Market was impossible to navigate.

But now I saw Marilee assessing me with a kind of enlightenment, even respect. I was, she seemed to be discovering, a quiet, shy, yet plucky American girl with that quintessential, somewhat naive but nevertheless admirable American virtue: a good and generous heart.

I can't say I actually got it that afternoon—what Charlene was up to, as far as I, or our friendship, was concerned. But certainly it was then that I had my first inkling.

It wasn't merely that everyone in the American community in Saigon, the other women at least, were sick to death of smarter-than-they-were Charlene. It was that Charlene was complex and I, to all observers, was simple.

Charlene plotted and schemed and traded on the black market; she pushed people around, drove like the devil, swept into rooms, popped pills, raised money; she was a dynamo. She laughed readily at other people's foolishness, and while she might suppress her anger at their stupidity—confining her fury to two impatient fingertips flicking each other under her cigarette like a flint against a stone—she did not let that stupidity pass. When her husband belittled her, good-naturedly, of course—it was the way all husbands belittled their wives in those days—she replied silently; she ducked her head demurely but managed nevertheless to make the gesture seem as defiant as a raised gun.

She was not, in short, a saint.

I was to be the saint. The saint in her cabal.

And all my naiveté, my shyness, my lousy French, but most especially my foolish, innocent plans to do good in this godforsaken place, could thus be accepted as a sweet faux pas that might nevertheless be indulged.

From across the white tablecloth, across our empty coffee cups and ice-cream dishes, across Charlene's ashtray and the sprig of bright bougainvillea in the centerpiece, I saw Marilee smile at me the way you smile at modest girl saints: ruefully, admiringly, amused by the poor idiot, yet sympathetic.

She said, to me, not Charlene, "I'm sorry. I guess I misunderstood. It's really a lovely idea."

Charlene turned to me as well. "Yes, isn't it?" she said. Now she and Marilee were allies in their admiration. "Tricia's out to repair the world," Charlene pronounced, as if I were a precocious child. "She taught me the Hebrew phrase for this: tikkun olam. Repair the world. It's her cri de guerre."

Marilee shook her head and breathed an admiring "Ahh"—won over completely, although, in truth, *She certainly doesn't look Jewish* was written plainly across her big brow.

THUS WAS OUR PROJECT not only conceived but made inevitable in that conversation on the roof of the Caravelle.

Charlene told me later that the whole idea, the idea to bring lovely new clothes to the lepers, had probably been somewhere in the back of her head, in her unconscious, she said, but it had only sprung to the forefront when she heard Marilee's perfectly rational argument against our altruism.

"My first impulse was to screw my cigarette into her face," Charlene said later. "She was so smug. Lecturing me about the Vietnamese economy. But then I thought, well, poor, homely

Marilee is as much a product of her birth, her genes, her confining circumstances, as she's right now saying the Vietnamese are. I thought, you know, she probably dresses this way—I mean, that blouse—because she doesn't believe her homely face and dimpled biceps deserve better. Probably married the major for the same reason. I thought, listening to her go on, that something in silk might improve her outlook. An ao dai for Marilee, I thought. Despite that face. Despite those linebacker's shoulders. And then I thought of the lepers. And then I was telling her about your wonderful plan, which, I'm afraid, I'd just hatched."

WE MADE THE TRIP to the leper colony on a Thursday—in late July or early August.

Lying, surely the first time I lied to him about my whereabouts, I told Peter I would spend the day at Charlene's, making doll clothes. Then I would stay to have dinner with the children while Charlene and Kent went out for a night on the town.

I didn't say—I didn't have to—that this diversion would be good for me, lift me out of my disappointment and sadness. I'd burst into tears the first time we made love after the miscarriage, and while Peter held me patiently, I had the sense, too, of some coolness in his touch, as if my tears had hurt his feelings.

The second time, he'd looked at me warily afterward. "You okay?" he asked. I answered honestly that I didn't know.

The third time, he asked me if I would ever again simply enjoy this, simply relax. In the days—I should say nights—that followed he seemed more and more like a man who was growing impatient with what he had thought would be an easy repair: a bit of glue, a bit of pressure, should have been easy . . . but the broken thing would not mend.

Shyly, he told me one night as I wept, "It's really not that important to me. A kid of my own."

I understood he meant to be kind. He was of that generation of men, among the last, I suppose, who opened doors for women, or gave up their seats on the subway, who stood whenever a woman walked into a room, and rushed to relieve any female companion of even the slightest burden—taking from her arms a bag of groceries, a basket of laundry, a briefcase, or a book. Instinctively. I recall an evening in New York when I looked out our apartment window and saw Peter walking home from the subway with the wife of our super beside him, her ungainly three-year-old, who had fallen asleep on the train, in his arms.

I understood that he wanted to take this burden from me, this burden to procreate, by telling me it really didn't matter. And I loved him for that kindness.

But I also feared my miscarriage had given him permission to tell the truth. Peter was the third of nine children. Five boys, four girls. One sister and one brother never married. Another sister became a nun. A brother became a priest. The other four siblings married and produced one child each. I guess they were all aware of the burden of an overcrowded household, too little money, too little space. Parents who seemed so fond of each other throughout the day and yet became so wary when evening approached.

Peter said his mother slept on the floor in his sisters' room for much of his childhood because—so the family joke went—their father's snoring could wake the dead.

The other family joke went that Peter and his brothers, and one of his sisters, joined the military straight out of high school in order to get some privacy.

HERE'S A STORY my sister-in-law, by then an ex-nun, told me: Late one night when she was a kid, their father came to the door of the bedroom the four girls shared, calling for their mother, and then, in an instant, before any of them was fully awake, he shoved open the door and flipped on the overhead light. Blinking and squinting, the four girls saw that the old mattress on the floor between their bunk beds, the mattress where their mother usually slept, was empty. Their father saw this, too, and bellowed.

He was not a drinker but they knew he'd had a few that night.

He demanded to know where their mother had gone. The girls shrugged, told him she had been there when they fell asleep. He stormed out, went to the boys' room, and then through the rest of the small house, calling for her. When he came back upstairs, he launched into a rant about their mother's obligation to him, her duty to him as ordained by God and the one, true, holy, catholic, and apostolic Church.

And then he said, somewhat unsteady on his feet, "I could divorce her for this."

By now all nine of the children were gathered, either in the girls' bedroom or out in the narrow hallway, all standing in their pajamas, in the strange, cold light of a household awoken suddenly at three a.m. They looked at their father in hushed fear—"divorce" was a terrifying word. You could hear the clocks ticking, Peter's sister said.

And then, from somewhere in the room, came their mother's

voice: "There's no divorce in the one, true, holy, *Catholic*, and apostolic Church," she cried. "You big lug."

There was another second of fraught silence, and then their mother peeked out from under the bed, from behind the pink ruffled bed skirt, and stuck out her tongue.

The kids, all nine of them, collapsed into wild laughter. The sound of it drove their poor father back to his own bed, alone.

He seemed quite ashamed of himself in the morning, Peter's sister said.

Another sister told me once, and this was only a few years ago, that menopause fell like a gentle grace on her parents' loving marriage, made them free to be affectionate once again.

In Saigon that year it occurred to me that with a childhood such as his, it was not inconceivable (forgive the pun) that Peter would be perfectly content to be childless.

My miscarriage had now given him permission to say so.

A tincture of self-interest mixed into his determination to be kind.

And yet, it was his kindness, I think, that made me lie to him about Charlene's latest scheme. With the innate, gentle solicitousness that was so much a part of who he was—a part of his upbringing, his self-esteem, of the time and place in which we were young—I knew he would not want me to be upset by what such a visit might bring. Not just the health risk—although Charlene had assured me, as Dr. Wally had assured her, that most of the patients at the colony were "dry" and that, despite the worldwide (not to mention biblical) misunderstanding, leprosy was not so easily transmittable—but the emotional risk of the visit, of the sight of such suffering.

I lied to him about my whereabouts that day because I feared he would, out of the goodness of his dear heart, want to shield me from that sadness. Relieve me of that burden. He would want me to look away.

A small evil, as Charlene said.

I LEFT THE HOUSE at seven that morning wearing pink pedal pushers and a sleeveless cotton blouse. Having amused myself the night before with the unspoken question: What do you wear to a leper colony? Wishing I had Stella nearby to share the joke.

Of course, even at that hour, the wet heat was oppressive. Peter put me in a cab with a peck on the cheek. At Charlene's, I was surprised to find Lily seated demurely in one of the chairs in Charlene's office. She sat on the edge of her seat, her hands folded before her. She stood, shyly smiling, when I came in. I thought at first—some version of the lie I had told my husband—that she was there to watch the children while we visited the lepers, but Charlene made it clear right away that Lily was coming with us.

We need a real seamstress, Charlene said, to take proper measurements.

And then she produced for us both—"I'm guessing you two are about the same size"—a set of freshly laundered army fatigues: pants and jackets and T-shirts. She had even procured two pairs of boots. This, she told us, was Dr. Welty's idea. He always asked Charlene to wear the same whenever she tagged along, unauthorized.

I recall that the name stenciled on my shirt was O'Connor. On Lily's it was D'Angelo. I pictured two teenage GIs, both of them short and skinny, sitting somewhere in their boxers and socks, awaiting our return.

We went to change—I to your bedroom on the second floor, a pretty room with a small Juliet balcony and a view of the yard. Your Barbie was there in Lily's ao dai, but I was amused, and appreciative, to see that she no longer wore the non la secured with straight pins. Rather, you had fashioned the ties so that the hat could be worn, just as authentically, on her back. There were two or three stuffed animals on your bed. I understood that should I ask you, you would recite for me their complex biographies.

We'd been, I think, the same kind of child.

I glanced in the mirror, felt ridiculous, and returned to Charlene's office in my new getup, fully prepared, of course, to endure Charlene's particular laugh. But she only shook her head. Charlene and Lily had both pulled their hair back into ponytails, but I still wore mine in my usual bouffant, flipped at the ends. I'd spent the night before sleeping in rollers, and I suppose I was reluctant to spoil the fruits of my discomfort.

Charlene said only that we looked like the Andrews Sisters on a USO tour. And then she gave us each a market basket of goodies to carry to the car.

OUTSIDE, AN ARMY TRANSPORT VEHICLE, not unlike the one Charlene often "borrowed," was waiting for us. This one had a large red cross painted on its canvas. As we came through the gate, long-legged Wally Welty unfolded himself from the passenger seat and Dominic, shorter and more solidly built, came around from the driver's side. Both men quickly took the baskets from our hands and stored them in the back. Then they helped us climb inside, holding open the canvas flap, taking our fingertips, and telling us to watch our step, as if we were three Cinderellas in army fatigues getting into our elegant pumpkin. Neither said a word about the fatigues.

I noticed Dominic did not drive with Charlene's maniacal aplomb. He braked more often and took the time to look over his shoulder—which she had never done. Of course the only view we had was out the back of the truck, and as we drove through the city I could see the puzzled looks of the Vietnamese—cabbies and bus drivers and boys and girls, even whole families, perched on cycles and motorbikes—when they pulled up behind us and glimpsed what must have appeared to them as three most peculiar GIs. Lily kept her head down and Charlene was leaning forward, speaking into Dr. Welty's ear, so I was left to meet these puzzled, sometimes amused, sometimes hostile stares. It was the hostile ones that made me finally flatten my careful coiffure.

While still talking to Dr. Wally, Charlene reached into her pocket and handed me a rubber band. "To tie up your bonnie brown hair," she said.

Once we were out on the highway, I could see Dominic's shoulders relax a bit—they'd been up around his flushed ears— as his hands on the wheel regained some color.

I don't know how much you traveled when you were there. Even in those days we were advised not to leave the city. I'm sure you saw all the usual tourist sights. (I do remember a conversation you and I had at one of your parents' parties, about the zoo, and the Xa Loi Pagoda, which you were very taken with.) You also had your daily commute to the American school, in your father's car or on the school bus. Certainly, you'd had your view of the place coming in from the airport. So I can't say how much you saw, no less remember, of the flat rice paddies shot with silver eddies, the bent peasants in the fields, the dark, slow-motion apparition of the water buffaloes, too large to seem real. From the back of the vehicle I felt I was seeing it all as I do now: in some vague, perhaps detached, retrospect. There were the slums and the ramshackle huts that bordered Saigon, and the thatched villages here and there as we moved farther from it. Away from the city scent of diesel and trash and waste, there was now the hot, damp smell of wet dirt and foliage, of the impending or left-over rain—a scent that mixed now and then with the truck's exhaust. I recall a sense of being underwater, what with the humidity, the low clouds, the passing downpours—as well as the filtered light of the canvas over our heads. Out of a dream once again, or so it seems now.

But this much I remember: I was truly happy—perhaps for the first time since the miscarriage. Happy to be bumping along through this lovely and exotic country, in the company of so many good people. To be Tricia in army fatigues and heavy boots. A young woman on an adventure that was safe (I'd been reassured) and yet daring (my husband had no idea where I was). A young woman who had never been shy. A kind of saint.

We had in the narrow space at our feet the baskets of usual treats for the children, tea and cigarettes for the adults and the Sisters. (Charlene had discovered on earlier trips that two of the nuns enjoyed an occasional smoke.) Wally had his medical bag with him up front, but there was also, in back with us, a green footlocker filled with the bandages and medicines he would need. In another basket, four whiffle ball sets for the boys and seven boxed Barbies in white ao dais for the girls. On her last visit, Charlene had counted only four girls, mostly young adolescents, but thought to bring along a few extra, just in case the numbers had changed.

I'd wondered if it was cruel to bring these doe-eyed and big-breasted effigies to the sick children, but Charlene was quite confident—needless to say. She thought giving the girls a Barbie now would only enhance their wonder when we returned in a few weeks' time with the same silk ao dais for the women.

There were also two rifles secured to the bed of the truck, just behind the front seats. A safety measure, I imagined. Not one I took very seriously.

ONCE WE WERE OUT IN THE COUNTRYSIDE, the road growing steep as we climbed into the hills, Dr. Wally turned to offer me, and Lily, a history of the leprosarium, giving us the names of the nuns and some of the lepers we would meet, each with a short personality sketch. "Sister Antoine will find us something to do the minute we say it's time to leave," he said. "So I always start saying goodbye an hour before we're gonna go. Vu, the caretaker, speaks in full paragraphs, sometimes pages. It doesn't bother him in the least that you don't understand a word."

I was reminded of the "rundowns," the biographical précis Peter always coached me with before a cocktail party or a company dinner, here or back home.

The difference being, I realized, that Peter's briefings always made my palms sweat while Wally's were putting me at ease.

He lectured us a bit about leprosy itself, repeating what Charlene had already told me about infection and contagion, wet and dry, treatments and prognosis and all the various myths about the disease. There was nothing conceited or condescending in this (no mansplaining, you would say now). Wally offered information the way another young man might casually hold out a pack of gum, a pack of cigarettes—from courtesy, yes, but also out of some shared taste. If he was interested, he was pretty sure you'd be interested. Apparently, he'd done some similar work with American lepers, in Louisiana, when he was in med school. It was a disease he had some interest in, he said, given how feared and misunderstood it was. "I'm always on the side of the misunderstood," he said.

I'd read a book about Father Damien and the lepers in college, and I spoke up, like a good student, to tell him so. Dominic said he'd read it, too. "Beautiful book. Made me want to be a missionary," he shouted as he drove. "For about a week."

Wally mentioned, too, a Vietnamese poet who had died of leprosy—someone the Sisters had told him about.

He said he'd hoped to find a French or English translation of the man's work but had been unsuccessful thus far. In fact, he'd been told the work was untranslatable. He asked Lily if she knew of this man, and she nodded.

Then he asked her, switching to slow French that was charmingly distorted by his drawl, if she'd ever seen versions of his poems in another language? Chinese, perhaps? She shook her head. She said, in English, that there were too many different words, in English and Vietnamese. Too many words that cannot be translated. She held out her palm, made a wall with the other, a chopping motion to indicate that there were some barriers words could not cross.

Wally shook his head at this. "That can't be true," he said, in English. Poetry, he said, is in the world well before a poet finds it. Its source is the unspoken. The unspoken is always translatable.

Charlene laughed, but it was not her usual sneeze of a laugh, with its aftermath of disdain and faux contrition. Or maybe the sound of the truck's engine, gears grinding, merely obscured the unkind edge.

"Dr. Wally," she cried. "You are a regular Confucius."

Wally laughed, too, abashed, I think. I don't know that I ever before, or since, saw him blush. "Of course I am," he said. "I'm a Southerner. Ancestor worship is in my blood."

"You build little altars to them?" Charlene asked. She waved her fingers in the air, coy and amused. I had never seen her flirt before.

Wally nodded. "All over town."

He went on to describe how the Sisters had told him that the man's early poems were beautiful, quite formal celebrations of love and the natural world—trees, sky, flowers, sunrise and sunset—but then, as his leprosy progressed, as he'd moved toward the end of his life, his work became wild and experimental, pretty much nonsensical.

"*Le chaos*," the Sisters had said. Wally shook his head. "Chaos poetry. I'd like to read some of that."

He was lanky, long-faced, with standard-issue dark-frame glasses, big ears, and a wide, ready grin. The calmest, most easygoing—these days you might say "centered"—young man I've ever met. Southern charm, I thought then.

Charlene repeated the term "chaos poetry." And then she asked him, "Is it poetry about chaos, the way a love poem is about love, or is it just gibberish? Chaos itself."

Wally had turned awkwardly in his seat, the long length of him, trying to see her fully, I suppose. He said he figured there was meaning in it somewhere. "The guy's dying of leprosy. His hands probably swollen. Fingers missing. His eyesight gone."

With all that pain, Wally argued, why would he torture himself with writing it down, putting it to paper, this chaos poetry? Why bother if the words were mere nonsense? Meaningless. Why go through all the trouble?

Charlene narrowed her eyes, still taking him in as she considered this. When she spoke, I heard that slight impatience with the slow-witted world she so often used with me. With everyone, I suppose.

She said, "A man who's been writing poems about love and the beauty of the natural world finds himself consumed by a terrible disease, racked with pain, ostracized from society. Finds his flesh falling from his bones. Who can blame him if he wants to amend his earlier praise? Take it back. Fling his own gibberish into the gobbling whirlwind?"

Wally turned away from her briefly, looking out through the windshield, which was now pocked with rain. I saw him exchange a look with Dom, who, ever conscientious, only briefly took his eyes from the road.

I suspect even gentle Wally Welty, a man of his time, was surprised to be talked back to in this way by a smarty-pants corporate wife.

Wally said, "If I remember my Old Testament right, it's God who speaks out of the whirlwind. Justifying his ways to man."

I saw that snap of lightning in Charlene's eyes. She was enjoying this.

"Yes, Job," she told him. "Of course. God telling the poor man to go scratch his boils and hush up." She was meeting his drawl with her own. "Throwing his eternal weight around. 'Where were you when I laid the foundations of the earth?' Isn't that right?"

Wally had turned to face her fully once again. He was grinning, admiring, even, but nevertheless chagrined. "That's it," he told her.

"Which is why I said 'into the whirlwind,' Dr. Wally." Despite the adamancy of her words, there was still what we used to call a come-hither in her tone. A tone, I suddenly imagined, that she must have put to good use as a teenager, surrounded by besotted boys. "You don't just give up when the whirlwind throws its nonsense at you. You shout back. Even if it's chaos for chaos."

Wally took her in, amused, engaged. In the fatigues—which did as much for her eyes as the green silk dress had done—and with her hair pulled back, she seemed to me younger, less feral, less searching. Some softening of the edges. Or maybe it was just the diffuse light of the canvas covering over our heads.

Or maybe she, too, felt the freedom from all we had briefly left behind.

"You might be right," Wally said.

"You know I am," she told him.

THE PLACE WAS AS BEAUTIFUL as Charlene had described. Breathtaking, I want to say. Lush and green with bright flowers here and there.

We arrived just as another rain had passed, when some indication of sunshine broke through the clouds and made everything suddenly steamy, streaming, glazed with light. We stepped out of the truck—Wally and Dom again acting as liveried footmen attending us princesses—and into the heat and the humidity and the sudden glorious glare: green shot with yellow, shadow shot with light, bursts of red and pink. The sandy grass at our feet flashed diamonds. The white and blue of the buildings before us (we shaded our eyes as we stepped out of the truck), the green foliage, the white sand and blue water, all seemed briefly unmoored. A floating kingdom by the sea. Immediately, figures began to emerge from the shade of the building's porticoes. I thought at first they were all children—it occurred to me that we had not brought enough Barbies—but quickly saw that I could not be sure how old they were.

It was that uncertainty, that sudden transformation of skipping innocents into hobbled lepers, right before, you might say, my squinting eyes, that unnerved me.

I was suddenly afraid. Suddenly doubtful of my own abilities here. My ability not to look away.

Behind the approaching patients, I glimpsed the white shape of one of the Sisters, coming forward as Wally and Dominic and Charlene greeted the first figures to reach us. Lily and I were still by the truck. I was happy to have her beside me, all uncertain as I was. But then a small woman, not a child, passed through the first group, coming toward us with increasing agility. She scurried crookedly, held out both her arms. One of her swollen hands was fingerless, the other wrapped in gauze. A supplicant from some nightmare. Her face—I lowered my eyes before I could take it all in. As I did, I heard Lily cry out, felt her brush past me.

And then the two women were laughing, and crying, holding each other in their arms. I saw the wrapped hand beating gently, steadily, against Lily's thin back.

Charlene was at my elbow, moving me forward. "Her cousin," she was saying. "They grew up together. Lily hasn't seen her since she was sent here. They were as close as twins, growing up. Twins shouldn't be apart for so long."

Charlene the dynamo.

"Lily's not here to take measurements, then?' I asked her. Thick as mud, as my father would have said.

"Of course she's here to take measurements," Charlene told me with her faux tolerance for the idiots in the world. "We all have work to do. It's just nice that she can see her cousin as well." And then she added, leaning into me, "Marcia Case thinks she's at my house all day, making doll clothes, then watching the children. Not sure she'd be delighted to know one of her house girls has been hobnobbing with lepers."

We were crossing into the building. "Same story I told Peter," I said. "He doesn't know I'm here."

Charlene pulled her head back a bit, made wide her green eyes. "You liar you," she said. I felt like a star pupil.

WE WALKED TOGETHER into what was something like a small dining room, where the Sisters had a table prepared for tea. Charlene introduced me all around, to the nuns—there were maybe six of them, as I recall—and to the two lepers who stood at the periphery, both lanky adolescent boys, shadow-thin, but without any outward signs of disease. Which I was grateful for, relieved not to feel again that initial failure of nerve, that panic. But I'm not sure I felt any pity, either, or compassion. I was holding myself back, I think, holding my fragile courage, as well as my fear, in a kind of defensive crouch, somewhere behind my ribs.

Dominic, on the other hand, was just open. I'm sorry I keep using that word, but it seems the one that suits him best: open-hearted, open-faced, open-handed, no guile, no self-consciousness or pride. I'd already noticed this about him in the children's ward, that he had no sense that he was watching himself, admiring himself, as he went about being a good and generous guy— that kind of clawing self-consciousness that I've observed over the years in many an altruist: priests, missionaries, ACLU attorneys, the leaders of certain charities, or all the well-dressed elites at black-tie global fundraisers. Performative bonhomie. Self-congratulatory demonstrations of their limitless agape.

Bestowers of favor, as Marilee might have put it, well pleased with the favors they bestow.

Maybe it was because Dominic was so young, and looked even younger, but everything he did—every polite and grateful gesture, his eager conversation with the nuns, his easy camaraderie with our teenage waiters—seemed infused with his own wide-eyed appreciation that he was here, having an interesting life. Like a newly released prisoner, perhaps, or, more apt, a young man newly escaped from a safe and boring middle-class childhood. Look at us, his blue-eyed joy seemed to convey, convey to everyone, even those poor young men whom he was somehow managing to make laugh. Look at us, here on earth, having an interesting life. Jesus. Aren't we something? Aren't we great?

I recalled how another GI on the children's ward had once called Dom the Buddha from Baltimore.

Before we sat down, we ladies were offered a visit to the nuns' small outhouse in the back. A primitive toilet with a cistern and an earthenware sink. French milled soap, lavender, on a string beside it. A luxury the nuns allowed themselves, Charlene told me as we walked back. Courtesy of Sister Étienne's family in Marseilles.

This was when she told me, too, about Lily and her cousin. Raised as if they were twins—they were born in the same month and year although Lily's mother did not survive the birth. The aunt and uncle who raised her were both employed in a tailor shop in Saigon, but when Lily's cousin began to show signs of ill health—she was about twelve or thirteen—her parents sent her to their hometown—hometown is how Charlene put it, although I gathered she meant some rural village. Away from the noise and dirt of the city. Of course, Lily had wanted to go with the girl—her twin, her heart (as Lily had said, telling Charlene the tale in bits and pieces as she fitted that green shantung dress)— but by then her aunt and uncle had grown dependent on Lily's skills, her good eye and delicate hands. It wasn't long after the cousin left Saigon that a local priest gave a name to her ailments and she was sent here. And then, two years ago, the aunt and uncle closed their shop—"There was an opportunity to follow some Frenchman out of the country," Charlene said—leaving Lily alone in Saigon. Marcia Case, "a clotheshorse if there ever was one," had been a customer at the shop and was delighted to bring Lily into her household.

So it had been nearly a decade since Lily had seen her cousin, her twin, her sister, her heart. Ten years since they'd been together. "Not acceptable," Charlene said.

When we returned to the table, I saw that Sister A already had Wally off in a corner, whispering into his ear. She was explaining something, or asking for something—her gestures were gentle, but tense, somehow. Wally, bending to listen, nodded and then shrugged, and then nodded again—reassuring her. The woman did not look reassured.

After our brief tea, while Wally and Dom and Charlene went to the truck for the footlocker of medical supplies, the nuns showed Lily and me where we could set up our little tailoring shop. It was a small, spare room that opened directly onto the outdoors so it got good light. There was a desk and a chair for me and, for Lily, a wooden crate on which our "patrons" could stand while they were measured. There was also a narrow bed in the shadows on the far side of the room, carefully made up. I gath-

ered it was a room waiting for its next occupant. Or recently
abandoned by its last.

Lily's cousin followed us in and took a seat on the edge of the
bed. She sat there in shadow throughout the morning, watching
us at our work, smiling and nodding—although it was not until
every other woman had been measured that she allowed herself
to be measured as well. Every now and then as we worked, the
two girls exchanged a happy look or a few words. And Lily's
cousin would then hug herself, her damaged hands at her bony
elbows, rocking with pleasure.

Charlene had to coax the first few women to our door. She
and Dominic were assisting at the outdoor medical station
Dr. Wally used, and our first few "customers" were women who
had just been seen. Some had new bandages, others newly applied
antiseptic gels on ulcerated wounds or infected insect bites.
Charlene steered them to us, touching elbows and shoulders.
She'd provided me with a small notebook, where I took down
each woman's name—Lily tried to spell each one for me, although in truth I wrote them down phonetically as well. I also
gave them, parenthetically, little nicknames, so I would remember who they were when we returned—names like Chubby
Cheeks, and Toothless. Not nice, I know. I then listed their measurements as Lily showed me the numbers on her cloth tape:
height, sleeve length, inseam, shoulders, chest, and waist. After
the initial (it seemed to me at first insurmountable) reluctance,
there was a good deal of giggling, especially when chest and
waist and inseam were involved. And soon we had a small crowd
of women outside the room.

At lunchtime we returned to the dining area, where the

Sisters had set out a simple spread: rice and a flaky kind of fish. Lemonade. More tea. It was so hot. Both Wally and Dominic were soaked across the back and under their arms. Charlene and I took off our socks and the ridiculous boots and waved our bare feet under the table. It didn't help. As we ate, another sudden rain moved in off the ocean. It was the kind of tropical rain that seems to build to a crescendo, and then, confounding some expectation that the worst has passed, builds again, builds further, louder, more intensely, so that you entertain the notion that it might never stop building, that it will, finally, overwhelm.

A sound to spark some primitive—or maybe only childish—fear. A flash of ancient, ignorant panic, tickling your spine. A brief awareness of how the natural world might, in an instant, reduce you to a brief, trembling, and utterly inconsequential detail of its larger machinations.

Somewhere at this point, this noisy pinnacle—I recall it as the intense height of the storm—a man stood briefly in the doorway, and then slipped into the room.

He was American. I knew that instinctively, before he said a word, by the way he moved. He was dark-haired, in need of a shave, as tall as Wally, as broad and fit as Dom, much older than them both. Fifties, perhaps. His khaki shirt and pants were wet with rain, especially across his shoulders and along his thighs, but nevertheless I could see that his clothes were also filthy. His pants were rolled at the ankles. His feet, splattered with wet mud, were bare, like ours. Sister A stood immediately to greet him, even as Wally stood, too, and, much to my surprise, saluted. Dominic, two seconds behind, did the same.

The man returned the salute somewhat casually, as if only to swipe the rain from his brow. And laughed, and said, "At ease."

He was handsome, no question he was handsome. Older than Wally, than the rest of us, but now I saw it was impossible to say by how much. He said, "Ladies," coming forward to offer us his hand. That's when I saw his shirt was unbuttoned and his chest bare, his pants low-slung—understandable in this heat, I supposed. His hairless chest and belly were filthy as well.

Being who I was in those days, I smiled up at him with my garden-party smile and shook his hand politely—I remember thinking his grip was weirdly dry, reptilian. I instantly disliked whatever change he had brought to the air in the room, to our company. Although he, too, was smiling, good teeth, his eyes skipped over me dismissively (too young, too plain, not interesting enough) and settled themselves on Charlene, who, when he offered her his hand, hesitated, unsmiling, brazenly assessing him for just long enough to make me embarrassed for her, as if she, of all people, was edging toward some terrible rudeness.

His name was Smith or Jones or Brown or Bates—something comically short and familiar and American. Perhaps you can ask Dominic if he remembers. I'll say Bates. A colonel or a major, I don't recall that, either. I learned over the course of the conversation that he'd arrived at the leprosarium yesterday morning at dawn, coming out of the jungle alone, on the black bicycle we had already seen propped against the wall outside one of the rooms. His room, I gathered, where he had been sleeping until now.

The Sisters had been saying their first prayers at the little outdoor chapel beside the path to the beach. He emerged from the trees, and as soon as he'd introduced himself, Sister A told him that some of his compatriots were due tomorrow. She was certain they would give him a ride back to Saigon.

I could tell even now that she wanted to be rid of him.

Up until this moment, she had been a gracious host, sitting with us at this morning's tea and now taking a leisurely lunch with us, clearly enjoying our company, Wally's and Dom's especially. She was middle-aged, I guess. Had come to Vietnam in the 1940s, working first at an orphanage in the north, then moving here just after the war (the French one). As she chatted with us in her accented English, I had the clear understanding that she knew she would never go home again. That she would live out her days here, die here—whether she died of leprosy, like Father Damien, or of old age, or of some other inevitability would be irrelevant, I supposed. She was here until her end.

This struck me, at twenty-three, as remarkable. I'd known plenty of nuns in my Catholic school days, but I don't know that I'd ever come face-to-face with any woman who had so thoroughly eliminated, erased (that's how I thought of it) every future option, every other possible life. Maybe because I was so young myself, I was amazed to think that she faced—had, in fact, willingly accepted—a future that was so stunted. She had finished with possibility, willingly. This astonished me. A kind of death in life, I thought. Admirable, I suppose. Suffocating as well.

I wondered: In a life so prescribed, so determined, what happened to the pleasure of expectation?

It had been clear to me this morning that the nun thought our little project frivolous. But by lunchtime I was sure she'd noticed how much laughter had sounded from the room where we took our measurements. And by now I'd concluded that Sister was willing to admit that even though she had taught herself to live a life—a holy life, no doubt—stripped of anticipation or change, or even some silly thing to look forward to, her patients did not necessarily need to do the same.

At lunch she told us that the ladies in her care would surely be counting the days until our return with their silk clothes.

But her entire demeanor changed when this American colonel or captain or whatever he was showed up. In my father's words, she wanted nothing better than to show him the door.

I thought at first this might have had something to do with his bare chest and belly, something obscene in it, in the way, as he sat, joined us at the table, his uncovered navel disappeared into a slight roll of muddy flesh. In front of nuns, no less.

He accepted some tea and wolfed down a bowl of rice. He told us where he was from in the Midwest—Iowa, Wisconsin, one of those places. He was a physician himself. Retired Army Medical Corps, but now here in the country on his own dime. Or on the few collected dimes of some Christian group associated with his hometown. A medical missionary of some sort, I gathered. (I'm sorry the details barely registered with me then and have long since been forgotten.) I know he said he'd spent some weeks in the highlands with the Montagnards, was making his way back to Saigon, stopping to do what good he could at orphanages and villages here and there.

He said, "Whatever small good." And then he grinned at us, at me briefly, at Charlene with more leisure, as if he knew he was paraphrasing her. Just short of mockery. I'm certain I remember this correctly. I'm certain Charlene looked as though she wanted to show him the door as well.

But Wally was his gracious self. And Dominic grew shy, I thought, listening to him. Maybe it was the presence of a superior officer, an older man. Maybe it was that he was tall and unshaven and movie-star handsome—despite how filthy he was, grime on his neck and hands, black fingernails in need of clipping, that bare, hairless chest under his opened shirt—a muscular chest, sculpted (I would say now) but streaked with dirt.

I wondered—being who I was in those days—if he even knew he was so unbuttoned. Wondered as he spoke if I shouldn't give him a subtle sign, as I would do with my father whenever he had a label sticking out of his collar, or his fly unzipped. I believe I even tried: my eyes to his face as I smiled at him, and then, with some small movement of my chin, my eyes to his breast— I might have nodded subtly—and then, trying to catch his eyes again, nearly mouthing the word "unbuttoned."

What a fool I must have seemed.

There was a damp, smoky smell about his clothes, as if he had spent many nights before an open fire—had doused the ashes and then rubbed them over his skin.

He seemed charmed by our little project—Charlene left it to me to explain it, which I did in a rush. And although at first he turned to me reluctantly (Charlene was the one he found attractive), as I spoke his expression changed. His dark eyes took me in, my face, my lips, then my hair. The name stenciled over the pocket of my green fatigue shirt. My hands in my lap. A slow-moving scrutiny that, strangely enough, soothed my nerves as I spoke, made me forget myself.

I confess I even, at one point, claimed that the project had, indeed, been my vision. Not my vision alone—I wasn't that bold—but, I said, my vision initially.

I sensed this pleased him, somehow. I sensed—no, more than sensed, understood clearly, as if he had spoken, whispered the word—that he was thinking of me as a morsel. As in a tasty little morsel. The realization flattered me, suddenly. (Things were different then.) Maybe because I'd already felt the sting of his dismissal.

Something of those delightful first-married stirrings—feelings that had grown so complicated of late—moved through me. An entirely physical longing. The man's mouth, I saw, was long and narrow, but his lips were plump. As I spoke, he touched them with the tip of his tongue. I thought of myself passing through them.

A saintly little morsel.

When I finished my spiel, he took his eyes from me and turned them to Charlene. I felt the loss of them. An irrational disappointment.

"The clothes maketh the man," he said wryly.

For an insane instant, I saw her as a rival.

Charlene only narrowed her green eyes. There was, you might say, some antipathy in the air.

He shook it off—if he felt it at all—and stirred in his chair, slow and languid, stretching his spine, rolling back his head. A prelude to leaving us, I thought. The dish before him on the table was empty, only a few delicate fish bones in a little broth. I was pretty sure the food was all he'd come in for.

He raised his shoulders, scratched at his dirty neck with those under-curving fingernails, asked for a cigarette in a general way. "Has anyone got a cigarette?" Something like that. It was Wally who reached into his breast pocket, offered his pack and a match. Behind the first exhaled smoke, he turned once more to Charlene.

"And where are your own children while you do your good deeds?" he asked her. He only glanced at me, as if he knew with just that glance that I was childless. "I'm assuming you have them," he said. "Children."

For a moment I thought for certain that Charlene would deny it, so much so that I was a little surprised by how easily she said, "I do. Two in school. One at home."

He held his cigarette close to his unshaven face, picked a piece of tobacco from his tongue. "Safe at home, then," he said.

She said, "Yes," although it was clear to me that he'd misunderstood her. Safe at home in Saigon is what she should have said. So I said it for her. Explained to him that Charlene was here with her husband, an oil engineer, and their three lovely children. Twins at the American Community School. A sweet baby.

"Safe," Charlene told him, cutting me off. I had the sense that we were now vying for his attention. "If not precisely at home."

He bowed his head as if to accept the correction.

And then he turned to Wally, began to ask him about his background and his training. I thought his interest in us had run dry. I glanced at Charlene. She was studying him with some thin anger playing about her mouth. As if he had recently insulted her.

When Wally told him pediatrics, the man asked if he'd had any experience with hydrocephalus back in the States. Wally said a reluctant no, like a student caught without the answer, and then our good doctor began to describe a baby he had just encountered at an orphanage in the hills.

Given the substance of what he said, his voice should have been a hushed whisper, but he shouted as he spoke. Perhaps he only wanted to be heard above the sound of the rain that still battered the roof.

He described a kid, only a year or so old, with a skull so heavy

he could not lift it. A body as thin and helpless, he said, as a rag
doll. Left on the orphanage steps as a newborn still streaked with
vernix, maybe minutes old. No question, he said, the monstrous
thing had killed the woman who gave birth to him, tore her
apart—"You can just imagine." Now it was moved around by the
women who ran the place, by the other orphans themselves, like
a limp package, a burlap bag of sawdust tied to a bowling ball.

Out of a shared bed in the morning, he said, onto the floor,
onto a mat in the shade, to the canvas hammock for feeding, to
the floor again, to the bed again. Eyes lively, sure, a word-like
sound or two on occasion, and hands and legs that would kick or
flail—even the other kids knew when it was trying to express
happiness or distress—but that was about it. No lifting that
monstrous burden of a misshapen skull. No sitting up. No future, really, although he discovered that the poor kid's heart was
strong, all vital signs strong enough to keep it alive indefinitely.
Unless cholera killed him, or malaria, diphtheria, or the mal-
nutrition that the people at the orphanage were barely managing
to keep at bay.

The doctor said the only humane thing for him to do was to
hold a gentle pillow over the poor monster's little face until he
stopped breathing—only a few minutes. Whatever muscles he
had had mostly atrophied under the orphanage's misguided
care. Not much fight in the kid. A corrective measure, he said.
What, after all, was the point of this thing still breathing?

Charlene said, "You did no such thing."

The doctor reached inside his shirt to put his hand to his
breast, or just to scratch at the streaked flesh over his heart. He
smiled. His lips were very smooth. "Of course not," he said. "But
I was tempted."

Wally stood abruptly—the only time I'd ever seen him be rude—the chair legs scraping against the stone. "If you'll excuse us," he said, "there's work," and as we all stood and thanked the Sisters for our repast, I lost whatever it was the dirty doctor then told Charlene. "A prayer for their safety" was what I made out, though I couldn't be sure.

As we left, he offered to join Wally and Dom and the nuns in their afternoon ministrations. Sister said, in English, "Much appreciated," with a dip of her head.

But no one could believe she meant it.

B Y ABOUT THREE O'CLOCK, we had measured all the women there and most of the men, so when the sun showed itself again, I told Lily I wanted to walk down to the beach before we left, to put my feet in the South China Sea. Just so I could say I'd done so. I'm not sure she understood, but she smiled and nodded. She and her cousin were now sitting side by side on the made-up bed. There was enough shadow that I could comfortably look at them straight on. Lily was holding the freshly bandaged stump of the girl's hand, stroking it like a beloved pet.

I followed the path. The place really was beautiful. Humid and buggy, sure, glinting puddles everywhere, but also so green and lush and, at that hour, so perfectly still, except for a movie musical soundtrack of birdcall and monkey screech. The small outdoor chapel was just off the path to the beach, a clearing with, at its far end, two rickety kneeling benches before a stone cross. Dominic was standing beside the cross, one hand on its base, looking out through the pines to the water. I didn't want to disturb him—he seemed not so much to be praying (there was a kneeling bench for that) as resting companionably beside the crucifix, which was made of some kind of white, weather-beaten limestone, streaked with green and black, moss or mildew.

Streaks of dirt, anyway, that recalled to my mind the American visitor's bare chest. I realized two things at once: For the past few hours, I had nearly forgotten him, his sudden arrival, his strange, unsettling presence. And now that I'd remembered, I wished I hadn't.

Impulsively, I called out to Dom. He looked over his shoulder, smiled (of course), and waved a bit.

"Isn't it something?" he asked, when I was beside him. He indicated the view through the trees: a curve of white beach, blue water, the sky.

I said I should have brought a camera, and he answered softly, "Next time."

I think it was then that I truly looked at him—something I hadn't heard before in his voice. I think it was then that I saw he was crying.

He shrugged, knowing I saw this. Apologized. Today it was all too much, he said. These poor people, the kids, especially. This was not his first trip here, but today, this afternoon, he said, it overtook him. All of it. He ran his hand over his eyes, apologized again. Said something about what a dope he must look like. Said, "Today, it's got me in the dumps."

I commiserated, of course. Terrible disease and the kindness of the nuns and—as if it were part of it all—this heat and humidity.

But my words only seemed to make his struggle more painful. I saw him swallow hard. His eyes, in the way of blonds, were already bloodshot, rimmed with bright red. His pale lashes darkened with tears.

He ran his wrist under his nose, like a toddler. Said, once more, that he was sorry. "Maybe it's because I have a kid of my own now," he said. "Maybe that's what makes it unbearable."

I said I could understand that.

He brushed his hand across the base of the mildewed cross, reminding me once again of the pale chest and belly, streaked with dirt. I wanted to offer that maybe it was the dirty doctor himself who had disturbed us all.

But somehow, I was reluctant to mention him.

Instead I asked Dom, brightly, if he wanted to walk down to the beach. Dip our toes.

He shook his head, put a brotherly hand on my arm. Told me it was not a great idea. "The VC probably have their eyes on us," he said. "They'll come in as soon as it gets dark, see what we've left for them. You know, in the way of medicine, supplies. They always do." He smiled. "The Sisters aren't on anybody's side."

I heard myself whisper a breathy "Really?"

Dom patted my arm, easily forgave my naiveté. He said the nuns will treat any sick or wounded Viet Cong soldiers who come into the compound. "What else are they going to do?" he asked. But they'll also give shelter to boys from the nearby villages, take them in and pretend they're lepers, in order to keep them from getting kidnapped when the VC make their raids.

"Keep them from getting *drafted* into Ho Chi Minh's army," he said.

The nuns took in healthy young boys, Dom explained, boys like our two teenage waiters at lunch, and let the VC believe they were lepers, shouldn't be touched.

"These kids," he added, "or probably their parents, think it's better to take a chance hanging out here than getting carried off by the communists." He laughed. "Puts a whole new spin on 'better dead than red,' right?"

And then a shaded regret in his blue eyes, as if he had disappointed himself with his joke. "State of the world," he said. "What are you going to do?" He shrugged, said again, "The Sisters aren't on anybody's side." Paused, smiled. "Or I guess they're on everybody's side—which is a hell of a lot more complicated."

There was the stirring of a breeze, a brief shower shaken from the trees above us. I was, for the first time that day, terrified. For myself. "Are we safe?" I asked him.

At that moment, my sense of my own stupidity—what had I risked for this little adventure?—was only the small chrysalis of the rising, thumping thing it would become later that afternoon and in the days that followed. I was very naive.

I told Dom I suddenly felt like an idiot. Like I'd been picnicking in a minefield.

But he shook his head. "No, no, no," he said, "You did good today, you ladies. Honest. It was biblical."

And then he spoke in that jivey, drawling, ghetto hipster / Southern redneck / Elvis-meets-Sammy-Davis-Jr. accent all the young GIs seemed to adopt, no matter where they were from.

"I mean," he added, "Jesus cured the lepers, but, come on, did he ever make them laugh?"

We'd returned to our familiar sibling routine.

"You ladies got the lepers laughing. I'm talking lepers here. Laughing. We all heard it. Laughing lepers. *Man*." He shook his head. "There should be some kind of medal for that. From the Vatican. From Albert Schweitzer. It's a frigging miracle."

AS WE WALKED BACK TO THE COMPOUND, I asked him how much longer he had on his tour. Another seven months or so, as I recall. He would miss his daughter's entire infancy.

I assured him as a former kindergarten teacher that he wasn't missing much: children only became interesting when they learned to talk.

I suppose I was searching for some Charlene-like authority I didn't feel, something to compensate for my silly *Gidget Goes to the South China Sea* beachcombing fantasies.

Or maybe it was some way to crack open and release my own clenched envy of the life that awaited him back home.

CHARLENE SAID, "HERE THEY ARE," as we approached. And then, to Dr. Wally, "I told you they'd be off visiting the chapel. Flies to honey."

Wally smiled, but I saw he was ready to leave. The footlocker had been closed and pushed up against the side of the building. Wally said we wouldn't take it back. He'd pick it up on his next visit. He wanted to make room in the truck for the American doctor's bicycle.

Lily and her cousin were arm in arm, and Lily was crying, elaborately wiping at her tears with the heel of her palm. For all the small good we'd done today, there were, nonetheless, plenty of tears.

I heard Charlene tell her, "You'll be back," even as she took Lily by the elbow and moved her to the truck, the cousin hanging on until Lily had no choice but to step up into it. Dom stood there, watching the two women, the saddest of footmen.

Her cousin held out her two damaged hands, just as she had done when we arrived, although now the bandages were fresh and white. I heard Dom tell her, "We'll all be back very soon," and then add a self-conscious "à bientôt."

Charlene and I gave our thanks to the nuns and followed

Lily into the hot and shaded truck bed. I slid in beside her on the hard bench, put my arm around her shoulder. "All will be well," I whispered. She nodded but then covered her face with her hands.

I looked to Charlene, who shook her head. Twins should never be apart for so long was what she meant. Through the opening in the canvas, I saw Wally once again giving his ear to Sister A, and then—I swear I had, once again, almost forgotten him, despite the muddy black bike standing where the foot-locker had been—our dirty American doctor, appearing out of the lush foliage, arising from a crouch, it seemed to me, and then sauntering toward us. He was pulling up his pants, tucking in his shirt.

Charlene said what I only thought: "He might have done his business a bit farther from the nuns."

I heard Wally offer him the passenger seat, heard the man say he wouldn't hear of it, and then he was in the truck with us—his big smoky-smelling self. He slid in next to Charlene, stretched his long legs out—he now wore a pair of run-down, laceless boots, which he placed right under the seat that Lily and I shared. As he did, I saw that his hairless ankles were littered with bug bites and scabs. He took up space with his smile. I was grateful to see that his shirt was buttoned now, at least to just below his breastbone.

Once again I was aware of some joy, or jauntiness, that had gone out of our group. Replaced now with a vague revulsion.

I turned to look out the back. Sister A had her arm around Lily's weeping cousin. Behind them, a few of the girls with our Barbies in their hands. I watched them recede, along with the compound, the glimpse of the sea.

Beside me, Lily was silent, her head in her hands. I patted her now and again, her khaki thigh. I stroked her arm. At one point, Charlene leaned forward and spoke softly in rapid French, comforting, reasoning. Promising, from what I could follow, our swift return to the place. Lily nodded as she spoke, made an effort to smile—even laughed briefly, over something Charlene said that I couldn't catch, except that it was about Marcia Case, Lily's employer.

Knowing Charlene, I figured it was something accurately catty.

Up front, Dom and Wally were mostly silent. I recall the sound of the engine, the whiff of diesel exhaust, the heat rising in the damp air.

When I glanced again at the doctor, his head was back, his mouth slightly open, and one hand had fallen to his side, resting palm up on the seat beside him, the other covered his crotch. I took in the sprawl of his legs, his open thighs. It struck me that he was a wholly physical being. One of those men who lived by the dictates of his body. He had slept through the morning, eaten voraciously, leered at us females, defecated, and now he slept again.

And yet, I reminded myself—I suppose after our own day of good works, I was trying to be kind—that he'd said he was here on his own. That on his own he had been going from village to village on that black bicycle, doing what he could.

We rode along in silence. Lily and Charlene both had closed their eyes, and I pretended to do the same, although I was, in truth, studying him in his exhausted sleep.

He was unpleasant still—he took some ease from our own efforts to do good—but now I wondered if his distasteful aura arose out of something outrageously, uncomfortably noble. I wondered if he had somehow pared down his own complexity, even as he dismissed our own niceties. If he had shed all the polite restraints that dictated our lives in order to give himself fully to the very basic, physical, animal needs of those he encountered here. Those who suffered.

The true measure of what it took not to look away.

We hit a rough patch on the road then, were bounced around a bit, all of us suddenly holding on. The doctor and Lily both opened their eyes. I put one hand on the man's stretched-out calf even as I grabbed Lily's arm with the other. I feared I'd be pitched out the back. Charlene hit her head on a crossbar, cried out an indignant "ouch."

Dom called, "Sorry, folks."

Wally asked, "Everyone okay?"

The doctor, fully alert now, was looking—peering, I should say—across the narrow distance. Peering because the light had grown dim: another rain had caught up with us—somehow, in my memory, I associate the two things, the rough patch, the rain, as if one were a consequence of the other. Another heavy downpour, heavy on the canvas roof, loud enough to drown our voices.

Dom shifted gears and slowed as the road quickly grew muddy. I realized I was losing all sense of the time of day. Was this darkness merely the lowering clouds, or had we left later than I realized? There was the dawning fear—senseless, but reflexive somehow—that the rising volume of the rain elicited (surely this crescendo would build to something destructive, overpowering), as well as the fear that we would return to Saigon much too late, that Peter would go looking for me, call at Charlene's, talk to Kent.

Dom downshifted again, seemed to struggle with the wheel, and then the truck came to a gliding halt. The sound of the rain was at its apex. I couldn't hear the engine as Dom attempted to start it again. Couldn't hear whatever words he and Wally were exchanging up front. The doctor pursed his plump lips. Charlene leaned toward Wally. Lily glanced at me. I could see my own worry on her plain face.

The rain let up, almost imperceptibly, and Dominic and Wally pushed opened their doors. They pulled up the hood. Reluctantly, our good doctor joined them, touching my thigh as he climbed out, crouching.

There ensued all the things that men do with stalled cars. No different than if we had been pulled to the side of the thruway. They looked and conferred and Dom climbed into the driver's seat again to try the ignition. Nothing. Not even a hopeless mechanical cough, an exhausted attempt to turn over. Just the click of the key in the ignition and silence. The engine might have disappeared altogether. Eventually, they closed the hood.

We three women sat still in the way women did in such cases—at least back then. Trusting and clueless. The world of auto maintenance a world of men alone.

Through the wet windshield, I could see the three consulting in the rain. Then Dom appeared at the back. "Sorry, ladies," he said. The water was dripping from the peak of his cap, staining his shirtfront. "Damn thing has just died on us. We're about ten miles from the airport. Lieutenant Welty's gonna ride. He's a long-distance biker. News to me. A man of many talents." He laughed. "He'll get us another vehicle. Shouldn't be too long." He climbed in. His clothes were wet as he brushed past us. He wrestled a bit with the black bicycle that had been wedged behind the two seats, then, lifting it above our knees, he maneuvered it out again, saying, "Sorry," "Careful there," "Excuse me."

As soon as he was outside, Charlene, moving quickly, followed. The rain had let up again. Outside, the two doctors were consulting over the bike, the captain no doubt sharing with Wally his familiarity with the flimsy piece of machinery, Wally nodding, moving the wheels back and forth a bit, as if he had already taken ownership, knew what he needed to know. Charlene stood watching them both with her hands on her hips. The two men shook hands. Dom gave a salute. Dr. Jones-Smith-Bones and Dom walked around the truck and stood outside the driver's-side door, talking. The doctor leaned, tall, over Dom. Dom nodded but only looked around.

When I glanced out the back again, I saw Charlene and Dr. Wally in conversation. Wally had one hand on the bike, resting it against his thigh, like some teenager on my street in Yonkers. He was bending toward her. They seemed to be speaking casually, no urgency, nothing to reflect our situation. He was even smiling. And then I saw her reach up to touch his cheek. He raised his free hand to touch hers. She lifted her face to him, and they kissed for what seemed a long while.

She stepped away; he shook the bike a bit, mounted, and took off. When I turned toward the front to watch him struggling down the muddy road, I met Lily's eyes. She smiled. She had seen what I'd seen.

Charlene climbed back into the truck and slid onto the bench beside me. Once again, we were hip to hip. She patted my thigh, and then, to my surprise, she put her arm around me.

Motherly. "Not to worry," she said, as if she and Lily had agreed to reassure me. "He'll be fine." And then she added, "I just hope he doesn't get busted for bringing us along."

DOM AND THE DOCTOR HAD COME to some kind of agreement, it seemed, because somehow they now each had a rifle tucked under an arm. I saw Dom perch himself on the front of the truck. The doctor was on the back bumper, leaning just inside the canvas doorway, one leg raised to the truck bed, one touching the ground. He held the butt of the rifle against his thigh. His body was turned toward Charlene, but he was facing the road behind us, the darkening trees on one side and a wide rice field on the other. I could hear the rain on the canvas, starting up again, although I couldn't see it in the encroaching dusk.

She asked him, "Should we be worried?"

He took a very long time to answer and when he did, he didn't turn his head. "What's the point?" he asked.

His voice was different now, less collegial, courteous. An edge of facetiousness, or, I don't know, contempt. Maybe with Wally gone—his only peer—he felt free to show his disdain for us women. I admit I'd seen other professional men, in more pleasant social settings, adopt the same tone when they found themselves alone among women, merely women.

I think we were silent for a while—perhaps sensing his distaste—until he, still scanning the landscape behind us, slowly began to describe a skirmish that had occurred some weeks ago. He named the place, a village somewhere to our west. He'd only come upon the aftermath, he said, days behind whatever had occurred. He shook his head and laughed as if to himself.

"You'd have thought someone had tossed a case of dynamite into a butcher shop," he said. In fact, he'd believed at first, in the falling darkness, that he had stumbled on a kind of jungle slaughterhouse, neatly staged in a narrow clearing. The stench of rotting meat, the tangle of bone and flesh, brown blood caked like mud, blood indistinguishable from mud. Some herd of small-to-midsized animals, he'd thought, sloppily dispatched, dispatched in some kind of frenzy. It was the tatter of clothing that gave it away, he said. Even before the clarifying sight of crushed skulls and swollen faces. Human, after all.

"You ladies will appreciate it," he said, still looking out. "It was the clothes that made them men." He paused, as if to admire the wordplay. "And women. And children."

I felt Charlene beside me, breathing deeply, absorbing the insult, if that's what it was. A belittlement, a reminder of how trivial we were. How silly our efforts. Her thumb and ring finger were doing their nervous circling above the khaki green of her thigh, but she had not bent her head, pretending to submit. She was staring at him, at his profile, though he still hadn't turned to face us. His eyes were on the bit of road we could see through the slit in the canvas. Had she been holding a cigarette, I'm pretty sure she'd have screwed it into his face.

"How very awful," I said. I felt someone should say something. And saw Charlene turn to me, surprised, I think. Perhaps because I sounded so politely curious. Like a McLean matron soothing tensions at her dinner party. I said, "Who were they?"

The rain was growing heavier again. He shrugged. "Innocents," he said.

We looked away from him, all three of us.

The rain began to stream down the sides of our canvas covering, pooling on the floor. This was the first time since our arrival that I actually felt a chill in the air. After all those months of relentless heat, it should have been a relief. But it wasn't.

"Poor Wally," I whispered to Charlene. "Out in this." But Charlene had her eyes on her hands. We were silent a good while.

Finally, she said to the doctor, "You should pull yourself inside," brisk and authoritative, her matron-in-charge tone. Whatever he'd been trying to do, whatever rise he'd hoped to get out of her with his insult, his disparagement, had not, her stern-mother tone told him, met its mark.

The driver's door was suddenly pulled opened—Lily and I both jumped—and Dom slid in, drenched. He rested the rifle across the passenger seat. Shook out his baseball cap. He smiled at us. "Things usually get worse before they get better," he said. And then leaned to roll down the passenger window, to see out as best he could.

The doctor was fully inside now, too, on the narrow bench, although he still used the rifle to hold back the canvas, still looked out. His odor of sweat, of doused fire, the wet leather of his boots. He seemed to take up so much space. We three squeezed ourselves together. The wind had picked up, and the rain was slanting this way and that, as if to try every entrance. For a few minutes it blew in the back and soaked my fatigues, Charlene's, too. I saw it gleaming on the dark shaft of the rifle. I briefly entertained the notion that the truck could be washed away. More worse.

We sat for a long time in silence, listening to the storm. At first I assured myself that whatever danger we were in was surely mitigated by the weather. Even Viet Cong guerrillas wouldn't chance being struck by lightning just to examine a stranded vehicle. A Red Cross vehicle at that. People out to do good.

But then I remembered that American GI killed in Saigon just before we arrived, killed by a grenade tossed into his cyclo. I began to imagine a grenade flying into the back of the truck or rolling under the carriage. The red cross on the canvas was, after all, meaningless in this falling darkness. And how would the Viet Cong here know that the Viet Cong back at the leprosarium were benefiting from the American medical supplies Wally was always sure to leave behind with the good Sisters who took no sides?

I thought of Peter, revisited another version of my father's mournful trip to Idlewild to collect what was left of me. Thought of you, Rainey, and your two brothers, left motherless. And then of Lily's cousin, waiting for her to return. I thought of all the patients, the poor lepers, waiting for us to return with their beautiful clothes, their little bit of anticipated joy. I wondered how long they would look for us.

I thought of Dominic's wife at home with his new baby. How long until they stopped looking for him?

I shut my eyes and bowed my head, trying to pray—how else do you prepare for what you can't control? Lily reached out and took my hand, as she had taken her cousin's this afternoon— it seemed ages ago.

It was not yet fully dark, but even with my eyes closed I was aware of the way the light was disappearing, gone from amber to brown to an enfolding gray. Behind my lids, I saw the faces I had seen today. Saw the swollen lesions, the distortions, the noseless cavity above the laughing mouth.

The revulsion I had kept in check all day, tucked under my ribs, stifled, ignored, smothered with a rigorous effort at compassion, at goonish, grinning sympathy, broke apart. I felt it flooding my chest, rising into my throat. I had risked my life, my happy future, for these gross and hopeless creatures.

I saw again Lily's cousin's awful face. Recalled the two of them—sweet Lily and that monster—side by side on the neatly made-up cot. Somebody's deathbed. A terrible death, reached only after the worst kind of pain. The gobbling whirlwind. The body in chaos.

I shook off Lily's hand. Wrapped myself in my own arms. I felt Charlene lean forward beside me, her elbows on her knees, our thighs touching, and, honestly, my skin crawled under my ridiculous outfit. A wave of nausea, revulsion. Contagion, I was thinking. Infection. I was thinking, *awful*.

I saw the slaughtered figures in the clearing. The clothes that made them men, he'd said. Pretty clever. The thought, my amusement and admiration, calmed me somehow. The clothes that made them women, made them children. Made of small animals, their flesh and blood and bone, something human.

What had we been doing all day but measuring those poor fools for their shrouds? Fools ourselves, risking our lives to dress the dead and the dying.

I thought of the pages in my little notebook, with my phonetic misspellings of each leper's name, my own cruel nicknames, followed by Lily's careful measurements: neck, arm, waist, inseam. No two of them the same. Should something terrible happen— a grenade rolled under the engine—those scribbled pages, that record in my own hand of our intention to do good, would end up blown across these wide, wet fields, meaningless to whoever might find them, notebook pages soaked in mud and rain and blood, my careful Catholic schoolgirl script—as indicative of who I was as my whorled fingerprints—bloated and indecipherable. In pieces.

I felt weighted, saturated, you might say. With what? "Revulsion" now seems too weak a word, but it was not as dramatic as despair. Not as vivid as hate. Or as self-conscious as disdain. A kind of resignation, a giving-in, nearly amused, to the paltriness of it, the human body, the monstrousness of flesh and bone. That seahorse-shaped collection of cells that had burned so easily.

I opened my eyes and saw with some weird detachment my hands folded in my lap, although by then I was certainly not praying. I studied the toes of my gross combat boots, the black sheen, even in the gloom, of the mud and the rain-slicked floor.

We were all very still. It was quiet, although I can't say for sure that the rain had stopped.

And then I looked up again. He was watching me. He was as he had been: across from us, his legs splayed, the butt of the rifle high up against his thick thigh, close to his groin, the barrel holding back a small slit in the dark canvas.

Through that opening—and I admit that this is perhaps the distortion of memory or the remnant of a dream—a kind of dull light came, like a muted phosphorous. Just enough of it to touch his neck and his bared chest, the sculpted limestone skin, wet now and still streaked with mud, or blood. He was slowly chewing something—gum or tobacco, a regurgitated bit of the nun's rice, I don't know—his jaw moving with some slow, savoring motion in that weird white light.

I felt, madness to remember it, a kind of fury. As if he, not Charlene, had led me here.

But I also felt, more powerfully, the tremendous attraction I'd been trying all afternoon to suppress. It was overwhelming now. A wholly physical thing, a longing.

I wanted to be rid of him, sure, but more than that I wanted to press myself into his flesh, to pass through that wry mouth of his. To be consumed. A morsel.

His jaw was moving. He was studying my face across the weirdly lit gloom, his eyes touched with delight.

I scrambled to stand, to move toward him, felt my feet go out from under me on the slick floor.

Three things happened at once: Dom shouted, "Outside," the doctor slipped from the truck, and Charlene whispered, "Tricia," her lips to my ear. She had, somehow, wrapped me in her arms. I saw that Lily, too, had caught me by the waist. Together, we three eased back onto the jeep's bench.

A vehicle was approaching from behind us, its headlights moved across our legs. I believe we all thought we were about to face the brief and violent end of our lives. Only a moment's blind despair, then resignation, even indifference.

Dom, too, had left the truck. He was just outside the passenger door, his rifle raised. We heard American voices. The doctor's voice, greeting them, calmly, "Gentlemen."

Through the bit of opened canvas, I saw Dom lower the gun and for the first time that evening I remembered that he was supposed to be a CO. When he put his smiling face into the truck again, backlit now by the headlights of our rescuers, he said, "The cavalry is here, ladies." And then, to Charlene alone, "We'll be okay."

She laughed, our arms about one another still. "For now," she said.

"For now's good by me," Dom said, and grinned his all-American boy grin. He made the sign of the cross over his green fatigues and put out his hand to help us from the truck. "Dominus vobiscum," he said.

MY MOTHER was an information operator at what we still referred to in those days as the telephone exchange, on Fiftieth Street in Manhattan. She worked the night shift, leaving the house every afternoon as soon as my father and I were home from school—our dinner already made, waiting to be reheated—and returning in the early hours of the next day.

(Does it surprise you to know she rode the subway and a bus at that hour without fear—knew, in fact, each bus driver by name? An antique past, for certain. Something out of a fairy tale, indeed.)

She was always there at breakfast with our lunches packed, the house clean, a funny story to tell about the night before: the crazy phone numbers people sought, the drunken confessions, even the "dirty talk" that she always met with an indignant "You are no gentleman, sir." There were recurring characters in her tales: a crooning hobo; a hapless, out-of-town businessman; a weary streetwalker; a lonely cop; even a guy at Riker's Island who always wanted the number for the mayor's bedroom at Gracie Mansion.

And on full-moon nights, she told us, Satan himself often

called, from a pay phone on some cold, blue-shaded street deep
in the stony caverns of Manhattan. My mother said she knew it
was the Devil by the sugary, sibilant way he always began, "I
once had this number by heart, but it's somehow slipped
away . . ." And by the chill in her spine after she'd given him the
number he sought—always with one or two digits transposed.

S O: A COUPLE MORE THINGS, weird things, to tell you about that night. Take them as you will. Just keep in mind all the superstitions, the apparitions, I believed in. In those days.

Our rescuers opened the hood and did the whole men-looking-at-an-engine thing again, this time with flashlights. Dom hopped into the driver's seat, turned the key, and the truck started up immediately, hummed as smoothly as the thing ever hummed. There was some good-natured kidding. One of the GIs used the term "submarine races." The other said it was a lot of effort just to get alone with some chicks.

And then Dom convinced them to take us chicks to Saigon in their jeep while he and the doctor returned to the base. The three of us squeezed into the back seat and rode a good part of the way with Dom and the doctor in the truck just behind us. We held hands, the three of us, like truant schoolgirls about to face the consequences.

I wonder now, in this long look back, what those two men found to say to each other as they drove.

◈

AT CHARLENE'S, YOU CHILDREN WERE IN BED and Kent was out. The villa was lit with low lights that somehow only increased my weariness—I don't know that I've ever been so bone-tired—as well as my uncertainty as to the time. I felt it should have been three a.m. It wasn't even ten.

Our clothes were hanging in Charlene's office, and Lily and I changed there. The morning's modesty, each getting dressed in a separate room, seemed silly now. I just wanted to get home.

The servant who had let us in came to the door, and Charlene spoke to him rapidly in French. I thought she was asking for some dinner, and told her I wouldn't stay to eat. I was just going to get a cab and get home before Peter began to worry.

She said, "I asked him to bring the car around. He can take you and Lily home." And then added, "Your French comes and goes."

"My French has yet to arrive," I told her, putting on my shoes. "I have no knack for it."

She was still in her fatigues, but she had let down her hair. I could now see how the sun had brought out the freckles on her face. "You understood him well enough," she said. "His butcher-shop tale."

It took me a minute to know who she referred to. "The doctor?"

She nodded. "You followed him pretty well."

"Why wouldn't I?" I said. I was wary, but only of Charlene's dismissiveness. I didn't know what she was getting at, but I sensed it would not reflect well on me.

"His French," she said.

I was still uncertain. "But he spoke English," I said. "He's an American."

She was smoking a cigarette, and I saw the fingers beneath it move together. "No, he didn't," she said. "Not in the truck. He spoke French. For Lily's sake, I think. To frighten her. Make her believe her fellow countrymen are barbarians. I was surprised you followed so well."

"He spoke English," I said again. And laughed at the absurdity of this conversation, of such a weird misremembering. "I heard him."

Lily was watching us both. She was very solemn. Or perhaps she, too, was bone-tired. Charlene turned to her and asked her, in French, if she had understood the man—that terrible man, she said. That much I took in. I don't know why her description so surprised me.

Lily said in French that she had understood him clearly. His Vietnamese and his French were both very good.

Charlene put the heels of her hands to her eyes. She stood like that for a few silent minutes, the cigarette burning between her fingers. I had the very brief notion—very brief—that she was going to cry. Some movement of her chin, I guess.

All about her feet, the indications of her efforts—crates and boxes and piled baby clothes. It all looked a bit forlorn to me, in my exhaustion, in the room's low late-night light. While she stood there, we heard a tap at the door, the servant saying the car was ready. She lowered her hands and flicked her cigarette in the vague direction of her ashtray.

She said, "I've got four bolts of silk to fetch in the morning. I'll bring them over to the Cases' by ten. I'm going to talk to Marcia about letting Lily get away from her domestic duties. Get these outfits finished quickly." And to Lily, "Let's see if you can get your friend Phan to help out."

If Wally was in trouble for bringing us along today, she went on, or reluctant to bring us again, she would ask one of the other corpsmen who'd been on their last trip. Or another medic she knew, an older doctor, always amused by her efforts. He'd find a way to get us back. She also knew a young American nurse at the station hospital. Had lunch with her just the other day. An adorable young woman. Head of nursing. She might be of some use if we needed transport.

The light was the light of three a.m.: vague and pointillist, colors washed thin, edges ill-defined. My feet ached after a day in those boots. My back was sore. I wanted to interrupt her to say, "We should go. The car is waiting. Peter is waiting." But I didn't. Couldn't. I knew we were watching Charlene at some essential work of her own. She was resetting her bearings, shoring up her confidence, reconstructing her faith in her own silly way of doing good. I understood without much thought that this faith had been toppled today, mocked and trivialized by someone whom we all, all unaccountably, had wanted to please.

Finally, Charlene said, "I refuse to say another word about him." And screwed out her cigarette in the silver dish, scattering ash.

LATE THAT SAME SUMMER, Jacqueline Kennedy's baby was born prematurely. All of us in the American community in Saigon—all of us women, anyway—kept breathless track of the news: the baby had been flown to Children's Hospital in Boston, as I recall. The president was with him.

For the Catholics among us who had waited for news of the dying pope, it was the summer's second sad vigil.

Finally, there was a press conference. Pierre Salinger told the world that the baby had died, the brevity of his little life making the details of such an announcement, the day, the hour, the minute of his death, all the more heartbreaking. There was a sympathetic intake of breath from the gathered press. And then a question: "Has Mrs. Kennedy been told?"

"No," came the answer. "Not yet."

No doubt this seems unbelievable to your generation, that she was the last to be told. But you have to understand what it was like in those days, for us, the wives.

❖

WHEN IT CAME TIME TO RETURN to the leprosarium with the pretty clothes, I told Charlene that Peter wouldn't allow it.

Things in the city were getting difficult. (The public record is reliable.) Late that August, Diem's secret police raided a dozen Buddhist pagodas throughout the city, cleared them of demonstrators, arrested hundreds. He closed the university, declared martial law.

I can't recall for certain if I cited any of these wider-world situations when I told Charlene that Peter wouldn't allow me to leave the city, but, in those days, I'm not sure I needed to. "My husband won't let me go" would have been sufficient enough explanation, even back home.

"Confined to quarters," Charlene said, amused but also, briefly, I thought, disappointed. And then annoyed. And then— all these emotions passed over her face in the time it might take a bit of cloud to obscure the sun—she shrugged, dismissed me with a wave of her hand.

I knew there were plenty of other women in her cabal.

O N A SUNDAY EVENING in mid-September a plastic bomb went off in the back of the Kinh Do movie theater. No one in the theater was killed, as it turned out—not this time, anyway—although there was damage to the surrounding buildings.

It was a Disney movie they were showing. *Lady and the Tramp*, I think. You and your brother were supposed to have been there.

I imagine you remember this, or at least remember being told about it.

Charlene and Kent were out that night. One of their servants had promised you both a trip to the movies. But at the last minute Ransom came down with a bout of Ho Chi Minh's revenge— "that boy will have his street snacks," Charlene said later—and the trip was canceled.

When word of the bombing reached the party your parents were attending, your mother left immediately—another guest had offered his car. Kent, calmer, as I imagine him, stayed behind to call the villa. Phone service in Saigon was often unpredictable, but eventually, he got through and discovered you children were there.

Charlene was already on her way to the movie theater, through the dark streets. Frantic, she said.

We were side by side at the edge of the pool at the Sports Club as she told me this. I recall how she spoke over her tanned and freckled shoulder, slick with baby oil, while our toes stirred the blue water. She had her hair pulled back in a girlish pony-tail—she had just played tennis—oversized sunglasses on her pert nose. So svelte in her black bathing suit. Sophisticated. I noticed then that her small feet had an unusually high instep.

She laughed—at herself this time. All around us the bodies of the children, American and European dependents, mostly: tod-dlers draped in beach towels, and their splashing older siblings—you and your brother somewhere among them—as well as jittery teenagers who tugged at wet bathing suits, eyed one another.

There were the bodies of women, too, the wives mostly at that weekday hour, in modest two-pieces and large sunglasses, Barbie bubble cuts and jaunty flips, scattered across the lounge chairs that ringed the periphery or swimming languid laps at the far end of the pool. That endless glare and heat and tinny transis-tor rock and roll that defined those long, idle afternoons. Idle for me; it was unusual to find Charlene here at the pool. You chil-dren usually came with a sitter or some other American family.

I remember flattering myself to think she'd come there that afternoon to seek me out.

Charlene said, "The most obnoxious shopkeeper in the Cen-tral Market couldn't have matched my bargaining skills that night. In the car to the theater. I offered God everything. If there's a spiritual equivalent to an eternal blow job, I offered it."

And she elbowed me until I laughed with her.

The street was in chaos, of course. The police and an ambulance or two. Barricades were already up so she had to run the last few blocks. Ruined her stockings, she told me, since she'd had to kick off her heels. Burning in the air. There was much shouting, and yet, in spite of it, a strange stillness as well. Confusion, of course. Broken glass. She thought she saw blood on the sidewalk. Probably mud. It was hard to tell in the darkness. Scraps of clothing, she thought.

Looking for her twins among the crowd—looking for the two of you in the chaos.

She ran through every street and alleyway she was not turned away from. Without luck—no clear sense of where the injured had been brought—she ran back to the car, limping now, her own feet bleeding. Kent was there by then, standing with the guy who had brought her. They were laughing together before they saw her. She must have looked, she told me, like a madwoman.

"They're fine," Kent said, when she drew near. "They're home. They never went. Ransom's got the runs. They never left the house." He put his arms around her, perhaps a little annoyed, a little impatient, a little ashamed of his blubbering wife in front of this other American male, the man who had driven her there.

And then he repeated, as if she were an irrational child, "They aren't even here, Charlene. Calm down." With feigned patience. "I told you they're safe."

The other American joined in, patting her shoulder. "Safe at home," he said.

Of course, I knew from the start who he was. I'd seen him around town in the days that followed our trip to the leper colony. He'd cleaned himself up, his nails trimmed and polished, shirt and trousers crisp. His hair, washed and combed, had more gray than I remembered. I hadn't spoken to him, and if he'd noticed me, or remembered me, he gave no indication as Peter and I walked past him at a crowded reception, and then again at another garden party, where I saw him absorbed in conversation with a small circle of men.

I'd glimpsed him again at a table at the Majestic. On the street hailing a cab.

Just another one of the tall, sunburned Americans you could find anywhere in the city, carrying a shopping bag or two, a leather briefcase, a golf bag.

"I've seen him around," I told Charlene. "He's clipped his nails."

Charlene nodded. "He has. He cleans up very nicely."

I thought, She's kissed him, too. I was that kind of innocent.

We were side by side in our bathing suits—hers a black maillot, mine a madras two-piece, modest compared to the French bikinis the European women wore.

I might have cried out with the envy I suddenly felt for all the good use Charlene was getting from her freckled flesh—three beautiful children, Kent, Wally, and now—I was certain—the dirty, handsome Devil himself.

"We have a negotiation going on," Charlene said.

We were looking out across the sun-struck pool, she and I, across the dark, wet heads of the calling children and the swiveling, fish-mouthed faces of the solemn lap swimmers—idle wives in their rubber swim caps festooned with starbursts of plastic peonies, daisies, tulips. For a moment, I imagined these splashing children and the women's determined progress through the water as somehow related. As if the kids had been spawned in their mothers' endless wakes.

Without turning to me, Charlene said, "Tell me what you think of this."

It was the same phrase she'd used in her office that day when she showed me the little non la. I knew by now that it wasn't really my opinion that she sought.

She asked if I remembered Phan, Lily's seamstress friend who was helping her out. I said I did: missing husband, ancient in-laws, two small children. Lily's generosity in giving her work. Sweet Lily, I'm sure I said.

"She's a widow now, this Phan," Charlene went on. "Word reached her. The husband was killed in a motorcycle accident. At least that's what Lily said." Charlene shrugged. "I didn't question. I'm pretty sure he was a sympathizer."

"Poor girl," I muttered.

"It gets worse," Charlene said. "She's pregnant. Nearly eight months on."

I feel sure I leaned away at this. Envy like a rusty fishhook in my throat.

"Phan came by the villa with some Barbie clothes. We got to talking. Her English isn't bad, but her French is impeccable. She told me she and her husband had been saving up to open their own little clothing business. They'd already arranged to purchase a number of Singers at a very good price—a result of Marilee's much-maligned Commercial Import Program, I gathered. Of course, when he disappeared, all their plans collapsed. And now she knows he's not coming back. And she has this baby due. And two toddlers already. His aging parents to take care of."

Charlene's big sunglasses reflected the sunlight, the bright pool water creased by black currents, by the bodies moving within it.

"So she asked me while we were chatting, rather shyly, if I knew any American couples who were looking to adopt."

I'm pretty sure I leaned away at this, too. But Charlene forged on, speaking to the air.

"He," she said, the pronoun emphatic somehow, utterly defining, "knows an American couple, quite wealthy, who are desperate for a baby. They would like a newborn. And they'd prefer a child who hasn't spent time in an orphanage, picking up disease."

Our bare arms were touching, our bare thighs.

Charlene said, "I want to get Phan five thousand dollars for her baby."

I could see my own fish-mouthed astonishment reflected in Charlene's big glasses.

The money would allow the girl to set up her shop, Charlene said, help her to feed her children and her old in-laws. It would buy her and her family a better future. "She's a very enterprising young girl. Not the seamstress Lily is, but more sure of herself, certainly more savvy. I can see her in business, if this government ever rights itself. I know she'd make good use of the money."

I swallowed some air with the same gaping expression of my lap-swimming compatriots. I think I said something like "You're kidding."

Charlene lifted the sunglasses from her nose, perched them on top of her head, and for a second her green eyes seemed as reflective as the dark lenses had been. She gave me her *Isn't that just like you?* smile.

Beyond the pool, a small swarm of wet children was playing a game among the chairs, searching for some hidden thing while a slim American teenager called out their names, saying who was getting warmer, who was cold. We watched them silently for a moment. I could feel Charlene's impatience with me as if it radiated from her flesh.

"Look," she said, finally. "It's not so rare. Do you know how much we had to dole out for Roberta's baby? A nice donation to the orphanage, to the church, to the powers that be for the paperwork. In fact, everyone along the way had a palm greased. Everyone was paid a little something. Except, of course, for the mother who gave birth to the child, who did all the work."

She shifted her bottom on the damp edge of the pool, stirred the water with her pretty feet. Raised her slick and freckled shoulders.

"Five thousand is perfectly reasonable," she said. "Don't you think?"

A small cheer went up from the searching children—whatever was hidden had been found. In truth, I'm not sure I knew what to think. She was talking about selling a baby.

Complicating it all—I would say, in retrospect, overriding it all—was the bitter, consuming envy I felt for the time she'd spent with our jungle doctor. For all the good use she was getting out of that body of hers.

I asked her, "What does he think?"

She didn't hesitate. She knew who I meant. "He thinks it's possible. If the baby is perfect."

I felt some further recoil—in the Christian part of my conscience, I suppose. I managed to say, "Couldn't you get in trouble for this? If word got out?"

Charlene was squinting at the children across the pool. The little ones were now kneeling in a row, their wet heads bowed, their faces in their hands. They counted together, sweet and breathless voices, as the lithe babysitter moved among the chairs, looking for another hiding place.

"I suppose," Charlene said without much interest. "But in some ways, that would be fine. If word got out." Even though she had turned away from me, I could see, as we used to say, the wheels turning.

"If we could set it up right," she went on, "we could make similar offers to other pregnant women. Maybe give them an advance on the final payment so they can afford to take care of themselves in the last few months, take care of their newborns. It could be a marvelous incentive. The mothers get a nice payoff at the end, and we get healthy babies to offer for adoption. At a premium."

"You're talking about selling babies," I said.

Charlene turned back to me with a laugh that just couldn't be suppressed. Her laugh. She pulled the shades from her head and once more placed them over her eyes, but still our faces were just inches apart, and I knew her eyes were on mine.

"No, I'm not," she said in her matter-of-fact Charlene way. "I'm talking about increasing their value—babies, children, their mothers, too." She grimaced, letting me know it was an act of supreme generosity on her part to take the time to explain to me what should have been perfectly clear.

"The streets of this city, Tricia, the orphanages, the hospitals, would not be so filled with lost and damaged children if anyone believed in their value." A brief twitch of contempt crossed her thin lips. "Imagine that every street kid you see, every orphan, every baby held up to us by a desperate mother is, instead," and now her smile was in appreciation for her own cleverness, "a

Hasselblad, a quart of Johnnie Walker Black, a Dior gown, a Rolex. Do you think such expensive items would be left to languish in parks and squalid institutions, neglected, ignored?"

She reached back to touch her spine, her trim torso, her small, firm breasts thrust forward.

"It's all about value assigned, Tricia. How in the world do you think we're getting twenty-five bucks for our silly little dolls?"

I suppose it was Stella's voice that I heard when I thought to say, *The madams in the whorehouses assign value, Charlene.* Or maybe, *Pimps assign value.*

But I was not Stella. And I had never before said those words out loud.

"It doesn't seem right" was all I managed to whisper.

Now Charlene's mouth beneath the dark glasses had aligned itself into a kind of thoughtful pity. Suddenly, she slipped her bare arm under mine—our hips were already aligned—and lifted my hand. There was the impression of the concrete edge of the pool on the fleshy heel of my palm, and she gently brushed it away.

She said, smoothing my hand with her own, "I made every bargain I could think of, the other night. When I thought the twins were there, at the theater. My own life for theirs was the first, Tricia, the easiest one to make. Take my life, but keep them safe."

She didn't look at me, only at our hands as she gently swept her fingers over my palm, heel, lifeline, fingertips. "It's the offer any mother would make. You'll see when you have a baby of your own. My life for my child's, my happiness for theirs. It's immediate. Instinctual, I guess. A mother will bear any pain, any loss, if it means her child will thrive."

She stopped stroking, but held on nevertheless.

"The women in this country," she said, "at home, too—don't kid yourself, it happens at home, too—are making the choice every day. Leaving their kids at orphanages. Putting them up for adoption. Offering them to us passing American ladies as we make our way to lunch. You know they are, Tricia. They're willing to have their own hearts broken if it means their kids will live. Any mother would."

She returned my hand and my arm to the concrete surrounding the pool, adjusted the glasses on her nose. "I'd just like to see them get paid for it."

I can't say now if Charlene knew what she'd done, or if she had done it with full intent, but she had nevertheless utterly defused my disapproval, my dismay, even my jealousy, with that simple phrase "You'll see when you have a baby of your own."

She had kindled my heart's keenest desire. No objection, no other thought, moral or otherwise, could survive that vision: a baby of my own. I was so disarmed, charmed, I suppose, by her easy conjuring that I failed to understand at first the way she suddenly shuddered, there at the edge of the pool.

All around us, there were the calls and cries of the children at their game, the thin music of transistor radios, the rhythmic lapping of the women in the water. And beyond these, that bone-on-bone rattle of palm leaves above the club's lush grounds, the gentle *plock* of tennis balls, the distant, oh so distant, clamor of the streets.

Your mother trembled beside me. Behind her grim, determined smile, her stylishly pale and carefully applied lipstick, her teeth were chattering.

Startled, I put my hand on her bare thigh. "Are you cold?" I asked her.

I saw her take in the placid scene, the children especially. Even with her dark glasses, I could see her eyes narrow. Her voice took on its own hissing breathlessness. "Do you mean am I nowhere near the prize?"

It took me a second to know she was referring to the children playing across the way. But she didn't wait, she never waited, for my full comprehension.

"Then yes," she said. "Still cold."

AS IT TURNED OUT, Phan wanted to keep her child. Or that's what Charlene told me when next I asked. She was vague about it, might have been lying. I had the sense that she regretted the scheme. Or regretted discussing it with me.

I think of this from time to time: Phan's baby would have been about twelve years old when Saigon fell. An adult now, perhaps with children, even grandchildren, of her own, wherever he or she might be.

And even all these years later, I can't say with any certainty what I hope for: that Charlene actually sold Phan's newborn to those wealthy Americans, got the child to safety—even prosperity—so early in the war, or that Phan kept her baby with her through all that was to come.

Disorienting, this not even knowing what to hope for.

A blessing, too, I suppose. The shrug that casts off guilt.

THAT NIGHT IN CHARLOTTESVILLE, when the mosquitoes became annoying, we went inside for coffee.

While Aunt Lorraine and the professor were in the kitchen, Stella gave me a tour of the artwork. I recognized none of the artists' names, although Stella assured me I should. Two or three of the smaller paintings were Aunt Lorraine's own—indistinguishable, I thought, from the ones Stella claimed to be "incredibly valuable." But I didn't say so. And, of course, after four years of Marymount, I knew enough not to say, "Why, I could have drawn that myself."

Although I do remember thinking that if I ever owned a house like this, I would want something warmer, friendlier on the walls. Nothing quite so chaotic and puzzling.

Aunt Lorraine carried the tray with the coffee service into the living room, the dogs trailing her. The professor excused himself and went to his study. Coffee at this hour, he said, was something he had, alas, outgrown.

Stella and I sat side by side on a low-slung couch as Aunt Lorraine handed us our cups, the dogs sniffing at our knees and then settling themselves around our feet. Once we were served, Aunt Lorraine straightened to her full height and walked languidly across the room. At the fireplace, she turned, her hands on her hips.

I was not to go to Birmingham, she announced. I was, in fact, to go straight back to New York in the morning. The professor would take me to the train. He would pay for my ticket.

Stella said, "Excuse me?" She executed one of her slow-burn frowns. "What?"

But Aunt Lorraine held up a hand. She herself, she said, would drive to Birmingham with Stella. They would take her car, not Stella's tiny jalopy.

"Fifal," I heard Stella say, resentfully, as if defending one of these smelly dogs.

It was not right, not right at all, Aunt Lorraine declared, for me to put myself at risk like this when I was "all the world" to my father. His only child, only family, sole companion and comfort for the coming years.

Stella laughed. "And what am I? Chopped liver?"

"You have a mess of siblings, darling," Aunt Lorraine pointed out. "Your parents have one another. An abundance of family." She shook her head. "Why, we have enough cousins on our side alone to fill a stadium."

Should anything happen to Stella, terrible as that would be, Aunt Lorraine said, there would be plenty of comfort, plenty of comforters, "for those who grieve."

Not so for my widowed father.

"He has his friend," Stella said, whining, suddenly childish. "Mr. Tannen."

Aunt Lorraine touched her forehead. "Oh, please." A flash of impatience.

Stella looked at me, crossed her eyes behind her glasses.

"This is nuts," she whispered. And then turned back to her aunt. "You're kidding, right?" she demanded. "This is a joke, right?"

The tumult inside my own head and heart at the moment was somewhat akin to the whirring that went on in the back seat of Fifal. I was confused, wary, flattered by the attention yet troubled by the directive. I retreated to my natural state: shyly silent, watchful.

"I am perfectly serious," Aunt Lorraine said. "I'll go with you. We'll do what we can. Put ourselves in harm's way if it comes to that. But"—she shook her head—"I'm sorry. I cannot in good conscience allow Patricia to do the same."

She repeated her logic, a little less imperiously this time. "We are all obliged to one another, of course, but Patsy is obliged to a single person in a very specific way. No one can replace her. Not in the least. She is not free to put herself in danger."

Her shoulders fell. She seemed, once again, genuinely sorrowful. "I know you girls want a heroic life. You want to show your courage. But self-sacrifice is never really selfless. It's often quite selfish."

Now she shifted her gaze, her deep-set eyes, to me alone—the distance from our sofa to the fireplace making me feel as if I had caught the attention of an actor on the stage, as if she'd memorized these words long ago and chose to direct them at me, at this moment, somewhat arbitrarily, for effect alone. A proclamation about the state of the world, the nature of life, that only incidentally applied to me. Like a horoscope, or one of the psalms.

"None of us is unfettered, dear," she said. "Each of us is fettered in some way. You are constrained by love and obligation. You are not free." And then, ending the discussion, "I will not allow you to leave here and put your father's life, the rest of your father's life, at risk. I have my own conscience to live with."

Stella argued. Not vehemently, as I recall. Undermining her own Joan-of-Arc-at-the-stake declaration at dinner's end, she told her aunt now that it really wasn't all that dangerous, what we were about to do. No one, seriously, was going to get hurt. We might get teargassed, but—she laughed—we'll hold our breath. We'll probably get arrested, but that didn't mean the electric chair. We would take the professor's advice and fill our pockets with dog biscuits, if that would please her.

But Aunt Lorraine was unmovable, and we were still young enough, still polite enough in the way of that time and place, to realize argument was futile.

When we went to our room that night, Stella was still angry. "We don't have to listen to her," she whispered. "We can leave right now. Tonight. She can't tell us what to do."

But I said it would be rude. To leave here like that, after our lovely dinner. She and the professor had been so very nice.

"You go down there with her," I told Stella gently. "I think she's really looking for an excuse to go. You know, to make her own restitution. For slavery. For Sonia."

Although I think I understood even then that Aunt Lorraine was not interested in going to Birmingham to make amends for her family's shameful history. She wanted to go only to keep Stella in check, to keep her safe from harm.

AFTER WE TURNED OUT THE LIGHTS, I thought about my father alone in our house, winding his bedside clock at this hour.

It was the sound I heard from my own bedroom every night of my life. Or every night but those I had spent at Stella's. I imagined him pushing off, toe to heel, toe to heel, his scuffed bedroom slippers. Lifting the blanket, drawing his legs underneath. A sigh—I always heard that, too—as he blessed himself, lying on his back. Then the click of the lamp. Soon he would be snoring.

In the morning, I knew, he would indeed press his shirt, as my mother had always done. The warm scent of steamed fabric in the air. He'd been proud, during all those years he worked at the school, of the neat crease in his uniform trousers, along the length of his starched sleeves.

He would make his tea in the kitchen, the sun coming through the window above the sink. He would boil an egg.

Earlier that evening, when I told Aunt Lorraine and the professor that my father worked at a high school in the Bronx, I knew they would assume he was a teacher. I knew this even as I said it. Knew I was, among these brilliant and interesting people, ashamed of him.

I turned on my side. Against the moonlight through the double window, I could see the silhouette of the lilacs in their vase. The crystal decanter of water on its silver tray. If I were to marry Peter (Please, God, I prayed), I might someday have a large house of my own. With a guest room such as this, redolent of flowers and clean linen. A room for my father—who would always, I understood, curtail my freedom, my independence, my flight. At least for as long as he lived.

I began to cry. Either at the thought of this constraint or at the thought of the hour and the day when it would be forever lifted.

Stella said into the darkness, "You crying?"

With my back to her, I managed a muffled "No."

And then she was climbing in beside me, into the narrow bed. She patted my shoulder, stroked my hair. She draped her heavy arm along my hip, entwined our fingers. I knew her scent. Knew the size and shape of her damp hands.

"We'll have lots of other chances," she whispered. "There's going to be a reckoning, wait and see. This summer is just the start." She sighed, her breath warm on my shoulder, her lips against the thin fabric of my nightgown. "We are on the precipice of tremendous change."

In truth, it took me a second to remember what she was talking about.

I SAW THEM BOTH OFF the next morning, the professor at my side. I felt, as soon as they pulled away in Aunt Lorraine's big wood-sided station wagon, a certain kinship with Fifal—who looked very small and foolish, abandoned as he was in their long driveway. Earlier, Stella and I had covered the open passenger window with the plastic sheeting and tape her father had provided.

The tiny car now looked as if it wore an opaque eye patch, as if it had taken a beating.

And yet it seemed happy, I thought. Sitting alone under the safe harbor of a fragrant magnolia.

Looking at that badly painted, bright green, battered yet becalmed little thing, I felt, somehow, absolved.

E VENTUALLY, THE GOOD DOCTOR disappeared from our midst.

Not so unusual in those days when Americans were always dropping in and dropping out: Robert McNamara and Maxwell Taylor, Hilsman, Rusk, Bundy, Forrestal. Men whose names, I suppose, are of fading significance to you, and of no significance at all to your children. Ambassador Nolting took his family on vacation to the Aegean, and the stalwart Trueheart took over. Then Nolting was replaced by Henry Cabot Lodge.

My husband always liked and admired Frederick Nolting. A gentleman farmer, he called him. A true Virginian, soft-spoken, deferential, patrician in a distinctly American way. Certainly, Peter approved of the way Nolting supported and encouraged Diem.

He was less enthused about Ambassador Lodge, who had arrived as Nolting's replacement late that summer. Not only because Lodge was a Republican, but because on his arrival, our new ambassador delayed presenting his credentials at the presidential palace until he had first visited the protesting Buddhists at Xa Loi.

As you can imagine, Peter thought this rude. Dishonorable. Naive.

I recall a story that went around that fall, how the visiting Maxwell Taylor, who was then the head of the Joint Chiefs, had played a vigorous game of tennis with the head of Diem's military, Big Minh. The rumor mill said both Ambassador Lodge and Secretary McNamara were much impressed by the American-size stature of General Minh, so different from Diem, the diminutive, aloof mandarin.

"We're going to sell out Diem for a guy who looks good in tennis whites," Peter told me.

I suppose we shared a working-class disdain for the sport.

IN MID-OCTOBER, another rabbit died, and I learned Dr. Navy did indeed wear a Rolex.

He assured Peter that I would be fine to travel through the early spring, so he could serve out his assignment. Or, the doctor suggested, I could go home by myself. Live with my father for a few months until Peter's work here was over.

Which brought me to another vision of my father meeting me at Idlewild. This time I was upright, but holding my breath, walking off the plane—in my imagination—with infinite care, tiny steps, eyes focused as if on a glass brimming to the top with, well, with something precious and precarious and easily spilled.

Days later, we had just turned off the bedside lights, the overhead fan was turning, the joss stick burning in its pail of sand. Peter told me he had purchased our return tickets that afternoon. With his own money. He had offered his resignation. He saw the handwriting on the wall, he said. Kennedy had spoken publicly about his willingness to see a change of personnel in Saigon. The U.S. was ready to let Diem fall. No good would come of it.

He said, "I want you out of here." He said, "I want us both out of here."

I said, "The three of us."

He looked at me in the mottled darkness. His eyes paused for a moment in their darting. I knew, I knew, it was on the tip of his tongue to ask, "Three?" But he caught himself. Patted my thigh. "Right," he said.

I sometimes suspect that even in those days, Peter never truly imagined full life for any child of our own making.

By the time we landed in Hawaii, Diem's overthrow was in the news. When we left for San Francisco the next morning, we heard he was dead. He and his brother both shot in the head, their hands tied behind their backs. Madame Nhu was on a tour of the States—something, I learned years later, Peter had helped to arrange; no one in the Catholic Intelligence Agency wanted to see a woman, any woman, murdered in the coup.

News reports said she was desperate to get her own children out of Saigon safely. The Dragon Lady was a mother, after all. Even she had managed that miracle.

It was in the hotel that night that I saw the first spot of blood. We stayed an extra few days until the miscarriage was complete.

Peter and I returned to D.C. on November 7. I remember the date because it was my father's birthday. The town house we'd barely moved into at the beginning of the year had grown alien in our absence, stark and, quite literally, without warmth. His sister had occupied the place so cautiously, it was hard to believe it had been lived in at all.

She and I left before dawn on the morning of November 25, and then stood for hours outside St. Matthew's Cathedral, in the cold and among the crowd, which was mostly silent except for some whispered prayers, some weeping. We glimpsed only briefly Jackie in her black veil, the powder blue coats of her two children. Or perhaps I'm confusing the photos with the event itself.

It took a few months—he should not have quit the navy so abruptly—but eventually Peter found a job with a small patent firm, where he spent the rest of his career. It was his pro bono work, for our parish, our diocese, various charities, that gave him real pleasure through the years. He was a good man with a generous heart.

I took over the kindergarten class at our parish school when the current teacher went on maternity leave and became a permanent fixture there when she decided not to return. I went back to college some years later for a master's in early childhood education—although there wasn't much I didn't already know.

I had three more miscarriages and then a hysterectomy at thirty-five. That's how it was done in those days. No other options were offered. Except for adoption, of course. The surgery, I was promised, would put an end to the depression and the insomnia and the wild, irrational tears that followed each miscarriage—all those merely biological reactions to hormones gone haywire. To my body's own animal insistence on life after life after life, more life.

We bought a small house. And then a bigger one. Our nieces and nephews visited to tour D.C., to look at colleges, to go on job interviews. One cheerful nephew lived with us for a year while interning on the Hill. I loved that.

Stella and I slowly lost touch—that mostly unintentional dwindling of correspondence that can happen with the friends of our youth. I suspect she was busy with her five kids, with the demands of her husband's career in what she had begun to call in her Christmas letters "global health." To be a helpmeet to such a man is, I suppose, yet another way to repair the world.

Our own marriage had the usual ups and downs, days of stasis, days of attenuated affection, days of gratitude, of the sometimes vivid, sometimes weary appreciation for a lifelong friend, lifelong lover. The only lover my body has known—strange as that must seem to your generation.

Of course, we never recaptured the astonishment, the magic, the delight of those newlywed days. Once, in the heat of some argument about something or other, I reminded Peter of the high romance of our first meeting—his dazed uncertainty there on Fifty-Ninth Street. "I'm going to spend the rest of my life regretting I never asked you for your name."

He said, "Well, I was right about the regret."

It hurt me to the core. I still feel the pinch of it. But of course there's no life without regretting.

When the house became too much for us, we moved to a condo. And when Peter died, I came here. Culling each time all that we'd accumulated. You're beginning to know the drill. I'm sorry I didn't keep your mother's letters. But delighted that you've tracked me down after all these years.

AND DOMINIC. Seeing his name again in your note felt like another sorting of souvenirs. That same jolt of recognition when something long lost, long forgotten, is suddenly retrieved. And then, of course, the familiar dilemma: What to do with it now?

Looking back, I suppose the last time I saw Dominic was at the hospital, although I can't say for sure it was my last visit. He had cleared out a storage room just off the ward and moved his puppet show in there so the music and the laughter would not disturb the sicker children. Your mother and I passed by the opened door, saw him bent over the little record player, maybe a half dozen kids, patched up, bandaged, around him on the floor.

He glanced at me over his shoulder. Smiled, of course. Those blue eyes. And then nodded toward a little girl at his feet. The child, maybe six, had a withered arm. But with it she'd pressed one of our small teddy bears against her heart. I then noticed that every one of the children gathered around him held one of our little gifts: a baby doll, a yo-yo, a stuffed puppy. Dom saw that I noticed. Gave us a thumbs-up. "You ladies done good," he called out.

"All credit to Saigon Barbie," Charlene said, but she pointed to me. A little joke.

We lingered a bit to watch as he put the record on, brought his purple dragon to life, and made it dance and turn and wiggle its hind end. The kids rolled with laughter. God, it made your heart ache, that lovely, childish laughter. At such a time, in such a place.

That's how I remember Dominic Carey—a good, open-hearted American kid. Lucky enough, I suppose, to get in and out of that place before so many kids like him were dying there in the awful years ahead. To get home to his wife and his baby and the rest of his life.

And now I'm picturing him once again on that road from the

leprosarium, backlit by the headlights of our rescue vehicle. His grin under the wet peak of his cap. The elaborate sign of the cross he made.

How his hand trembled as he helped each of us down from the truck, and then into the back seat of the jeep that would take us home, a tremor across the length of his palm and into his fingertips. The dull reverberation of what I, too, had felt that night: a disturbance worse than fear—colder, more penetrating than fear.

An understanding, perhaps, of what a paltry, personal matter it is to lose your life.

Now, tell me how you two met. Tell me everything. I have, these days, as you may have noticed, time on my hands. As much time to read as to write.

II

P ART OF DOMINIC'S PROPERTY ran adjacent to our smaller lot, and I first met him through the beige reeds and spindly weeds that defined the divide. This was July, early morning, hot. There was the haze of sun and heat and the sound of buzzing things, and he was walking down a slight incline of tall grass with his youngest child—a squat, square boy with Down syndrome, whom I guessed to be ten or twelve but later learned was twenty.

"His shadow," I once called him.

Father and son wore white fisherman hats and each carried a child's plastic bucket—on their way to a patch of wild blackberries, Dominic said, shouting over the tangled vegetation. "You must be our new neighbor."

He told me he'd bought his own house when he retired from teaching—history and social studies in a small parochial school in the district. It was another old farmhouse, larger than ours but, judging from what I'd seen of it from the road, defaced by a number of decades' disparate additions. He still had the fair, full face you described, and though his eyes were in shadow under the brim of his hat, his bright mouth and his broad cheeks were expressive enough—of a certain good humor, an openness, as you said, a willingness to be known.

He was fit for his age. He wore a gray T-shirt and khaki shorts. A military sort of bearing, but without the humorlessness that phrase always evokes, for me at least. I found out about his time in Vietnam much later.

A friendly guy, I told my husband when I walked back up to the house.

Having been introduced, his son Jamie stood patiently by, his head bent, his hands worrying the rusty handle of his pail as his father and I talked. When the conversation was interrupted by the crisis of a yellow jacket landing on one of the boy's fingers—he let out a small anxious squeal—Dominic said, softly, "Just be still, honey," and then waited with his son, all three of us watching in perfect silence until the thing took flight again.

And then Dominic resumed the conversation, holding the boy's incurred-upon hand with the lightest grip.

Well, of course it would touch anybody, the sight of the two of them—the damaged child and this aging man. You didn't have to be softhearted to be moved by the sight of the two of them walking on across the field, Dominic in front—not tall but towering compared with the stature of his child—the son deliberate in his every step, deliberately matching his father's footprints in the trampled grass.

As we parted, Dominic said, "We'll have to have you over to the house," and I told him that we, my husband Doug and I, had just driven out for the day, to check on our renovation. I said we wouldn't be spending any time out here until, at best, August.

Dominic touched the brim of his cap. "In August, then."

THE PARTY WAS SIMPLE ENOUGH: Sunday-afternoon cocktails under the corrugated roof of the patio behind their house, Douglas and I, and a pair of retirees from down the road, who asked me, as we were introduced, "Haven't we seen you at St. Raymond's?"

"Not likely," Douglas replied for me. "Not if the church is still standing."

I had to tell them, "We're not churchgoers."

Dom's oldest son was there, too, with his wife and their three small children, and Jamie, of course, at his father's elbow, and Ellen, Dom's wife. She was warm, maybe a little overweight but with a nice face, rosy skin, strong bones, dark brown eyes. She had that ability to follow any introduction to a stranger with a conversation that seemed a continuation of something you'd already shared. She and I had just been introduced when we found ourselves laughing about the sullen, heavily pierced kid who manned a nearby farm stand. Ellen said Dominic called him Saint Sebastian.

There was a spattering of rain, more sound than substance, on the pale green roof. The floor of the patio was poured concrete, the furniture eclectic: molded plastic outdoor chairs, wooden picnic tables, a sagging hammock. Evidence of the grandchildren: scooters and trikes and basketballs, a Little Tikes log cabin and a pint-sized kitchen sink had been pushed to the periphery, but there weren't many other signs of party preparation—only a dozen citronella candles in small tin buckets, and maybe twice as many lit votives scattered across the two picnic tables.

The food was delicious: crab dip, a large plate of baked brie, a tatin of cheese and eggplant and fresh tomatoes, all of it served warm and a little haphazardly, one dish at a time, as if Dom and Ellen were just improvising, fetching each one from the kitchen on a whim.

Jamie had been given the task of refilling glasses, and he moved among the guests with shy determination, saying each time he poured another splash of wine, "Not all the way to the top."

"Good job," I told him as he topped off my own. "That's just right. That's perfect." I saw him turn to show his father how well he had done.

His father's eyes were pale blue, and like the rest of his broad, pleasant, sun-pink face, well suited to showing affection.

"Be careful," Dom told me. We were sitting side by side in those molded supermarket chairs. He wore a blue denim shirt, open at the collar, rolled at the sleeves. "Jamie can be overattentive when he likes someone. Elaborately generous, if he has the chance. He'll get you plastered."

I laughed. "He's a gracious host."

Dom shook his head. "Oh, yeah, a real charmer."

It was the same proud, fond, sarcastic tone I'd heard other fathers use to deflect praise for talented sons.

"We volunteer down in the city," he said. "A meals-on-wheels type of thing. For our church. Jamie manages to get even the most cantankerous types to eat up, drink their milk. They can't refuse him. He's got the gift."

"I can tell," I said. Dom, too, had the ability to make me feel we were renewing an old friendship. "Good for you," I added, "volunteering like that."

He shrugged. There was something of Jamie's shyness in the motion.

"I've had a lot of answered prayers," he told me. He said it quickly, and with a kind of crookedness to his smile, as if to assure me that he well understood the wariness such talk might elicit, especially in the likes of me, who had—as my husband had made so boisterously clear—no use for churches of any kind.

Dom nodded toward Jamie as he walked among the guests. The wine bottle was wrapped in a pale dish towel, and Jamie held it before him proudly, with both hands, as if it were an unfurling flag.

"We didn't think he was going to make it when he first arrived," Dominic said. "Heart problems, lung problems, you name it. It was like there were no minor hurdles. You wanted to be wearing a flak jacket." He shook his head, admiringly—the admiration all for the boy himself, not for whatever he and his wife must have endured.

Then he raised his voice so his son could hear him. "We lucked out. We got our own in-house sommelier."

Jamie's attention was instant, as if as he'd made his way among the guests he was waiting only to return to his father's side. "What?" he asked, squinting, already pleased.

"Sommelier," his father said. "A wine expert. You."

"Me?" Jamie said.

Everything uncomplicated and elemental about a boy's worship of a father was there in his face. His small dark eyes were shining. A tremor of pleasure shook his shoulders.

"I am?" He moved closer, touched his thigh to his father's knee, and, laughing, suddenly reached across his lap to pour more wine into my glass.

"Absolutely," Dom said. With the subtlest and most practiced of movements, he reached out to tip the bottle up, averting an overflow.

Jamie grinned, raised the wine bottle triumphantly into the air. He put his free arm around his father's pink neck, and all the little flames of the votive lights behind them suddenly leapt and flared—a trick of my own wine-fueled tears.

IT WAS IMPOSSIBLE, I told Douglas later, to fully understand what it meant to be a family with such a child. Impossible not to feel, ultimately, that you can't imagine their pain or their love or their resilience. Did they ever grow numb to the disappointment? I wondered. Did they ever grow immune to the daily tug of regret, the wish, hour by hour, that the poor kid had been formed otherwise? There was the older son, for instance, who had Jamie's same fair coloring, who might even be said to resemble his little brother, except for the fact that he was healthy and smart, an Emory grad, a scientist at NIH, with a lovely wife and bright children.

Could Dom and Ellen ever stop seeing what might have been for their youngest, damaged son, in the beauty, the wholeness of their first? Could they ever stop thinking about what might have been if genetics, Mother Nature, hadn't failed them?

The bitch, as you say my mother put it.

"I wonder if they had amnio," Douglas said. "They should have. She must have been fifty."

"I don't suppose it would have mattered," I told him.

We were having scrambled eggs in our own kitchen after the

cocktail party. Moments before, Douglas had been disgruntled, as whiny as a child, much as he always was after cocktail parties where he hadn't eaten enough to call it dinner but had eaten too much to want a real dinner once he got home.

In all the years of your own long marriage, in all your years of "getting things done" at cocktail parties and garden parties, I bet you went through this, too. Doug complained when I offered to throw some steaks on the grill—it was too late, he'd be up all night with acid reflux—and complained again when I suggested scrambled eggs: "I enjoy dinner. I hate missing dinner."

In a variation on the same plea I'd been making against his minor but inconsolable dissatisfactions for forty years, I told him, "I can't change the hour and I can't change your appetite." I waved a carton of eggs in one hand, the steaks still wrapped in butcher paper in the other. I'd begun to notice how Doug and I were sounding more and more like our own two kids when they were young and always bickering. "Work with me here."

"Well, they're very affectionate," Douglas added now—the buttered toast and the warm eggs working their charm on his mood. "Those Down syndrome kids. It's possible they wouldn't change him if they could."

"I can't believe that," I said.

The table where we sat, the ladder-back chairs with French country cushions, our utensils and plates and the placemats that matched the cushions, were all new, part of all the new things we had purchased for this house over the course of the summer—as if we were just starting out.

Not that we were ever the kind of wide-eyed and joyous newlyweds you and your husband were. Another era altogether, as you said.

The house itself, our new country house, was more than one hundred years old, but the renovation had left it all spit-and-polish on the inside. It still smelled of paint and new rugs, fresh plumbing supplies, and refinished wood.

Before we'd found this house in western Maryland, just sixty miles from Roland Park and the four-bedroom, four-bath colonial where we'd raised the kids, we told ourselves we were looking for a place to retire to, but I think we already knew we wouldn't retire this far from home. We'd spend parts of the summer here, and occasional winter weekends, and when we were both ready to quit working, in another couple of years, we'd sell the big house and buy a condo, probably around the Inner Harbor.

This would remain our "country place," a place we should have bought decades ago when our kids were young, when it could have provided the backdrop for fond childhood memories of glorious summers.

But we couldn't have afforded it when our kids were young. And we'd only bought it now, impulsively, because my father's death had left us flush with cash. Money we no longer called ill-gotten.

Problem was, now our children were grown and gone and reluctant, thus far anyway, to upend their own routines to come visit.

I found myself thinking during these first few days in the finished house that I would be much fonder of the place if it held some memories.

As you say, no such thing as a life without regret. Maybe because we fortunates have far too many options.

DOUGLAS STOOD, made his final pronouncement on our scrambled-egg dinner: "Let's throw those steaks on the grill tomorrow. It would be nice to have a real meal for a change." And then he carried his refilled wineglass into the little hearth room to watch TV.

"We've had real meals all week," I said. But I lacked the energy to argue. So many of our conversations over the past year had involved a host of other people—the carpenters, the plumbers, the roofers and landscapers, the architect and the contractor—that I now felt the loss of them.

Thrown together again, in our brand-new but no less empty nest, it seemed we had little left to say.

"What the hell number is CNN?" Doug called out.

"You've already passed it twice," I said, and saw him pass it a third and then a fourth time, until his attention settled on a show featuring a young couple who were searching for a vacation home in Cabo San Lucas. I knew he would be asleep in his chair before it ended.

I carried our plates to the kitchen sink. Through the open window I could hear, faintly, the voices of Dom and Ellen's grandchildren as they played some game in the fields behind the house, catching fireflies, no doubt. Mixed among their piping was Jamie's hoarse voice, deep, delighted, and punctuated every now and then with an excited call to his father.

I leaned toward the window screen to listen, but I couldn't catch Dominic's reply, only the vague tenor of his voice, reassuring the boy that he was there.

I called to Doug, "How many children did they say they have? Our new neighbors?"

There was a pause. He might have been asleep. But then he said, "Seven. He must have knocked her up in high school."

Through the screen, I heard Jamie's voice calling again, followed by his rough and delighted laughter when his father called back.

"What a mistake," Douglas said from the hearth room. "House number two was the deal. The place is a money pit." His voice was rising. "You stupid fools."

I tried to laugh. "You sound like a crazy old man," I told him.

"I am," he called back. "I'm a crazy old man. But they should have taken the house by the beach."

A SPATE OF WEDDING WEEKENDS kept us from driving out to the house through most of that fall, although the beauty of autumn in the country had been a selling point.

Happily, the weddings were all tasteful, with good wine and food. Not a clunker among them. A marked improvement over what had gone on when Doug and I were young, when tacky tradition still vied with loopy counterculture. When one friend's wedding might feature tulle and morning coats and another's batik peasant dresses and embroidered tunics. Music from Mendelssohn or the Carpenters or Ravi Shankar. Long-haired grooms, visibly pregnant brides, first dances to a schmaltzy 1950s rendition of "More," even as pot smoke drifted out of the catering hall bathrooms.

Your generation escaped all that confusion. My own kids find it laughable.

At my mother's insistence—you can imagine Charlene planning a wedding—my own had been traditional enough, except for the few, unattributed lines from *Lady Chatterley's Lover* that I'd asked the best man to read from the pulpit. Except for the hash-laced brownies that had passed from knee to knee under the head table.

IT WAS MID-NOVEMBER before we got out to the house again. I saw Dominic and Jamie crossing their field on Friday morning, both bundled in identical down jackets, and then met them that afternoon in the tiny grocery store at the crossroads.

When his son wandered down one of the narrow aisles, Dom leaned closer to say that the boy had had some surgery last month, a heart valve issue that had turned out fine.

I apologized for having heard nothing about it. We'd been away so much. He touched my elbow.

"We're fine," he said. "It was practically routine. But I'm pretty sure he'll want to tell you all about it before we leave here, and I wanted to give you fair warning."

Sure enough, as we waited in line together, Jamie described the ordeal, making a little cross over his heart as he told me about his operation, and then assured me, as his father had done, that he was fine, fine, patting my arm. But something aged had come into his round and boyish face since last I saw him. I recognized it in his mouth first, the smacking of his lips over his small teeth, the pucker that caused his chin to protrude, and in a new sunken darkness about his eyes. There was the black stubble of beard on his throat—I hadn't noticed this before—and seeing it now in the ugly light of the store, I felt the weariness of his parents' long haul, loving this child.

Jamie touched my elbow, his father's gesture. "It wasn't bad at all," he said.

I told him he looked great. And was very brave. And then smiled at Dominic behind him, who seemed, too, older than I remembered him. In need of sun and rest. And a haircut, I thought. A wifely habit.

THE NEXT MORNING I made two lemon pound cakes and brought one over. When Dominic came to the door, he insisted I come in. Ellen was at her yoga class. He and Jamie were finishing up the sandwich-making for what Dom called their "D.C. run," but there was fresh coffee brewing in the kitchen, I really had to come in . . . and then he stopped himself, shaking his head and looking as if he knew I understood that he was making too much of the invitation, while at the same time acknowledging that he also knew I would forgive him for it, his awkward offer of friendship.

"Just come on in," he said finally. "Jamie will love to see you."

I followed him into the kitchen, which was broad and cluttered. Jamie was sitting on a stool at a long, high butcher-block table, carefully spreading peanut butter on a slice of wheat bread, his tongue caught in the corner of his mouth. His concentration was so great that he didn't look up until his father whispered, "Jamie. We have a guest." Then he grinned and slipped off the stool and came to me, putting his arms around my waist without the slightest hesitation, resting his head against my coat. Touched and surprised, I kissed his fair hair.

I asked to help. It seemed only polite. And was set up at what they called the jelly station, where I was to swipe each piece of bread with grape jelly and then match it to Jamie's peanut butter side. I saw as I placed the first that the boy had traced a heart into the thick peanut butter with the tip of his knife.

"That's so nice," I said, and he grinned, but whispered, "No one will see it," as if to assure me that he understood this.

I said, "You never know."

His father was wrapping the completed sandwiches and piling them into the empty bread bags. When we were finished, he poured the coffee and sliced the cake.

In the way of new neighbors—"country living," Doug liked to say—we talked about our renovations, comparing plumbers and electricians. I asked him who he used for snow removal and he said, "Us," volunteering to hit our drive with his own plow whenever—if ever—we had an accumulation. At some point, I followed him through the house to see the skylights they had added to brighten a back stairwell, and as we passed through a narrow corridor lined with bookshelves, I saw one of our own Saigon Barbies—white ao dai, faded non la—propped inside a plexiglass case.

"You have one," I said.

It took him a minute to see what I saw, and then he laughed. "My daughter's," he told me.

I said, "My mother made these. Or had them made. The ao dais. Exactly the same. She sold them. In Saigon."

Dominic said, "Charlene?"

I know it's ordinary magic at best, this kind of weird coincidence. But I think we both felt the astonishment of it. I mean: to find ourselves standing together in the narrow corridor of that crooked farmhouse, under the early winter light of—let's face it—the early winter of our own lifetimes—two utter strangers, hardly even neighbors, and to discover—amazing—this long-ago and faraway thing we had somehow shared.

Dominic shook his head. "She gave me this when my daughter was born," he said. "Nineteen sixty-three. Jesus. She's your mother? She's some lady, Charlene."

He turned to Jamie. "Isn't this something, honey? We just found out we were in Vietnam at the same time, like a million years ago. When I was younger than you and"—he glanced at me—"you were a kid. One of Charlene's kids."

He reached up to take the doll from the shelf, lifting it out of its careful display case—Ellen's idea, he explained—and placing it in my palm. The white silk had yellowed, and the hat had grown brittle but was still intact. Mine had dried and crumbled years ago when my daughter confiscated my own Saigon Barbie, joined her to a slutty pile of bimbo versions in cheap hot-pink clothes—all of them now gone to Goodwill.

I brushed my fingers over Lily's perfect tiny stitches at the neckline and the waistband.

I felt suddenly overwhelmed—with heartache, regret, nostalgia, who knows? Blindsided by it: lost time, lost childhood, lost years. I let out a stifled sob.

Sweet Jamie put his arms around my waist once more, and Dom, poor Dom, patted my shoulder.

"Has she passed?" he whispered.

I tried to laugh, at myself. "Over twenty years ago, for God's sake," I managed to say. "You'd think I'd be over it."

Dom returned the doll to the shelf, gently apologizing. I shook my head—"Not your fault"—and sucked back those unshed tears. A trick I had mastered—as you noticed—in Saigon.

LATER, I HELPED JAMIE zip up his jacket, and then I walked with father and son as they carried the bags of sandwiches to the car. Once again, Jamie put his arms around my waist to say goodbye.

Dom said, "I remember your mother so well." And then he put his hand to my cheek. A gesture that both startled and pleased me. I felt a rush of affection—another kind of memory restored to me in that instant. The memory of what I once would have identified as a new infatuation.

"You take after her," he said.

It was only the long habit of the years that made me tell him, "I hope not."

WHEN I WAS IN BOARDING SCHOOL—exiled there in my turbulent teens—each of us girls had some image of our mother, some broad caricature, that we wore pinned to our lapel, so to speak. Like those little political buttons of the era. There was the warm but clueless mother, easily fooled. The ambitious working mother, easily avoided. There was the social snob, easiest to ridicule. There was the mother who hovered and manipulated and made her daughter cower—the source of many late-night tears. The homely mother envious of a beautiful daughter. The beautiful mother disappointed by a homely child. And always, it seemed, a mother who was ill, or fighting some illness, whose story (whose daughter) made us pause briefly in our boisterous ridicule of our own, but only briefly. Mine was the "mother's little helper" mother, and our own obsessive pursuit of hash and grass and stolen Valium did nothing to mitigate how funny I could be about her Manhattans and tranquilizers.

The fact that she was also a church lady made my comic riffs even more delightful to my peers.

I knew plenty about the Librium and the Manhattans, but

the night terrors were news to me. Maybe she got over them once we got home.

WE RETURNED FROM SAIGON in the summer of 1964. My father, like your husband, didn't want any more overseas assignments after the chaos of those final months in Saigon: the bombings and barbed wire, the appearance of armed American soldiers on our school buses. The feeling that our servants might as easily slit our throats as make our beds. At least that's how my father put it.

He told me his new title back home would be General Manager.

I had my own image of generals by then, those confident, talkative men who had come to my parents' parties at the villa.

It was the generals who filled our house with the smell of cigar smoke; whose manly voices rose up above the twittering sound of the other party guests and whatever music was on the record player.

I remember Doris Day singing "Que Sera, Sera."

On those many nights my parents entertained, I loved to fall asleep listening to the bright voices that percolated through the floor—bursts of laughter or chitchat or sing-along: "Whatever will be, will be."

But it was the voices of the generals that set the floorboards humming, that sent a metallic thrum through the frame of my wrought-iron bed and all along my spine.

And yet, once we got home, I associated my father's new title not with the military but with the manager at our local A&P—

a plump, affable man out of central casting who always had some interesting treat for us kids: sample packs of cookies or tiny loaves of Wonder Bread.

I thought a general manager meant a watchful guardian, a genial shepherd. My father exactly.

I guess we were both devoted daughters. Or maybe we both preferred men to women.

IT'S MY BROTHER RANSOM who has made a study of our time in Saigon. He's got a Facebook cohort of former dependent kids, all old geezers by now, who compare memories of the American school or the Central Market or the odor of nuoc mam with a kind of desperation—a contradiction in one post can set off a flurry of insistence, speculation, indignant documentation, and the combative parrying of Wikipedia timelines, historical accounts, eyewitness testimony from parents now dead.

I'm not sure, exactly, what this pursuit of collective confirmation does for them all. What they're afraid to lose, or hoping to retain.

My own recollections of Saigon are distinct but disorganized. I'm happy enough to keep them uncorroborated, mine alone.

I remember the bedroom you described.

The room had been Ransom's when we first arrived. He'd claimed it for himself as we made our first crazed run through the villa—jazzed by exhaustion and excitement and all the candy our mother had doled out over the endless flights.

It was a pretty room, with its two windows and French doors

and the Juliet balcony. I remember how badly I wanted it for myself.

But my parents agreed that since it was the larger of the two guest rooms, it was only reasonable it should go to Ransom because he was a "big boy," although barely an inch taller than I was then.

I was disappointed, but as the world turns, male privilege gets put to the test. Or so I like to believe. Only a few days or weeks after we settled in, the moon rose over Saigon and a swath of lunar light spilled through the French doors. A path of light that was alive with the diving, veering, flitting shadows of the bats that lived under our eaves. Big, brave Ransom lost it. Woke up the entire household with his screams.

The next morning, the room became mine.

My father told me that I should take this as a stroke of luck—the bats, he assured me, were dive-bombing the mosquitoes outside my window, keeping them from my tender flesh.

But my mother gave me only an assessing glance when I assured them both I was not in the least bit afraid.

Still, I kept my bedside light on that first night in my longed-for room.

When I woke up—who knows what time it was?—the lamp was off. It took me only a few seconds to see that the path of moonlight cast across my floor was swarming with the small black silhouettes of darting bats.

I know I sucked in a breath—preparing to scream, or to cry out.

My mother was in a chair at the foot of my bed, just beyond the moonlight, awake, watching me. I caught the flash of her eyes, a nod that said, "Good for you. You're terrified. You're keeping it to yourself. Good for you."

It was all I needed: her smile, her nod, her wordless attention, there in the terrible darkness.

I ALSO REMEMBER an afternoon when Ransom and I were called in from the garden by the servants, an abrupt flurry of commands, a rush of Vietnamese and French and harsh words in English: "Now, now."

I was coloring, making my way through a pile of Halloween candy. My brother was gluing together one of his models—a PT boat.

Although we had by then grown accustomed to the street noise that reached our little yard, that day we heard something else in those moments before the servants shouted us inside. Something unusual, heavier, louder, was in the air. Ransom and I looked at each other, not in fear but in giddy anticipation. By the time the servants appeared on the patio, shouting and waving, pushing at our shoulders, we were poised to run. We nearly danced into the house. The radio in the kitchen was on, the same American music the servants always played while they worked. Weirdly placid now, in the excitement.

They herded us under the dining room table. Some fun. And joined us there—two of the housemaids and the amah who had baby Roger pressed against her chest. By now there were explosions rattling the windows and ringing the glass and crockery, smaller, jangling explosions all around us as things fell from shelves. The retort of distant, whining fireworks.

I looked up at the underside of the table, the struts and dull hardware and unvarnished wood marked with chalk, all of it familiar to me from rainy-day games of hide-and-seek. I wasn't afraid. There was Ransom, who, uncharacteristically, had his arms around me, and the two servants and the young nurse-maid who was holding Roger. I don't remember where my mother was.

I wasn't afraid. I'd always believed that as long as I wasn't alone, I'd be protected, cared for, immune from all harm. A confident if untested faith that there was safety in numbers. I'm sure this had something to do with being a twin.

At some point my father came into the house—through the kitchen, which he never did—calling for the housekeeper, for Ransom, for me. And then he was peering under the tablecloth, grimacing like a backstage comedian peeking out before curtain call. He lowered himself—he was six feet two and broad shouldered—so that his torso, at least, was under the table with us, his legs still sprawling, unprotected, into the rest of the room. Somehow he managed to get his arms around both of us, my brother and me. I could smell the Brylcreem in his hair, feel the stubble of his cheek under my hand.

We listened together to the sound of gunfire, explosions, the rattle of window glass and crystal and the table legs themselves against the tile floor. The sound of Roger's little amah weeping as she held him against her chest.

My brother identifies this as the morning Diem was overthrown. I have no reason to disagree. It's the vivid memory of my father that usurps politics and history for me. I wasn't afraid. My father was with us. I remember the strength of his arms.

❖

AND OF COURSE, those colorful market baskets filled with treats—my mother kneeling on her office floor, packing each so carefully, arranging and rearranging until she had a gorgeous display. Calling on me to admire the bounty, especially when her funds were flush.

I knew never to ask if I could take something for myself. I knew I'd be told I had no lack of toys and candy of my own.

And I remember my mother's joke: that Rainey loved the rainy season in Saigon. But I also loved going into her bedroom or her office on those days when she was out. I loved going through her dresser and her desk or standing before the neatly arranged dresses in her closet like a lonely stargazer.

I can't say even now what I was looking for.

WE SETTLED ON LONG ISLAND, in Garden City, on our return, and my childhood proceeded normally enough until my teens, when I got a little wild. Busted, at sixteen, for smoking a joint with some friends on the roof of the community room of our church. We were there, in fact, to make sandwiches for the homeless—my mother's idea, of course—and we thought it would be hysterical to do so while high and fighting the munchies.

The other kids were reprimanded, grounded, sentenced to even more useless good work, but I was exiled to a Maryland boarding school.

I wasn't there three months when I was busted again for getting high with two other girls in the woods behind the house we'd gone to—AWOL—for a party. We should have been expelled, we wanted to be expelled, but we were sent instead to drug counseling, hosted by the county. A motley class of smartass kids who spent the time between educational filmstrips and lectures and breakout sessions about self-esteem exchanging dealers' names and head-shop locations, or how to get a phony driver's license that said you were twenty-one. That's where I met Douglas.

He was a skinny, clever kid, a voracious reader, sarcastic and smart. I thought he was the funniest boy I'd ever met. His family was solidly middle-class and feared that his "habit"—he was caught only once, a joint at an outdoor concert, but it was by the police—would jeopardize his chances for a college scholarship. It didn't. After six weeks of keeping company with the worst and most thrilling of our peers, we all had our "records" erased. Douglas went on to the University of Maryland. I followed him there, much to my parents' dismay. My father wanted me at Cornell, his alma mater. My mother wanted me at one of the Seven Sister schools, her fantasy of where a daughter of privilege should go. Although she never went to college herself—did you know?

In many ways, I envy the simplicity of the era you were married in. Douglas and I had a rockier start—breakups and hookups and wanting so desperately not to become our parents. We slept together and then lived together and then fled to different cities where we slept with other people and were miserable. And then we endured our big traditional wedding as if it were a joke only the two of us were in on. A joke on his parents, who believed he had married into great wealth.

A joke on mine, who paid the bill with what we were still calling blood money. Oil money.

Doug believed even then, when conspiracy theories were not so easily disseminated, that it was my father's pals—Esso, Standard Oil, the oligarchs—who had funded and extended the war in Vietnam. Who had sent so many poor, working-class fools to get fucked up over there—as we put it—kids from his own neighborhood if not from mine.

It was all very detailed, Doug's indictment of the guilty parties. He gladly would have explained to you, for instance, why so many engineers were needed in Saigon. The depth charges that the navy was dropping into the South China Sea in the early sixties—World War II surplus, Doug would have told you— were not meant to dredge Vietnamese ports as the dumb— bovine, Doug would have said—American public had been led to believe but to explore that small country's offshore oil reserve. To have it all mapped out and ready to steal, "export," whenever American-owned democracy prevailed.

He was quite articulate about it all, and, at the time, I took it all, every outraged accusation, as revealed truth.

Truth salted and sweetened, of course, with the arrogance of youth. That is to say, all our ideas about the world made absolutely delicious by what we were certain no one before us had ever known or understood—not the way we did: mendacity, greed, hypocrisy, the corporate world's hunger for profit, the political world's hunger for power, the prevalence of evil intent, even among the people we knew, the people we loved.

Had I told Douglas then that you and my mother encountered the Devil in Vietnam, he would have asked me, shrugging, "Who didn't?"

YES, THE THINGS THAT GET SAID over the course of a long marriage: Doug sometimes accused me of having pursued him too desperately when we were very young. The extent of my infatuation overwhelmed him.

I always told him he flattered himself. I married him mostly to piss off my mother.

I n 1975, the U.S. began to airlift children and babies out of Vietnam. Operation Babylift, it was called. Not very clever, but how much poetry can you expect from the Department of Defense? Chaos poetry at best.

Maybe you remember this: The first of these flights, filled with infants and small children and the aid workers who accompanied them, was fired on by the advancing Viet Cong right after it took off from Tan Son Nhut Air Base. The pilot attempted a return, and the plane crash-landed. Seventy-eight children died in that crash, along with something like thirty-five of the adults who were accompanying them.

I was home from college. It must have been spring break. My mother was reading the newspaper account. Morning in our breakfast nook, in verdant suburbia, rain-washed sunlight streaming in. A cigarette burning between her fingers. Her careful grooming—hair and nails and pale lipstick.

My mother's mouth was grim as she read. The escorts on that plane were mostly women, women hired by, or already a part of, various charities, orphanages, government agencies. Women out to do good.

My mother said she just hoped no one she knew was among the dead.

I said something snotty. Something about the children— why she thought first of the helpers who were killed, who were volunteers after all, rather than the kids who were being snatched from their homeland. Probably to be sold to the highest bidder once they arrived here.

I asked her, speaking with Doug's stoner voice, if she even understood that it wasn't freedom all those poor and middle-class American boys had died for in Vietnam. The United States didn't give a hoot about some peasants in rice paddies laboring under a communist regime or a democratic one. The peasants didn't give a good goddamn hoot about it, either.

It was the oil companies, my father's company, that had sent all those hapless kids to their deaths. For the sake of the Mercedes and the Cadillac in our driveway. Our plush two acres of grass. My father's portfolio. Her addiction to Chanel and St. John.

At some point, my father came into the kitchen. He stood between us in his golf clothes. Told me to hush. My mother said nothing.

Or, actually, she began to speak, but then stopped herself and let her eyes drift away, turning from me as if her attention had been drawn by something far more worthy of her concern. Some absorbing, invisible thing.

Ransom called this her *Wait a minute, why do I care about this?* look.

I thought it was *Why do I care about* you?

I suppose she was doing, too, that thing she did with her two fingers, thumb and ring finger, that agitated circling.

Finally, my father told me to get out of his house. Which I did. I went back to Maryland. Fought with Doug when he praised me for standing up to them. Left him some weeks later when he called my father a mass murderer. Moved in with another boy. Then quit school for a semester to follow yet another to New Orleans, where I broke an arm in an alcoholic blackout.

No point in sorting through that mess.

Then back to College Park to finish my degree. To reconnect with Doug. A homecoming—we used the word with some irony—for both of us.

One thing we were certain of, looking to the future: we didn't want our parents' lives.

And then we did.

I hope I won't cause you any grief by saying that the birth of my first child, my daughter, and the second, my son, made me happier than I'd ever been, more certain, more secure. Maybe it was the whole safety-in-numbers thing. Maybe becoming a mother made me feel somehow twinned again.

Or maybe it was just that insistence you described: life, more life.

I was saying something about this—my happiness—on another morning in my mother's kitchen, my new baby asleep in my arms. Telling my own mother, as if no woman had ever discovered this before, what it was to be in love with your child. Your own.

Suddenly, Charlene leaned toward me and put her thin hand under my chin. She turned my face to the French doors that looked out on our elegant patio, our green garden, our lofty, sunstruck trees: our family's gorgeous little universe built on compromise, of course; ill-gotten gains, I suppose; bargains with the Devil, no doubt.

But also luck, grace.

Whatever it took to get us, to keep us, safely home.

S HE DIED OF KIDNEY CANCER. She was nearly sixty. An annoying ache in her back that in what seemed merely a few nightmarish days was pronounced incurable. The placid everyday becoming, in our astonished retrospect, the last hours of her life.

We spent many of those hours, my brothers and I, in long, cautious telephone calls, mostly reassuring one another that her prognosis was good, or improving, and praising Dad's patience with her demands. I see myself now with the phone tucked against my shoulder as I chopped vegetables, or unpacked groceries, or held up a hand to a colleague who had come to my office door with a question or a contract.

I wish now I had gone to her immediately, gone home to her, but I didn't. I told myself I had my family, my career, my daily demands. I told myself she would be fine.

She died well before any of us had shaken off our disbelief at the swiftness of it all—before we fully lost our childish faith in her ability to set anything, including her body itself, to rights. Or maybe it was only our faith in our own fortunate lives.

Doug had his Ph.D. by then—drug and alcohol counseling, what else?—and my brothers were settled in their careers. I was managing a title company out in the suburbs, wrangling real-estate attorneys and anxious home buyers. We had the two kids, our nice house.

Aunt Arlene, her resourceful sister—they were Charlene and Arlene; we were Rainey and Ransom; people did that to twins in those days—the provider of those purloined cigarettes, tranquilizers, baby clothes, and Barbie dolls—swept in for the funeral wearing a beautiful beige cashmere wrap coat with some kind of long-haired fur collar, soft, white, speckled brown—an angel's aura, or a stripper's feather boa—that moved with her lipstick-scented words.

"My darlings," she called us. We thought her ridiculous. "My motherless darlings."

Back at the house that evening, my father sequestered himself in their bedroom—which was still filled with the detritus of my mother's fundraising efforts: auction items and donated gifts, prettily arranged "baskets of cheer."

My father had been transformed, physically, by my mother's illness. He was thinner now, stooped. A kind of tentativeness in his gestures and his gaze, something he never really lost in the two decades he lived without her.

Like your father, he became susceptible in those years to a startling weepiness.

Aunt Arlene sat up with us on the night of my mother's funeral, my brothers and me and our spouses, smoking cigarette after cigarette, drinking bourbon, her brocade dressing gown over her silk slip, her stockinged feet on our coffee table. We were telling stories about my mother, making gentle fun of the Librium and the Manhattans and the well-groomed piety. The fundraising: card parties, galas, fashion shows for the dispossessed, for the dark-eyed children in dusty "Indian schools," for the motherless darlings who through no fault of their own had been born in countries that simply could not measure up.

In the early eighties, when she looked and dressed like Nancy Reagan, my mother had started bringing gifts to AIDS patients at two hospitals in the city, never letting on to her church lady donors what the money she'd gotten out of them was meant for.

She didn't ask us to go with her—my brothers and me—but we'd sometimes help her load up her car with beautiful baskets filled with fresh flowers, glossy magazines, Swiss chocolates, French soaps, brightly colored cashmere socks, and silk hand-kerchiefs rolled to resemble plaid or paisley roses.

She'd schlep it all to Manhattan, where she'd breeze into the rooms of the dying young men, offer them the fabulous array.

Her lepers, my father had called them.

"Poor guys," we said on the night of her funeral. "Beset by Charlene, the whirlwind." We thought we were being witty. Clear-eyed and unsentimental, even in loss.

Aunt Arlene suddenly asked us, "Didn't you love her?"

We said of course we loved her. She was difficult sometimes, with her demands, her old-fashioned propriety. She was often a pain in the ass, exhausting—"Let's face it"—but we loved her.

"You wouldn't know it, to hear you," Arlene said.

We were silent then. Reprimanded, I suppose. Or maybe searching our memories. Even then, my memories of loving my mother were all tactile. Her freckled arms, her cool hand grip-ping my chin, and her slim fingers locked under my jaw as she recalibrated my attention, directed my gaze.

Her thin body—how thin she grew over our lifetime to-gether, not merely in those last days—leaning into mine as she joined us at the hip in order to strong-arm me into something she wanted me to do, or to be, or to understand. Directing my eyes, literally and figuratively, with the iron grip of her thin hand.

It occurred to me that evening that my love for my mother had been wholly physical: the familiar quick fingers, the green eyes, the rough texture of her hair, the curve of muscle in her calf, and, yes, the high instep of her small feet—those were the images that came to mind when I argued that I loved her. Had loved her. That: the physicalness of her, the familiarity of her sharp-boned embrace. That body of hers was what I mourned for. Still mourn for now.

Arlene's eyes were a soft, rich brown, overdrawn with eyeliner and shadow, without my mother's green intensity. She said, her nose in the air, "Your mother might have left you all, when you came back from Saigon. There was another man. She might have gone off with him. I told her to. I would have. But she didn't. She didn't."

We took a cautious minute to absorb this. "Why not?" one of us asked.

Arlene didn't hesitate. She spoke, in fact, as if the answer were clear.

"She would have lost you," she said. "You three."

She said, "You have to remember how it was in those days. For women. For wives."

Children, she claimed, were a married woman's golden handcuffs. "As we say in the corporate world." With a Career Girl sniff. "If your mother had left, she would have lost you."

Once more we paused, took this in, silently.

And then we laughed, all three of us. Arlene the drama queen.

"Come on," we teased her, "Tell us who it was. Who?" A general? A secretary of state? A muscular GI? A saffron-robed monk?

But she dismissed us. "Not for me to say," she whispered, mysterious, but satisfied, we could tell. Satisfied that she had, perhaps, made our mother's life interesting.

"Someone who would have allowed her to do great things," Arlene told us.

"Another oil guy," Doug whispered.

The next day I asked Ransom if he thought this could possibly be true, that our mother might have left her marriage, left us.

He said, "Don't kid yourself. If Mom wanted to walk away, no one could have stopped her."

Wally Welty, you say. Or more likely that bare-chested doctor whose name has been forgotten. I haven't a clue. Certainly there were no letters from men among my mother's things.

I'm inclined to agree with Ransom here: I'm pretty sure my mother had the life she wanted—I'm pretty sure no one could have made her live otherwise.

WHEN MY BROTHERS AND I put together my mother's obituary, we cited all the usual affiliations: her church, her country club, her various charities, her love of tennis. Reviewing what we had composed, my father asked if we could add something about "how fashionable she was."

I slapped an introductory phrase onto one of the sentences,

"An inveterate clotheshorse," I wrote, "she loved a good game of doubles, a lavish silent auction, her five grandkids . . ."

Since "clotheshorse" was a term she'd used often, my father and my brothers were satisfied with the wording.

But you and I both know my mother had never used the phrase as a compliment. She had used it to indict, to reproach. To point out another woman's shallow ambitions, her foolishness.

Maybe it was a lingering bit of adolescent rebellion on my part. Or maybe the sudden loss of her had briefly revived my childish sense of abandonment. Maybe I thought I was settling some score.

It was a small betrayal, anyway. Petty. But one I wish now I had managed to resist.

Months passed before Dominic and I spoke again. The holidays came. They were the last we were going to spend in the Roland Park house—we'd decided to put it on the market come spring, and so the kids made an effort to be there for Thanksgiving and Christmas. Our own sorting had begun.

It was mid-January before we were back, and on our first weekend there the forecast suddenly turned from rain to snow. Douglas and I drank a bottle of wine by the fire in the hearth room, the snow coming down, a kind of muffled patter against the windows. We were feeling pleased, at last, with ourselves and our decision to buy this isolated old house. The loneliness of the place, something that had struck us both, somewhat naively, certainly belatedly, when we first moved in, we now called, after the frenzy of the holidays, its greatest gift.

Just the two of us and the night falling with the slowly accumulating snow.

Early morning and I was standing at our front window with my coffee when I saw Dom's tractor turn into our driveway. Jamie was hunched beside him in the cab, intent, serious—bouncing from side to side with his mouth hanging open and his round black eyes staring straight ahead. In his cap, behind the glass, there was no mistaking him for a child. When they got to the top of the driveway, I waved. Father and son waved back.

I heard Douglas coming down the narrow stairs behind me. He'd been snoring something awful last night—the wine—and I'd finally gone into the second bedroom just before dawn.

"Who the fuck's clearing the driveway?" he asked.

I turned around to say, "Dominic," realizing as I did that he didn't recognize the name. "The guy next door," I added. "I told you he said he would. He offered." And then, when he still didn't comprehend, I said, "Dominic. Next door. With the Down syndrome boy."

Douglas was in his boxers and a T-shirt, his thinning hair still tousled. It was unusual for him to come downstairs before showering.

"What Down syndrome boy?" he asked. Nearly angry. He kept his hand on the banister, and I found myself suddenly wishing he would let it go. He looked, with his morning beard and his bed head and those skinny legs, very old.

I rolled my eyes in the sibling way of the long-married. I tapped the glass. "Jamie," I said. "The boy next door. Ellen and Dominic. Next door."

He made his way across the pretty room. He was barefoot, too. He leaned to look out the window. The tractor with the plow was down at the far end of the driveway now. There was a long two-lane stripe of cleared asphalt next to a neat wall of what might have been half a foot of snow. I was tapping the window, one hand on my hip to convey *Now do you see what I've been trying to tell you?* The marital arrogance that I had long ago given up trying to withstand.

He peered out into the brightness for a few minutes, the sound of the plow growing louder, and then he raised his unshaven face to mine. He smelled of sleep. He looked at me, and then his eyes darted away, across the room, touching, it seemed, piece by piece, all of our newlywed trappings, fruits of my inheritance: new couch, new lamps, new paintings on the wall. Then he turned back, and all that was familiar about his face, the still-identifiable traces of that skinny, funny stoner kid I had known and loved for most of my life, was transformed. By time, of course, but by fear, too. Something I knew in an instant I'd never seen in his face before.

I was certain he didn't know where he was.

He said, casually, "Oh yeah. I remember." He ran his hand over his eyes. "I'm still half asleep," he said.

And then, this wasn't much like him, he leaned against me, put his arm around my waist. A mere remnant of last night's fun—the brief lights-off lovemaking of the long-married. We watched the tractor move down the drive. Doug said, "At least we never had to deal with anything like that. A kid like that."

I thought to ask him, but didn't: What do you mean "at least"?

He turned back toward the stairs, and just as I was about to return to the window—I was going to wave to Dominic again, signal that he and Jamie should come inside for some coffee, some cocoa—Doug's arm shot out. He knocked over the ceramic lamp on a small end table, swept off, in a fury, the glass and a book that had been left there. "You didn't tell me," he cried—suddenly bellowing—"you didn't tell me anything about someone plowing our drive." For the first time in my life, I thought he would hit me. "How much is he charging? Why the fuck didn't you tell me?"

I should have soothed him, cajoled him, even asked him gently why in the world he was yelling about this. But that wasn't my way. My mother's daughter. I met his anger with my own. Perhaps because I realized, vaguely, how much I'd been looking forward to seeing Dominic again, to hearing his voice. Perhaps because I thought Doug's strange outburst was some reaction to the vague romantic notions I'd begun to attach to Dominic in the dull loneliness of this new life we were heading toward.

"Why are you yelling at me?" I asked. "Our neighbor is plowing our driveway for us. For God's sake. What's wrong with that?"

He ran his hand over his face once again. Said something about never telling him what he needed to know.

"You must be hung over," I said and turned back to the window—Dom's tractor was now making its last pass—until I heard Doug go back up the stairs. I was too angry, then, to invite the two of them in. I should have been frightened, I suppose, by Doug's outburst. It wasn't much like him, but, then again, it wasn't so unlike him that I was moved to suspect something other than a bad mood, too much wine.

We spent the rest of the weekend barely speaking and drove home on Sunday without seeing Dom and Jamie again—although I did drop a thank-you note in their mailbox before we left. And then the long winter, getting the house ready to be put on the market come spring.

IT WAS MARCH WHEN I RETURNED. I went alone. Our arguments, our impatience with each other, had become burdensome. Again, I saw this only as a consequence of the changes we were bringing on ourselves: selling the house, "downsizing," feeling old age encroaching. We'd begun the stupid habit of tagging everything in our past with an equal and opposite glance at our future: ten years ago we did that bike tour in Napa. In ten more years, we'll be . . .

Observations that always left us both in a bad mood.

I arrived at the house in the late afternoon. Made a quick trip to the little store at the crossroads and settled in. I'd imagined fixing a simple dinner for myself, eating it alone by the fire, with a book and a bottle of good wine. I imagined myself luxuriating in my rebellion—there had been a bit of a scene when I told Doug I did not want his company for the weekend—basking in my daring solitude. I was not the sort of woman who did many things alone.

But I ended up watching television, the same shows I would have watched with Doug, and then feeling when I turned off the set and began to turn off the downstairs lights both foolish and vaguely afraid. I climbed the stairs to our bedroom feeling I'd been called out on my independent-woman charade. I climbed the stairs dreading the night ahead.

Sleepless, I spent most of it in the guest room, in a pretty little chair I had selected with our decorator, one I had never actually sat in before. It was very dark—a moonless night. I would have welcomed that terrifying bat-wing lunar light show of those nights in Saigon.

I would have welcomed as well my mother's certainty that there was something contained in the darkness. Something I was supposed to know.

The one window in the little room slowly reappeared: an intimation of gray, then pinkish dawn. I dressed as soon as there was light enough to see by.

Outside, our property displayed only the shyest indications of spring: that furred shade of red about the barely budded branches, and the sharp early morning scent of March, some whiff of fading snow in it, some hint of sun. The sky was brightening behind a distant copse of trees, turning from fiery pink to watercolor blue. Across our back field, there was mud and new growth, green among the dry stalks. I heard the spring-again sound of rushing water, a sound that made me remember the stream at the back of our property.

I set out for it, dressed in duck boots and barn jacket, playing the part.

We'd had a talkative real-estate agent when we first toured the house. A back-to-nature type, Doug had called him. As we walked this field, he suggested that while we were out this way, we take the time to visit a spot some miles to our west. An ecological reserve, he said. Rare and fascinating. A few hundred acres of swamp formed ten thousand years ago by the runoff of the continental ice sheet, and full of certain plant species—tamarack trees, he said, cotton grass, cranberry—as old as the Pleistocene itself.

"You can walk right through it," he told us. "There are paths and raised platforms."

He said it would be a good way to remember how brief life is, how little time we have on this roiling planet. "It'll give you the long view," he said.

Douglas was walking ahead of us, his head down, but he slowed his pace at this and then, as we caught up, he glanced my way. I knew that grin. My husband's own sarcastic, too-cool-for-school, smart-ass grin. The one that said he would not be taken in.

"That's some sales pitch, buddy," Douglas told him.

But the man was unfazed. He went on to say that the area was what the scientists called a relict. "Like relic, but with a t." A word that connotes, he told us, something that has survived the death of another.

Douglas smiled again.

"Name me something that hasn't," he said.

I SKIRTED THE WETTEST PARTS OF THE FIELD by walking along our property line and saw a small wooden swing set at the far side of Dom's land, and then the ramshackle remains of a tree house, weather-worn boards gone askew and a knotted climbing rope. There was another small outbuilding, doorless with a shadowed interior, far enough away that I couldn't be sure if it housed both the tractor and the plow or the plow alone. And near it, a part of the field shorn of undergrowth, which indicated, I knew now (country living), the heavy cover of the septic tank.

Both properties sloped down toward the trees, and I veered right and then found a path through them.

I can't say I was feeling any better out and about, in the morning sunlight. In fact, I grew more wary, walking through the woods, imagining what might happen should I trip on a bit of fallen branch or twisted vine, should I suddenly be seized with a heart attack, or stroke, or even just, simply, lose my way. I was beginning to realize that what frightened me about being alone, last night in the empty house and now as I made my way down a barely discernible path toward the rushing creek, was that no one was within the sound of my call.

I could as well be here as nowhere at all.

Their voices reached me as I came into the clearing that marked the stream. Dom and Jamie, talking together.

I came upon them easily enough. Dom was seated on a fallen tree trunk, his back to me. Jamie was about ten yards away, in knee-high galoshes, a switch in his hand. He was following something in the water, and Dom was offering advice and bits of caution.

I called out a hello, hoping not to startle them. But neither, of course, was plagued by my own desperate encounters with solitude. They greeted me with no more surprise than they had when I'd seen them at our little grocery store. They were perfectly at ease in the world.

Jamie waved and called, "Hi." Dom looked at me over his shoulder, called "Good morning," and then stood, politely— some remnant of that impulse your husband's generation was so steeped in. An instinctive response to a woman's, any woman's, appearance, anywhere. All rise.

"You're up early," he said. He had seen my car in our driveway. "I was wondering if you guys would be back with the spring."

We sat down together on the fallen tree. He told me that one of his sons and a daughter-in-law and their two small children were visiting. They'd arrived from Atlanta just last night. Sleeping in, he said, as normal people are happy to do. He and Jamie had started out on their hike first thing this morning to allay their impatience. Both of them—father and son—were counting the minutes until these little ones were awake and running around the house.

He said it was a habit of theirs to walk out here on those mornings when neither of them could sleep—usually because they were impatient to get a good day started: those visiting grandkids awake and ready to play, for instance, or a trip to the ocean, a promised meteor shower, tickets to an Orioles game.

"You name it," he said, "Jamie and I are the first up and looking out the window. We're both antsy in the same crazy, insomniac way."

Jamie was some distance from us, walking along the edge of the stream in his boots, but not so far that we couldn't see him looking back now and then—despite the intensity of his focus as he searched the shoreline of what was just a creek, a meandering bit of silver in this light. Now and then as he looked back, he waved.

Dom never failed to wave back, even as the two of us talked about my mother.

She was, Dom said, "something else." He knew her, of course, from the hospital work, and remembered clearly the morning she had brought him the Barbie doll in the ao dai for his newborn daughter.

He'd been a little afraid of my mother, he confessed. At first, anyway. She was so beautiful and confident. "Kind of bossy," he added, and I said, "Tell me about it." He had his eyes on Jamie as he spoke, who was crouched now, inspecting and sorting the rocks and pebbles at the stream's tiny shoreline.

He remembered her market baskets filled with toys, and the other women who trailed her. You among them, I suppose. He said she had come along on occasion when a contingent of American corpsmen visited rural orphanages, even a leper colony outside the city. He recalled that she had once brought silk clothes for all the patients.

"Any boyfriends?" I asked. I told him briefly about Aunt Arlene's mysterious man.

Dom shrugged. He might have blushed. "I could probably think of three or four guys who were in love with her," he said.

He said one time, there was a kid in really bad shape, malnourished when he was brought in, full of worms and then, as happened too often, a cascade of troubles: the moment when they might have saved him suddenly, somehow, irretrievable. Gone too close to the edge. Slipped over the cliff. He said Charlene was holding the kid when he died. A simple, barely noticeable passing. Shallow breaths that merely paused and did not start up again.

He said one of the American doctors who was with them put a stethoscope to the kid's heart, and told my mother he was gone. And then Charlene looked up, like he'd just insulted her.

"I'll never forget it. She was pissed as hell. She said, as if we could do anything about it, 'This is unacceptable.'"

Dom shook his head, his eyes still on Jamie. "I'd been going around with this basket she'd brought, helping to give out her little treats, and I was standing there with them both, Charlene and the doc, feeling like a fool—this big empty basket on my arm. This poor kid in hers. And her so frigging angry. Outraged. I heard myself say, I swear, I meant to be nice, you know, comforting, 'What are you gonna do? These things happen.' Or some such-is-life kind of thing."

He paused, shook his head. "And then the doctor turns on me. Sort of matching her fury. Jesus." He laughed, remembering. Jamie was now carrying something to us in his cupped and dripping palms.

"'Do this,' he tells me."

Dom leaned over his knees, hunched his shoulders, dropped his voice, and turned his face to mine.

"This guy points to your mother, with that poor wreck of a kid on her lap. He says, 'See if you have the balls to do this.'"

In that early morning light, Dom's blue eyes had something of the silver flash and sparkle of the running stream beside us.

"I was in love with her myself at that moment," he told me. "I loved how angry she was. Like that kid was the most valuable thing ever made."

And then Jamie stood before us, his galoshes sparkling with spring water, his flannel shirtsleeves rolled up to the elbows and his hands wet and spotted with mud. "What you got?" Dom asked him.

Shyly, the boy held out a shining stone. It was a chipped black rock veined with silver, fused to two smaller stones with what seemed a wreath of pink pearls.

"Look at this," Jamie said simply, full of simple wonder.

Dom placed his own hand under his son's. "That's a beauty," he said. He waved a gentle pinky over the stone. "Onyx, I'm guessing," he whispered. "Maybe mica. Sandstone, pink quartz."

He told Jamie to bring the stone up to the house, show it to his brother. "He's smarter than either of us about rocks."

But Jamie closed his hand again. He looked at me from under his fair brows. "It's for you," he whispered, and offered me the fused stone. I took it, thanked him.

And then he turned back to his careful inspection of the pebbled shoreline.

THE THREE OF US walked together back through the field. As we approached Dom's shed, a truck pulled slowly into the long drive. The men, Dom's workers, I assumed, waved to Jamie, and he ran to greet them.

Dom and I lingered. The sound of the truck, the bustle of the men as they left the cab, broke open somehow the day's fresh beginning. We might both have been reluctant to let the quiet go.

I asked how Jamie's health was, his heart.

"Great," Dom said, and, as his son had done, made with his thumb a little cross over his chest. "Turns out, his first heart surgery, which he had before he was ours, was pretty amazing. Every doctor since has said so. Guy who did it was some kind of magician." He laughed, but I think he was aware that he was telling me something I might not have understood.

It was like a piece of the new sunlight, golden pink as it was, had fallen on that casual phrase "before he was ours."

He spoke in a rush. "A pediatric cardiac surgeon working gratis on an abandoned premie with Down syndrome at a third-rate hospital—so good that twenty years later other surgeons are saying, Wow." He shook his head. "How's that for believing in a benevolent universe?"

I said, "He's adopted."

And Dom nodded. Ellen's sister had been a nurse at the hospital, told them about the abandoned child. It was supposed to have been a fostering situation, given their ages. But adoption got Jamie on their medical insurance. A few strings were pulled, Dom said. "A lot of answered prayers in order to make him our own."

BACK AT THE HOUSE, I placed the pretty stone on the windowsill above our kitchen sink. It was there, in the periphery of my vision, when I looked out early the next morning, after another mostly sleepless night.

I was deciding whether to join them again at the stream—wondering, in an adolescent sort of way, whether I would seem foolish, infatuated. Or if I should simply throw my bag in the car and drive home to my husband—to what turned out to be the difficult closing years of our own American romance.

Years when our own flawed, fortunate past slipped out of memory.

But then I heard voices from Dom's yard. Ellen's voice first, I was certain, and then the deep, commanding voices of men that quickly became a confusion of shouts. And then a siren.

I pulled on shoes. I was out the back door and running over the uneven ground. I could see the scarlet indication of an ambulance's flashing lights at the far end of their driveway.

I ran along the dried tangle of bush and branch and reed that divided us, feeling the ground had suddenly pitched itself at a steeper, less manageable angle, until I glimpsed them all. Jamie was wailing—I don't know when I realized it was Jamie wailing, but I know I felt some odd relief, the familiar mother-logic: if he's wailing, he's alive.

I saw Ellen, her back to me, crouched on the ground, with Jamie in her arms. He was kneeling before her, his head against her heart. She was rocking him as he sobbed. And at some distance, a trio of men knelt over a splayed figure. Work boots nearly shapeless with mud, all his clothes, in fact, shapeless with mud except for a gash of color where his shirt and jacket had been torn open.

His pale chest, also streaked with mud, so white against the rugged earth it might have been illuminated from within. It took me a few seconds to see that it was his son who was doing CPR, saying evenly, I could hear it now, "Stay with me, Dad, stay with me."

I suppose I fought my way through that brambled divide. The medics had taken over, were bringing a gurney. I went to Ellen. She and Jamie both were covered in mud, their clothes heavy with it, their cheeks and hands. Jamie's head was pressed against his mother's heart. He was wailing still, his eyes shut. I saw Ellen looking beyond him, to where Dom was being lifted onto the gurney. She began to stand as her older son came to her, saying, "We'll follow."

Then I had Jamie in my arms. He was no longer crying, only holding on to me. We were holding on to each other. The mud that covered us was thick. The air smelled of damp earth, waste, decay, as well as the lingering diesel exhaust of the ambulance.

We crouched there, holding each other, until some wan spring sunlight rose over the trees.

◈

THEY'D BEEN UP EARLIER THAN USUAL, before dawn, and it was barely light enough to see when they'd made their way toward the stream. Jamie hoped to find another gorgeous stone to bring back to his mother.

Running ahead of Dom in the bare morning light, he'd somehow stumbled into the open septic tank, left uncovered by the workmen the day before. Dom had climbed in after his son, hoisted him on his shoulders, raised him up until Jamie scrambled out. He'd run to the house for help, poor kid, but by the time they returned, Dom had been overcome. I think he was gone even as his son struggled to restart his good heart.

WHEN WE CLEARED OUT my father's house in Garden City, my brothers and I were surprised to see how many letters my mother had saved from people she'd known during her time in Saigon. Names you would probably recognize. I guess you're the last of the letter-writing generation. Handwritten or typewritten, even mimeographed notes, catching up on where they were living now, or moving to, and how old their kids were, references to more exotic postings, or the refusal of them, to aging parents, or brushes with illness, brushes with hurricanes or blizzards, happy vacations, accidents, second homes, various charities.

Always some mention of charity work: galas, card parties, clothing drives—perhaps the trailing remnants of their time in her cabal.

No letters from men. Certainly no love letters. A few photos, mostly of the Christmas-card type. Here and there a Vietnamese child among the smiling family portraits.

I remember a photo of a cute little boy standing beside his blond brother, both of them holding hockey sticks. And a pair of girls at Disneyland. A skinny kid on crutches, both legs in small white casts—a good prognosis, the letter had said. And another family group on a tarmac somewhere, in the now-faded Kodachrome of the era: father in khaki, squinting into the sun, an arm around his pretty wife, who holds on her hip a Vietnamese toddler in a party dress, the shadow of a birthmark across her plump cheek. A few handsome graduation photos of completely Americanized Vietnamese kids. I suspect you might have known some of these families.

Whatever mention these women made of the days they'd all spent as dependents in Vietnam was usually of the *Little did we know* sort.

I carried a box of these letters from Long Island to Baltimore after my father died. I had some vague idea then that I'd try to find these old friends of my mother, or their children, perhaps even return their letters to them. Never got around to it. Busyness, and demon time.

As we began our first sorting that spring, I decided it was senseless to hold on to these letters any longer, mundane as they were, the record of a disappearing generation's efforts at inconsequential good.

As I mentioned, I'm not religious myself. My churchgoing life, my parents' Episcopalian traditions, fell away with my childhood. And I'm pretty sure I'm free of most superstition. I certainly don't think it was the Devil you encountered at the leprosarium, no American Satan that my mother bargained with in Saigon. I think he was just a man—a man like my father, like your husband. A man out to repair the world.

◈

AMONG ALL THE USELESS THINGS we'd accumulated—the knickknacks, yes, the souvenirs, the detritus of a long life, a life within a family—there was a smooth gray stone etched with the smiling face of a bodhisattva, the figures of small children carved into his robe.

I can't recall now what my mother said when she placed it in my hand as I went off for my boarding school banishment. I know I was disarmed by the gift. Not because I knew the story behind it, but because Buddhism was so cool. And my mother was not.

I found that little stone again in our own first sorting and carried it to the country house. I placed it on the same window-sill where I later placed Jamie's gift.

And as I write this, I feel my mother's thin hand clutching my chin, directing my gaze even as she forbids easy tears: an un-crossable river, an endless task, demons, yes, but also one benevolent being. Just one.

D OUG'S DEMENTIA WAS DIAGNOSED in the months after Dom died. I took the Roland Park house off the market. A move would have been too difficult for us both. I sold the farmhouse and focused on taking care of my husband and our kids, on getting through the days.

I don't recall seeing your letters to my mother; no doubt they were there—there were so many. But I always remembered your name and how attentive you were to me. I imagine we both sometimes felt unseen in my mother's churning wake.

I resolved to find you, if only to ask if you remembered me, if you remembered Dom.

It wasn't difficult. There was that article in the metro section when you retired—the beloved kindergarten teacher. I only had to call the school and wait until they found someone who had your current address.

Everyone there was very friendly.

III

NOT LONG BEFORE WE LEFT SAIGON, Charlene appeared at our villa unannounced, breezed into my room one morning while I was still in my housecoat, damp from my bath, covered in talc.

She told me to get dressed. Nothing fancy, she said, a shirtwaist would do. "But put on some lipstick"—with her laugh—"pin up your hair." Hers was in an immaculate chignon. "It's hot as Hades out there."

She said, "I have a little excursion in mind, since you're going home."

She said she'd wait for me downstairs.

In truth, I didn't know then that we were going home. Peter hadn't told me yet. I still don't know how she knew. Another mystery of our time and place.

On that morning, as I had so many times before, I simply bent to her will. Got dressed. Pinned up my hair. I suppose I assumed she needed me at her side for some bit of coercive fundraising—me, her saintly sidekick.

When I came downstairs, Charlene looked me over in her way and declared my outfit "fine." And then Minh-Linh came out of the kitchen. She was wearing one of her Sunday ao dais, a pale blue flowered print, her square patent leather purse over her arm.

Thinking she was off on her own excursion, I started to tell her, "Charlene and I are just going out." When Charlene took my arm.

"Minh-Linh's coming, too," she said.

As a translator, I thought. Or because Charlene had arranged some tearful reunion for Minh-Linh and a long-lost cousin or two. It wouldn't have surprised me. It seemed to me in those days that Charlene had her fingers in everyone's lives. I've heard the phrase of late, "white savior." Charlene, despite her freckles, would have fit the bill.

I was relieved to see there was no jeep at the curb. Instead, Charlene languidly raised her arm and a little Renault instantly appeared. She climbed in. Minh-Linh gestured that I should follow and then squeezed in beside me, her stiff purse on her lap. Minh-Linh was the one who gave the instructions to our driver in a stream of Vietnamese.

"What's the plan?" I asked, when we had veered out into the chaos of Saigon traffic.

Charlene lowered her freckled eyelids and smiled wisely. You would think we were reclined in the back seat of an air-cooled limo, she looked so crisp and composed. "Wait and see," she said.

Both women turned to their windows as if to take in some placid view. I stared straight ahead, past the driver's narrow shoulders and the curling ducktail at the back of his head. Soon I was utterly lost.

I think I knew we were in Cholon and then we'd gone through it. I recognized but could not place the ramshackle houses, the teeming streets, a section of the city that was surely poorer than any I'd been to before. Pressed as I was between Charlene and Minh-Linh, I struggled to find a landmark. I assumed this was a through-passage to some other, safer spot where we might be having lunch. Making a pitch to some major's wife. Perhaps the likes of Madame Nhu herself.

I wondered if I should remind Charlene that Peter had forbidden me to leave the city.

The cab stopped at the mouth of a terrible-looking street. Minh-Linh and the driver exchanged more words—he was gesturing down a narrow alleyway, then nodding, shrugging, until something was resolved.

"He'll wait," Minh-Linh told Charlene, and Charlene patted the man's shoulder.

"Merci," she said. Too brightly, I thought, for our environs.

We got out. Charlene and I reflexively brushed out our skirts. Minh-Linh led the way. Down this impassable alleyway, the shacks on either side looking as if—it seemed to me—they were not so much constructed where they stood as piled, piled up, like debris after a storm, an aftermath, an afterthought, haphazardly stacked and pushed aside. There were a few cooking fires, the odor of their charcoal smoke, a few Vietnamese men and women crouched over them. Some of them glanced up at us warily. We wended—that's the word—wended our way right, then left, following a course Minh-Linh seemed to know well.

Once or twice I was able to see into some of the gloomy rooms that lined the alley. I could see beds draped with netting, a table or two. At another turn we came upon two young GIs— sweat-stained T-shirts, dog tags, their trousers low-slung on thin hips, standing together at the mouth of one of these rooms, smoking and laughing. They seemed as startled to see us as we were to see them. One of them even stamped out his cigarette as we approached, like a teenager caught by the school principal. In truth, he was a teenager.

"Afternoon, ladies," the other, a bit more brazen, said, with a little salute.

Charlene returned the greeting, smiling, but then called to them over her shoulder as we passed by, "Write home to your mothers, boys."

Of course I was thinking now that we were not here to raise more funds, Barbie or otherwise, but to spend them. Although Charlene had no basket of goodies on her arm. I wondered if there might be a colony of lepers hidden here in these tangled streets, unfortunates in need of Charlene's care. I grew more uncertain about my role in this excursion, but I think I suspected this was Charlene folding me back into her cabal after Peter had confined me to quarters—absolving me of my wifely obeisance.

I recall a slight shift in the humid air. A touch of salt, mold, old dampness. We were near water, the river, perhaps, although I could not have said how near.

A courtyard of some sort. A collection of junk—crates, piles of rags, the smell of waste, urine, something burned. And then a somewhat larger building. A doorless entryway. "Please," Minh-Linh said, indicating we should go inside. And "please," again to urge us to climb a narrow staircase, each tread marked with a bright, though peeling, slap of scarlet paint.

We entered a large room. Filled with a family, I thought on first impression, multigenerational. There were a number of children of various ages, two crawling babies and a tall girl in early adolescence, an old woman sitting up on a narrow bed and one crouched over a small stove. Another, middle-aged, who crossed the room immediately to take Minh-Linh's hands. They seemed to be old friends. I thought: a lost cousin, a separated twin.

After a kind of introduction, two chairs were offered to Charlene and me—tufted red seat cushions, worn but clean. We were offered tea, and watched as the tall girl, perhaps about eleven or twelve, ceremoniously brewed and poured. She was a serious child with two braids over her shoulders, pigtails as I thought of them, intense in her focus on the small stove and the brass teapot. Minh-Linh and her friend chattered together all the while, and the other children watched us, the older ones somewhat shyly, but the younger ones with the same curiosity and openness of children everywhere. A toddler with a new stuffed toy, a little cat or a dog—I recognized it as one of our own, and guessed then that this was some kind of nursery school or orphanage that had already benefited from Charlene's good works—made her way across the room and placed the doll in Charlene's lap. Another, crawling, seemed to make a game of moving toward me, intent on my shoes, and then sitting with a plop, laughing, crawling away.

The tea in the china cup was hot when the girl handed it to me, a tingling in my fingertips, and I recall raising it, turning away, as the child once more approached—an instinctive caution to my mind—what anyone would do when supplied with a hot drink and a friendly child. But the gesture made Minh-Linh and her friend laugh. Charlene reached up to take the cup away as I lifted the crawling toddler to my lap, to the edge of my knees (now an ingrained precaution), and ran my palm over his dark head. His seat was a little damp, but no matter. It was lovely to hold him, to smile at his chatter.

I was back in my kindergarten classroom again. I was Anna again in *The King and I*. Getting to know you.

The conversation between Minh-Linh and her friend stopped briefly. I saw them watching me, smiling. Wondered if this somehow was my role here. When the two women started talking again, Charlene joined in, in French.

A command was given to the girl who had made our tea, and with her head down she quickly left the room. Two more middle-aged women, who wore cheaply made pastel ao dais—I was beginning to notice such things—suddenly moved toward Charlene and me in our chairs, scooping up the other children as they did.

One leaned down to take the little boy from my lap. I asked for his name, in French, but I don't think she heard me—he began to cry—or maybe she didn't understand.

She took the boy into the next room, through the same doorway the pigtailed girl had used. Her companion followed with two more of the smaller kids in her arms. Without the smallest children, the room seemed suddenly still. Minh-Linh and her friend stood together with their arms folded across their chests. Charlene said, "Well now," and the other, older children, the two old women, peered at us both.

I sensed we were about to begin whatever bit of business Charlene had devised.

But then the tall girl returned. She was carrying a baby, perhaps six, seven months old. A plump little girl in a very Western pink party dress, a pink bow in her little bit of black hair. The girl crossed the room and gently placed the baby in my lap. And then backed away, her head bowed.

I cooed—of course I cooed. It seemed the child had just

been bathed. In the heat of the room, her sweet arms and legs with their little rings of flesh were cool to the touch. She smelled of talc and baby shampoo. She looked up at me, curious, alert, lovely. Of course I saw immediately the long birthmark that covered the left side of her face—what we used to call a port-wine stain. It ran like a broad brushstroke of dark paint from her scalp to her plump jawline; there were scattered remnants of it along her neck and into her dress.

I heard Charlene ask, "Isn't she sweet?"

I held her. She seemed perfectly content in my lap, even reached up to touch my face, my lips. I raised my chin, laughing. I knew with a sudden confidence—the confidence I had sought that afternoon at the garden party with little Roger in my arms—that I would, indeed, be a wonderful mother, eventually.

Holding the lovely child, I felt that gentle, familiar stirring of the blood, that physical tug—a literal movement, it seemed to me, of heart, of breath. I felt that gentle, persistent stirring, longing, that hunger—the insistence no disappointment or sensible reordering of expectations could ever evade. I would have a child of my own.

"What's her name?" I asked, as I took her hand and kissed her little palm.

Minh-Linh's friend said, "Suzie," nearly a shout. Charlene and I both laughed.

And then Charlene said, "She's yours."

ONCE MORE, the memory transforms itself, obscures itself, into the fanciful. I can't say for certain if the room spun or if I reeled,

if the entire scene—Charlene, Minh-Linh, the old women, the
solemn children scattered along the walls—actually took on the
amber light of a stage set, of a historical photo of some world-
changing event, but that's how it seems to me now, in memory.
In memory, the heat has fallen away, the noise from the street
has fallen away, the objections, the logistics, the years ahead, all
have fallen away. There is only the baby's sweet babble, her cool
limbs, the achievement of my body's surest desire.

"She's yours," Charlene said. "Take her home." And then, as
if she had read my mind: "Free of charge."

I suppose I offered some objections. There was Peter to consider, I said.

Charlene said, "Oh, I know. You wouldn't go to St. Christopher's without his permission. For God's sake, girl. Think for
yourself."

I said something about legalities, passports.

"I'll arrange it," Charlene said.

There was also my own as yet unspoken hope—a missed period not quite two weeks ago—that we had hit the mark again.
That we would soon have a child of our own.

"Insurance," Charlene said. "You said yourself you hated being an only child."

I didn't doubt my capacity to love this girl. Even as Charlene
ran a finger along her birthmark ("I've talked to Wally about
this," she was saying. "There's much they can do now, back in
the States"), I felt a mother's furious defense. "She's perfect," I
said.

Charlene smiled, said something in French that made Minh-
Linh lean toward her, whisper a response.

"Where there is love," Charlene told me, patiently translating Minh-Linh's words, "a smallpox scar is as charming as a dimple."

WHAT FOLLOWED was something like the bundling of a package. The bustling preparation of a gift. The two middle-aged women returned, one with a sheet of fabric that they wound us both in, mother and child, securing my new baby against my chest.

(I confess I recalled for a moment the leper women with their arms raised, Lily's tape measure going under their arms. Some vague recollection of my own bitter conclusion that we were preparing their shrouds. I rejected it as best I could, with this baby in my arms.)

And then Charlene, Minh-Linh, and I were once again navigating the noisy, narrow alleys of that strange neighborhood. Now Minh-Linh held my purse and I held the child bound to my chest, her fragrant head just under my chin, my hands cupping her round bottom.

But when we reached the street, we saw that the taxi had gone.

Clearly, Charlene declared, the driver had been bribed by those two GIs we'd seen earlier, smoking and grinning after getting their rocks off—"Fine boys," she said. We waited on the street for a few minutes, but there were no other cabs to be seen in this part of town.

Minh-Linh was confident we wouldn't have far to walk before we found one.

And so we trekked for a while in the heat and humidity. The

noise. Lost as I was, I simply followed Minh-Linh and Charlene. Before long, I felt the perspiration funneling down my spine. I brushed my thumb over the poor child's forehead, her black hair with its little bow now grown wet. She looked up at me, awake but quiet. I imagined she smiled. There were a few times when I had to pause, to catch my breath, or to stand for a few minutes in the shade of a scrawny flame tree, a ramshackle lean-to. My lower back had begun to ache, and my shoes were uncomfortable.

Charlene said, "We'll find a cab. It won't be long now."

I was thinking, on one level, about Peter. How he would re-act. Surely he would recognize my own joy. Surely he would be unable to resist the beauty of the child, the sweet folds of flesh, the toothless smile.

I was thinking about all I would need to purchase—a crib, more clothes, diapers, baby food from the PX.

But looking back I also want to believe that this journey, its utter unreality, the physical pain that in memory seems merely incidental, was somehow equivalent to a long and difficult labor—an entirely physical birthing. Silly, I know. And yet, look-ing back, I think Charlene felt the same. Once when I paused, she produced a fragrant handkerchief, wiped my brow with it, and then the brow of the child.

Minh-Linh led us toward the river. I heard what had become the familiar soft clanging of sampans and fishing boats be-fore I realized where we were—not so far out of the city as I'd imagined.

Looking back, I wonder if Charlene, or Minh-Linh, or only the disloyal taxi driver had taken us on a circuitous route in or-der to make my return impossible.

We stopped at a small café for Cokes. I dipped my finger in

the cool drink, wet the baby's lips and tongue. Once more Charlene put a napkin to the sweat on my lip, motherly, attentive.

When taxis began to appear on the streets once again, I saw Charlene touch Minh-Linh's raised hand. They exchanged a few words and then Charlene turned to me.

"Shall we keep walking?" she asked.

I could see the delicate beads of perspiration above her parched lips, the way the stray hairs at her forehead were plastered with sweat. Minh-Linh, too, was looking weary. We might indeed have been three women caught in a long labor. The child, the delicious weight of her, was now sound asleep against my chest. I said, "Let's."

At one point, Charlene bought a paper parasol from a sidewalk stand. Minh-Linh held it over me the rest of the way. Making something triumphant of our little sweat-stained and foot-weary procession.

At our town house gate, Charlene said, "I'm off." She told me there were a few things to take care of, she'd be in touch. And Dr. Wally had promised to stop by in the morning. "He'll tell you everything you'll need to do in the coming days."

Standing at the curb, poised to hail a cab, to get on to her next project it seemed to me, Charlene added, "And she doesn't have to be Suzie. She's yours now. You can call her whatever you like." But I needed to decide quickly, she said, for the adoption papers, the passport.

"You'll want everything in order before you leave," she said.

I wanted only to get inside with my treasure. To unwrap her, so to speak, and consider my life ahead. I told Charlene we still had months to go on Peter's assignment in Saigon.

She gazed at me. As disheveled as she was with the heat, she should not have managed such a cool, an icy, appraisal. "You," she said. And paused to let a particular loud band of motor scooters pass by on the street. "You can't go to church without his permission, yet he doesn't bother to tell you he's quit. He's booked your flight home."

I absorbed this, Suzie in my arms. Felt, perhaps, the first real sense of humiliation at my own childishness, the same humiliation, I suppose, that moved me to describe for you, to invent—I apologize—that earlier version of our deliberations, Peter and mine, our late-night plans to leave.

In truth, there had been no whispering in the dark, no shared consideration. We'd never discussed it at all. No fault of Peter's, really. What it was like for us, in those days. Us wives.

I have to laugh when I think about it now: how much easier life must have been for certain government agencies—how much easier for secrecy to be maintained—in those days before men felt any obligation to share their lives with the women they loved.

INSIDE, MINH-LINH PRODUCED from her quarters a large market basket lined with a fresh blanket, a bassinet. It was filled with diapers, and plastic pants, some baby clothes, a couple of bottles, and cans of formula. She and Charlene had been planning this for some time, it seemed.

Together, we bathed the child in a tin dishpan. As I cupped the water over her plump shoulders, and turned away laughing as she splashed, I was reeling—it seems the only word—reeling with delight, happiness, astonishment. How many words are there for joy? I've heard other mothers say it, you said it yourself: the world begun again, in beauty and innocence, in goodness and hope. And entirely in your care.

I changed the child into a little sunsuit that Minh-Linh, or Charlene, had already procured, fed her the bottle Minh-Linh had prepared. With Minh-Linh watching over her, I took a quick bath myself, changed into something pretty and cool. I was imagining all the ways I would introduce Peter to his daughter—realizing as I did that Charlene, scheming Charlene, had given me a way to respond should Peter object that I had not consulted him first: When were you going to tell me we're leaving?

A fresh, even combative response that would surely surprise

him. Something new for me, but available now. A defense for my own secrets.

I resolved on an immediate introduction. I would take the child to our little veranda at the front of the house, where we sometimes had cocktails in the evening if the heat wasn't bad. It was a good place to listen to the sounds of the street and to glimpse through our locked front gate the cars and pedestrians that passed by. The gate was far enough from the porch that we wouldn't have to worry about anything "unpleasant"—as Peter once put it—being lobbed through the bars, but close enough that we felt a part of the city.

It was the gate Peter would come through when he got home—this morning, he'd promised a routine day, home in time for dinner—and so he would see me, with Suzie in my arms, right away. I recall that I had this very strange notion that the sight of us, Madonna and Child, would evoke for him his fondness for the Blessed Virgin, a devotion instilled by his own mother. That the familiar image, much adored, would overwhelm his sensible objections.

I imagined how I might tell him, as he approached down the little path from the gate, "She's yours."

I changed her diaper again—she was a good, placid little thing—she would grow up to be shy, I thought, like me. Minh-Linh brought in another bottle, but I brushed it away. I didn't want her puking all over my dress as I waited for Peter, what with the heat. Lesson learned.

Because of the heat, I waited inside until perhaps ten or twenty minutes before Peter's usual return. Then I carried Suzie to the veranda and settled her prettily on my lap.

I heard them before I saw them, the children. One of them

crying—only one at first—and the others hushing. It was not unusual to hear the voices of children on the street in front of our house. I made nothing of it at first. But then—in memory it seems absolutely choreographed—they appeared, one by one, outside our gate. I recognized the pigtailed girl first, taller than the rest. And then I knew the others from that cluttered and capacious room.

They called out, pushing their hands through the bars. Now every one of them was crying, calling. The name they called was some accented version of Sue, Suzie.

I had barely figured out who they were when Minh-Linh appeared from around the house, running headlong toward the gate, nearly skidding on the stone path. She was shouting, a thin, high-pitched stream of angry words. In her hand was a tea towel; she had been in the kitchen getting our dinner, and when she reached the gate, she swung the bit of damp cloth in wide arcs, back and forth, striking as she did the rungs of the gate as if to drive away a swarm of flies.

I saw the children quickly withdraw the hands they had thrust through the bars, recoiling from a hot stove. And yet they made no other effort to step away, to run away. In fact, they instantly met her cries with their own—raising their voices against hers, the way, it seemed to me, an arm might be raised to defend a face. A wall of sound to match and deflect whatever it was she was telling them, to answer her outrage and her anger in kind.

The towel she was wielding, striking the bars, might have been a choirmaster's baton, the way the children replied with their own chorus of shrill complaint.

I gathered the baby in my arms and walked quickly toward the gate. I had to shout to be heard. Minh-Linh was sputtering with anger, her lips wet and her eyes truly blazing. "Stop," I heard myself say in my schoolteacher's voice. "What's going on here?" I shouted, "What do they want?"

The children's hands slipped through the bars again as soon as Minh-Linh stopped her swatting. "Go away," she shouted at me, caught up as she was in her fight with the children. She corrected herself. "Tell them to go away."

They were crying, all of them, weeping now with abandon. All, I saw, but the tall girl with the pigtails, who stood behind the other, shouting children, glaring into the yard. Glaring, in truth, at me with plump Suzie in my arms.

I stepped back, frightened somehow by the girl's steady reserve. I told Minh-Linh to let them in.

She objected, said again, "They must go away. You must tell them. They don't belong here."

I moved past her to lift the lock, pull open the gate. The movement was enough to suddenly silence them. They stepped back, uncertain now that the way was no longer closed to them. I knew this from my kindergarten days: the best way to subdue an adamant child is to hand her whatever she demands—possession being, I'd found, the best way to confound desire.

"Come in, children," I said. "Come inside."

Shyly, suddenly silent, they stepped in single file through the gate, sniffing up their tears, looking carefully around. There were five little ones, and then the tall girl, who came in last—she had her head down, her eyes to the ground, and yet there was something regal about her. Something that reminded me of Lily's self-confidence, a hidden but no less assured belief in her own quiet abilities.

I asked Minh-Linh to fetch the children some lemonade. She

paused for a moment, the damp dish towel now limp in her hands. Her dark eyes were indeed ablaze, but now her fury was directed at me. "Go away," she said again. Her voice no longer shrill, but solid, solid steel. "They must go away." She added, "You must tell them."

I said, "The children are thirsty. Please do as I say."

They remain, to my mind, the harshest words I'd ever spoken to anyone the whole time we were in Saigon.

And I supposed I received the harshest appraisal—her eyes moving in turn from my face, to the child in my arms, to my waist, my infertile middle.

Minh-Linh spun away from me and walked angrily into the house.

The five children surrounded me now; they were touching Suzie's plump legs, cooing, and—my heart sank at the sound— beginning to cry again, but softly, grief without outrage. Gently, I herded them toward the veranda, pretending a graciousness, a resilience I didn't feel.

The tall one trailed us, reluctant, sullen. Something of the heat and the humid air in the quality of her sullenness.

I indicated the chairs around our little wrought iron table. The children sat, two to a seat, squeezing together, sitting on one another's thighs and knees the way children do. The tall girl took the last chair and lifted one of the smaller ones, the only boy, into her lap. As I sat with them, Suzie leaned in my arms, laughing, reaching for the children's outstretched hands. I smiled, holding her around the waist, feeling how she strained toward them and trying to believe it was not affection or even instinct that pulled her, only infant curiosity. She might reach for sunbeams in her crib in the same way.

I smiled at them. "You walked?" I asked, or some such, walking two fingers across the tabletop. They did not turn their attention from the baby. I might not have spoken at all.

I know I glanced toward the gate, wondering when Peter would appear. Any minute now, I knew.

I asked again, this time addressing myself to the tall girl. "You kids walked all the way here?" And then it suddenly occurred to me. "Did you follow us?"

Her chin puckered and her lips began to quiver. Although she might have been the oldest among them, her struggle, her helplessness before her own suddenly rising tears, made me realize she was no more than a child herself.

Minh-Linh came through the door with a tray of short glasses partially filled, grudgingly, I thought, with cloudy lemonade. She put the glasses on the table, nearly elbowing the children's heads as she did, and then, with the tray dropped against her thigh, she began to berate the tall girl in swift Vietnamese. Now I glimpsed something of the girl's coming adolescence, that secret strength she carried in her long spine, as she replied in her own bitter stream, over the head of the little boy in her arms. For a moment, I feared Minh-Linh would begin swinging the bamboo tray as she had swung the dish towel. I touched her arm. "Stop," I said. "Enough. Please."

She looked down at me with so much disdain that I feared for a moment the tray could well be aimed at me.

"What do they want?" I asked her.

Before she could reply, the tall girl turned to me. "Please, lady," she said.

But Minh-Linh shouted over her. "They want to make trouble," she said. And then directed another torrent of words at the girl. As she spoke, the other children began to cry again, one by one, a domino line of sprung leaks.

I felt Suzie stiffen on my lap. I bounced her a bit to keep her from crying as well. "How are they going to make trouble?" I asked Minh-Linh. "They're just little kids." I asked her again, more insistent now, "What do they want?"

The tall girl's chin, her puffed bottom lip, trembled so, it was all I could do not to reach out to her, to touch her cheek.

"They want trouble," Minh-Linh said. She really was a wall. "You must tell them to go away."

But the tall girl suddenly squeezed her eyes shut and tilted her head back, shouting over her. "Our sister," she cried out. Nearly moaning it. "Come home." And then a cloudburst of tears.

Once again, the volume of their collective lament rose and rose. Now Suzie in my arms joined in, clutching her own little hands together in an ancient gesture of womanly helplessness and sorrow. I bounced her again. And then lifted her to my shoulder, patting her back. I glanced again at the gate, looking for Peter to appear.

Minh-Linh was shouting at them to stop. I didn't know the words, but I knew her meaning. Patting Suzie's back I asked her, "Is she their sister?"

"No," Minh-Linh said. Now she was indeed gesturing with the bamboo tray. Lifting it by one handle as if she'd whack every one of us. I'd never seen her so angry. I don't suppose I'd ever seen her angry at all.

"They're lying. She has no sister. Her mother is dead." She raised the tray toward Suzie. "No one wants this ugly child. You take her out of here. Give her a good chance." And then, as if to clarify something, "These are bad kids."

Added to all this agitation was my awareness that Peter might at any minute come upon this scene, the chaotic din. Proof positive, I thought, of my ineptitude, my childishness. What kind of mother I was going to make.

I heard myself shouting, "Stop it. Stop it. All of you." Which had the only real effect of transforming Suzie's whimper into a howl.

Once again Minh-Linh turned her back on me, stormed away.

I patted the child, moved her again to my lap. Brushed her tears from her cheek, her long birthmark, the edge of her chubby chin. Now that the shouting had stopped, the other children's tears seemed merely companionable, as if their sobbing were simply a language I didn't understand.

I asked the tall girl, "She is your sister?" And the girl nodded. I looked at the little boy on her lap. "Sister?" I asked him, but he only stared back. I turned to the two little girls squeezed together in the chair on my right. "Your sister?" I asked, and saw them both glance at their tall companion. Slowly, they, too, nodded, clearly with no real sense of what they were agreeing to. Their tears had made long trails along their dirty cheeks, rivulets in a sandy stream. I turned to the other two, who had their arms around each other. They were nodding already.

They were so painfully thin, all of them. Bone-thin arms and wrists and narrow hips sharing a single chair. Their shirts and dresses and shorts were, it seemed to me, cobweb thin as well. And yet my little Suzie was plump, well-fed. She had been bathed and powdered and presented to me in her frilly American dress— irresistible despite the stain that marked her as an ugly child.

For the first time I wondered how long it had taken Charlene to arrange this; how long ago had she set her eyes on this little girl, directed the women to fatten her up for me. Dress her up. I wondered if the pink party dress itself had perhaps been procured by Charlene's clever sister.

Or if Charlene and our doctor friend had paid the mother a good price.

She had bypassed me completely in her scheme. Minh-Linh was in on it, the women in the wide room were in on it, even these children—the taxi driver, for all I knew—but I had been left in the dark. What kind of logic had Charlene employed to leave me so out of it? *Don't ask Tricia to decide. Tricia will never decide. Tell her, Here you are. All your heart's desires in a fait accompli.*

I indicated to the children that they should drink their lemonade, using words I knew they didn't understand. "We'll figure something out," I said. "Don't cry," I said. "All will be well." I indicated again that they should drink up. I asked them if they were hungry. Gestured the question. They merely looked at me, sucking in their tears, glancing at the tall girl.

Suzie began to settle a bit, hiccuping, swallowing air, although once again she was clasping her own plump fingers, hand in hand with herself, understanding, I suppose, that no surer comfort would arrive. I ran my fingertips along her little spine.

If I made a decision, I made it then, although I had no awareness of it. As if I had no more volition here than I had had all along, in all of Charlene's planning.

Standing slowly, I lifted the baby, the children's eyes on us both, and then lowered her, without a word, into the lap of the tall girl, right beside the little boy she already held on her knee. They both moved quickly to accommodate the child.

And then I held out my hand, as you would to a pack of dogs, newly, precariously, trained.

"You stay right here, please," I said. "You stay. I will send out some food." Once again, I made an eating gesture.

And then I turned my back on them and went into the house. I suppose I was fully aware that they might all, Suzie included, be gone by the time I returned.

I called to Minh-Linh. She came from the kitchen. "Bring those kids something to eat," I said. "And fill their glasses to the top, for God's sake."

Upstairs, I pulled a pillowcase from the linen cupboard in the hall. I stuffed it, quickly, with the little wardrobe Minh-Linh had produced, the diapers and the plastic pants and the small T-shirts. There really wasn't much. And then I added the Saigon Barbie that Charlene had given me, a souvenir of our efforts.

I tossed the pillowcase into the market basket Minh-Linh had made into a bassinet, and then lifted the thing by its rope handles. Carrying it all out of our room, I paused at the dresser, considered, and then reached for my little stone bodhisattva beside the pail of sand and ash, tossed it into the mix as well.

I grabbed what money was left in my wooden box carved with the Xa Loi Pagoda—dollars and piastres both.

I made my way downstairs.

When I try to recount what was going through my mind in all this, I can think only of hot and cold—hot with anger, at Charlene, at Peter, at everyone in my life who had considered my opinions inconsequential, who had lied to me or ignored me or manipulated me for what they considered my own benefit. Hot to think of those who'd set out to do good on my behalf.

But cold, too. I would not allow myself to consider what I

would lose in giving up this lovely child. My insurance against childlessness.

Minh-Linh had set out on the table—was it in spite?—a bowl of potato chips, another of pretzels, a plate of Oreos. She had dumped a few tins of Vienna sausages—Peter's favorite—into a shallow dish. American food, straight from the PX. The children were making a feast of it. The little boy had taken my chair and was reaching happily for everything spread before him. The crying had stopped. Little Suzie was sitting contentedly beneath the tall girl's chin. There were potato chip crumbs in her dark hair.

Once again, I looked warily toward the gate, imagined Peter's astonished entrance onto this scene.

I waited, watching them all, holding the bassinet before me with both hands, like a schoolgirl with her satchel.

My thoughts were hot and cold, and the unreality of it all— the heat, the noise of the street, these strange creatures around my little table—left me both disoriented and bitterly impatient.

I wanted this whole sojourn to be over. I wanted to go home. I wanted another kind of life, my own life. My own baby.

Suddenly, I cried out, "Home." I barely recognized my own voice. "Home," I said again and moved toward our gate. The children paused, looked at me warily. I said, "Now. Go home," and moved the wide basket toward the gate. "Take your sister home."

If I had been on the precipice of something just seconds ago, I was, surely, free-falling now.

The tall girl was the first to stand, and I saw how she struggled a bit to get up with Suzie still in her lap. I knew—my mind both hot and cold—that were I to take the child from her skinny arms, if I were to hold that plump child against my heart, I would have no choice but to keep her. I would, once again, have no choice in the matter. I would be bound forever to what had been arranged for me.

And so I held back, the rope handles of the market basket clutched in my hands, binding my wrists.

One by one, the children got up from the table and followed my command. Or, more accurately, they followed their tall sister, who was now moving warily, Suzie on her hip. I saw how each of these smaller children grabbed a few more cookies, stacked them in their little hands, and palmed them against their thin chests, like shoplifters, tiny smugglers, greedy and inept.

I recalled my kindergarteners back home. It was the same sneaky gesture I had seen among them at snack time—or at least among those who knew, innately perhaps, or perhaps from some experience of want, never to ask permission.

I opened the gate and let them file out in front of me, the stolen cookies clutched to their hearts.

I followed them onto the sidewalk, hailed a cab. The tall girl ducked in first with Suzie in her arms, and the others quickly scrambled in as well, stacking themselves one over the other. There was childish laughter, as if the day had transformed itself into a grand adventure. Only the tall girl turned her head toward the window, away from me.

I had stopped her tantrum by handing her her heart's desire. I do believe she was stunned by her achievement.

With some bizarre, maybe cruel, indifference, I squeezed the bassinet into the back seat, on top of them all, as if merely stacking goods, stuffing it in. The children grabbed at the basket, at the tumbling little baby clothes, giggling. There were broken Oreos scattered among them, over their limbs, and on the floor of the cab.

I handed them as well the wad of cash, the dollars and pias-tres I had taken from my jewelry box.

When I turned away, Peter was approaching on the sidewalk behind me.

He had taken to going to work in just a short-sleeved shirt and dress pants—ties and jackets had been abandoned by the American workforce at some point during our stay. In ret-rospect I guess you could say it was an indication of our set-tling in.

The new informality made him seem so boyish. He might have been a thin Catholic schoolkid with his white shirt and his leather satchel. He might have been that puzzled young man who had called to me out of the rushing crowds on a cold after-noon in midtown Manhattan.

"What was that all about?" he asked.

I shrugged. "One of Charlene's projects," I said.

He looked beyond me, although the cab had already turned the far corner. "Was she here?"

I shrugged. "You know Charlene," I said. "Everywhere and nowhere."

We exchanged our usual quick homecoming kiss, and I said, "You're later than you promised."

He looked again into the middle distance where the taxi was long gone. "I was needed," he said with a smile. "You know how it is. Everywhere and nowhere."

"Oh, I know," I told him. "I know how it is."

As we went back inside the gate together, Peter paused to consider the iron bars, narrowly spaced. He could fit his fingers through them, but not his whole hand.

"I'm thinking some chicken wire here," he said, wiggling

his fingers to demonstrate. "Might be safer. With all that's going on."

We walked together across the path. Under the veranda, Minh-Linh, fury in her every gesture, was now cleaning off the little table.

I said—hot and cold in my voice and my heart—"What does it matter now? Charlene tells me we're going home."

INCONSEQUENTIAL GOOD, you said, describing your mother's life, all her little efforts.

A phrase less pertinent, less painful, to us, I think, since neither one of us, as far as I can tell, has claimed any gift for altruism, no outsized generosity, no impulse to shout back at the gobbling whirlwind—no furious ambition, for that matter, to do more than is reasonable about the chaos in the world. The awfulness.

We hoped only, I think, you and I, to stay safe: to close as tightly as we could the circle of our affection—blood-deep, insistent affection for our own, for the few we could bear to love.

ONE MORE THING to tell you about those days.

Although, as I said, I begged off, Lily—I never learned to call her Ly—returned to the leprosarium with Charlene and the lovely clothes. Charlene told me later how remarkable it was that so few adjustments had to be made: every ao dai fit so beautifully. I wasn't surprised and knew it had little to do with my careful note-taking. I had my memory, even then, of sweet Lily wielding those comically large scissors, her concentration and her skill as she bent over the tiny bit of white silk.

You needn't apologize for the dizzying delight you felt, finding the doll on Dominic's shelf, seeing again Lily's careful handiwork. I would have felt the same. Something to take home. Something to preserve. Something of the girl in every small bit of thread, who she was, may still be.

Lily returned a third time when she and Charlene brought the silk tunics for the men. She'd made silk pillow slips, too, Charlene told me in a letter. A gift for the Sisters.

"Something cool for their cheeks at the end of the day," she said in her inimitable way. "You know, after they've shed those hair shirts."

I do believe Charlene envied them, those confident Sisters with their circumscribed, industrious, single-minded lives. Women who, as Dom said, were on everybody's side.

On this third trip, Lily stayed behind.

She would not be parted from her twin, your mother said. Her heart. Her own. And the Sisters gave up trying to dissuade her.

Marcia Case, your mother wrote, is absolutely furious with me. Lily was her favorite girl.